*To my wonderful husband
who always believed I could,
even when I wasn't so sure.
And to my beautiful daughters
who say they want to be just like me.
I hope they're kidding.*

Crazy
Little Thing

Crazy
Little Thing

TRACY BROGAN

Montlake
Romance

Published by Montlake Romance
P.O. Box 40081
Las Vegas, NV 89140

ISBN-13: 9781612186009
ISBN-10: 1612186009

CHAPTER 1

MY HUSBAND HAD A TALENT for putting the dick in unpredictable, so I wasn't entirely surprised to catch him at an office party with his hand up the skirt of a giggly, jiggly redhead. Or that he had mistletoe dangling from his belt buckle. Even though it wasn't Christmas. Suddenly eight years of wondering if I was paranoid or intuitive were finally answered. Richard was cheating on me, and I couldn't ignore it any longer.

I probably should have left him sooner, but I was dumb in love, plus my mother thought divorce was tacky even though she'd been through one herself. Maybe she worried I couldn't do any better. Turns out, I couldn't have done much worse.

Exactly one year, six days, and fourteen hours later, Richard and I signed on the dotted line and our marriage dissolved, like margarita salt on the tongue, leaving behind the bitter aftertaste of something that started out sweet but ended sour.

The details of our sordid divorce prompted a feeding frenzy for the local Glenville press. Richard was the city's favorite son, after all, and everyone wanted the juiciest morsel for their evening headline. His job as anchorman of Channel Seven news earned him a quasi-celebrity status and a sycophantic following. I, on the other hand, was painted in a single stroke as a gold-digging Real Housewife just after his cash. No one but me seemed to remember the incident with the redhead, and somehow I became the pariah, a one-dimensional villain trapped inside the reality show of my own life. So when my aunt Dody called to invite the kids and me to spend the summer with her in tiny Bell Harbor, Michigan, it was an offer too good to refuse.

"You need a good psychic cleansing, Sadie," Dody told me over the phone. "It's time to purge all of Richard's nasty karma right out of your system."

I had zero faith in her tarot-reading, angel-guided, crystal-waving nonsense, but I was desperate for a vacation. And a chance to hide. Her pink clapboard house, perched high on a hill overlooking Lake Michigan, was the perfect spot to rest, reboot, and figure out what the hell to do with the next fifty years of my life. Sure, I'd probably be dead long before that, but I hate leaving things to chance.

I guided my SUV along the narrow, elm-lined avenues of Bell Harbor. Lowering the window, I breathed in deeply. The scent of hot sand tinged with tanning oil and lilacs reminded me of carefree summers, back before I cared about damaging UV rays and toxins in the lake. The buzz of cicadas nearly drowned out the sound of waves splashing on the nearby shore.

What a drastic change from the shimmering heat and road-warrior mentality of Glenville's asphalt raceway. Bell Harbor seemed frozen in a moment that never existed anyplace else, untouched by the tawdriness of life outside its borders. Like enchanted Brigadoon, except around here people didn't randomly burst into song and dance. Or maybe they did and I just never noticed.

I drove on, past pale houses with spindly white porches draped with American flags. A scruffy yellow dog sporting a red bandana trotted down the sidewalk, his tail swinging high as if he had someplace important to be. Then around the last curve in the road, Dody's yard burst into view. Like at a discount garden store, flowers were everywhere, some real, some silk, some faded and plastic. Overgrown azalea bushes crowded around birdbaths, iron benches, and assorted stone statues of angels and gnomes. My heart thumped unexpectedly against my rib cage like a firefly trying to escape a glass jar.

"Wow! Look at all the junk!" gasped my daughter, Paige. At six years old, she was a master at stating the obvious.

"There's dorfs," added four-year-old Jordan. "One, two, free, four—"

"Those are gnomes, dumdum. And anyway, you're not supposed to call them dorfs because it's rude."

"So is calling me dumdum, stupid head."

"That's enough, you two. We don't call anyone dumdum or stupid head," I said.

My children had spent the better part of our two-hour drive from Glenville in heated debate over such inane topics as whether or not a pixie is bigger than the tooth fairy, if all giraffes have the same number of spots, and where one might find, and I quote, "the poop hole on a mermaid." Jordan, being his father's son, could not resist taking sides in an argument, no matter how arbitrary the topic. My head was numb from their banter.

I parked the car in Dody's driveway and pulled the keys from the ignition. Paige pushed open her door and exploded from the backseat like popcorn, with Jordan fast on her heels. They sprinted into the dense growth of the overburdened flower beds and began running zigzag patterns around the sculptures.

"Be careful in that mess of weeds!" I called out. "There might be prickers in there!"

They went on, heedless of my warning. I'd be pulling slivers from their feet tonight for certain.

I climbed out of the car and headed up the faded wooden steps into Aunt Dody's house. I hadn't been there in more than a year, but I opened the door without knocking. The trusting folks of Bell Harbor didn't knock—or lock their doors either. And they liked it when you called them *folks*, which is a word I don't normally use, but since I was there for the summer I should try to fit in.

The moment my strappy sandal touched cracked peach linoleum, the wild disarray of mismatched everything landed a gut punch to my minimalist sensibilities. Clutter, both dazzling and unnerving, rendered me breathless. A macramé owl with beady wooden eyes peered vacantly from across the room. A ferret cage, long missing its musky occupant, overflowed with dusty silk roses. A memorial gesture to his passing, no doubt. Porcelain ballerinas competed for shelf domination with Elvis bobbleheads. And a moose head, with its enormous antlers spanning the distance of the mantel over the stone fireplace, had a Detroit Tigers baseball cap dangling rakishly over one ear.

My chest squeezed tight. Dody's garage-sale decor always disoriented me.

No one would ever accuse her of being a meticulous housekeeper. No one ever accused me of being anything but.

"Dody? Hello?" I called out.

The clickety-clack of doggy claws on the floor offered a brief warning before I was slammed unceremoniously against the wall as Lazyboy and Fatso, two burly, uncouth hounds of indeterminate breed and negligible manners, slathered me with wet, sloppy kisses. Their love was unconditional, their drool indiscriminate. I raised a knee to nudge them away, but they persisted as if I had bacon in my pocket. They quivered with adoration.

Oh, to be a dog and experience such uninhibited joy.

"Dody," I shouted again. "Call off the dogs!"

"Sadie? Darling, is that you? At last!"

My aunt careened around the corner, flailing her tanned arms high above blonde curls. Either she was excited to see me or the house was on fire. Her turquoise kimono was covered by a pink flowered apron. Expertly shoving the dogs aside with one plump hip, she gathered me in her robust, anaconda-like hug.

"I thought you'd never get here! How was the drive?" She pushed with the other hip as the dogs tried to assault me again. "Did you come down Main and see the new post office? Aren't the gargoyles fabulous? Thank goodness you didn't have to worry about snow. But then it's June so of course there wouldn't be any. Lazy, get off my foot." She pushed him with her hand. "Well? Where are the children! Are they here?"

My aunt was a tsunami in fuzzy slippers. And for some reason, a kimono.

"They're outside counting gnomes."

Her eyes sparkled. "Oh, I can't wait to see them. Have they grown? Of course they have."

She pulled me back toward the door and smacked the screen with such force it swung open, whacked against the side of the house, and slammed back shut.

She shook her head. "Drat, I wish Walter had fixed this door before he died." She opened it with more caution. Stepping into the sunlight, she pressed both palms against her face at the sight of my mischievous offspring. "Oh, there they are! The children. Sadie, aren't they precious?"

Paige was holding a fistful of foliage, root balls still attached, while Jordan was attempting to shove a grapefruit-sized rock into his tiny pocket. My children flinched as the dogs bounded over for more kissing.

"Lazy! Fatso! Behave yourselves!" Dody clapped her hands and the dogs dolefully meandered away.

"Kids, come say hello to Aunt Dody."

Paige trotted over immediately. "Aunt Dody, I got you flowers!"

"Paige! Mommy has told you not to pull things out of other people's gardens!" I scolded.

"But you said it was all weeds in there."

Dody squinted at me from the corner of her eye, then leaned forward to touch Paige's cheek, as if it were fragile as a bubble.

"You pick all the flowers you want, darling. That's what they're for." Dody took the impromptu bouquet, tapping the clumps of dirt against her silk-clad leg. "These are simply lovely. And who is the tall fellow over there?" Dody gestured toward Jordan. "That can't be your baby brother."

Jordan hesitated. He knew Dody, but he had become very shy since the divorce.

"I'm not a baby," he grumbled.

"Of course you're not. Why, you're nearly tall enough to punch Jasper right in the kisser."

My son's lips twitched as he fought to hide a smile.

Jasper was Dody's oldest son and, at six foot four, by far the tallest in the family. He had recently graduated from cooking school but was quick to inform people it was called the *Institute of Culinary Arts and Hospitality Management.*

"Did you know Jasper got a new job at Arno's! Swankiest restaurant in Bell Harbor, thank you very much. He can tell you all about it. Jasper!" she hollered over her shoulder.

"Is he here?" I asked.

"Oh, yes. Didn't I tell you? He moved back home to save money to buy a restaurant."

My brain pinged in alarm. She knew perfectly well she hadn't told me, because if she had, I might not have come. She knew I wanted a man-free zone for my summer vacation. If Jasper was there, I'd have to share a bathroom with his whiskers and his toilet seat neglect. He'd fart at random and blame it on the dogs. And I'd have to wear a bra all the time! What the hell kind of vacation was this going to be? My trepidation over coming resurfaced.

It hadn't been an easy decision to pull the kids away from everything familiar. Any extended visit with Dody had the potential for mayhem. So did most short visits. But the tipping point came when Richard forbid us to go. The passive-aggressive glee I got from telling him he couldn't stop me was worth having to put up with Jasper.

I walked over to my SUV and opened the back to unload. It was loaded to the brim. I was a notorious over-packer and brought everything we could possibly need for the summer—and several things we wouldn't. I liked to plan for every potential contingency. You just never knew when you'd get stranded in a remote place and need a ball of twine or rubber cement. Richard always teased me, but he had no idea how much of *my* effort went into making sure *his* vacation ran smoothly.

Dody turned to my children. "Darlings, there are toys for you in the kitchen. It's mostly old junk from my friend Anita Parker. She just cleaned her attic."

Paige and Jordan squeaked and immediately ran inside. The promise of toys, even crappy old toys from some stranger's attic, was enough to get Jordan over his shyness.

Dody turned back to me. "Anita's bird died. Did I tell you that? What a tragedy." She lowered her voice in solemnity. "Gobbled up by her own cat! Can you imagine?"

"You mean the bird that bit me when I was little?" I was terrified of that bird.

Dody nodded. "Probably." She hugged me again. "Oh, I'm so happy you're finally here! Three years is too long."

I reached out from her embrace and tugged on another suitcase.

"It hasn't been so very long, Dody."

"Pish-posh. Those times you stayed at a hotel don't count." She brushed a strand of hair from my cheek, as if I were three instead of thirty.

"We didn't stay here because Richard was allergic to the dogs."

"Bullshit. He just didn't like me."

I didn't argue. She was right. Richard thought Dody was rude and invasive and that her house always smelled like cabbage and patchouli. Which it does.

Deliberately moving on, I said, "I signed the divorce papers last week."

"You did? Thank goodness!"

I received another effusive embrace.

"I never liked him either, you know." Dody wiped her hands together as if her memory of him were a greasy smudge. "Now that's over and done with, we can find you a better man."

I jerked out another suitcase and nearly slugged her with it. "Why would I want another man?"

Her expression of bewilderment suggested I'd just turned down chocolate cake. "Because, silly, you can't stay single forever."

I dropped the luggage with a thud into the dirt of the driveway.

"Technically, I've been divorced for five days, Dody. Uncle Walter died six years ago and you're still single."

"But you've been alone for over a year now. And I'm playing the field. As a matter of fact, I met a simply delightful man just the other day. Didn't I tell you? We met at the shooting range."

"The shooting range? What were you doing at the shooting range?"

"Target practice, silly. You shouldn't own a gun if you don't know how to use it."

I nearly slammed my hand in the trunk.

"Use it? When did you get a gun?"

This was not good news. My aunt wasn't responsible enough to own a squirt gun, much less something with real bullets.

"A few weeks ago. We have that skunk, you know."

"What skunk?"

"The one who keeps getting in our trash. Last week he sprayed Lazyboy right in the face."

"So you're going to shoot him?"

"Of course not!" She reached down and picked up the smallest suitcase. "I'll shoot over his head to scare him away. Anyway, his name is Harry."

"You named the skunk Harry?"

She looked at me as though I was the one talking crazy. "Why would I name the skunk Harry? That's ridiculous. Harry is the man I met. He's a dentist. Lovely teeth, I must say. And his granddaughter works at the new Starbursts."

"Starbursts?"

"Yes, the coffee place."

"Oh, you mean Starbucks."

"Yes, that's the one. I love those Ralph Macchios, don't you?"

"She means macchiato," said Jasper, coming out from the house at last. He gave me a fast hug then scooped up several suitcases. "Welcome to Casa de Loco."

"Thanks."

My cousin hadn't changed much since the last time I'd seen him. Taller, skinnier, if that was possible, but still a boyish version of my aunt, with curly blond hair and light blue eyes. And he wasn't particularly hairy. Maybe he wouldn't leave too many whiskers in the bathroom.

"Anyway," Dody said, "Harry is Italian. He has a mustache, like the Italians. And there's the gun too, of course. But do you know the very best part?" She gave a girlish giggle. "He looks just like Dr. Phil!"

Seriously? That was the best part?

"I met him, you know, Dr. Phil," she went on as Jasper and I carried my stuff into the house. "At a taping of his show. He told me my scarf was very unique. It was the one Walter got me at Fort Knox. You know, the one that looks like a giant hundred dollar bill? Anyway, that Dr. Phil was the most charming man ever, even if he was staring at my bosoms." She straightened her shoulders. "Walter always did say I have an impressive rack."

"God, mother," Jasper winced.

"What? I do."

∗   ∗   ∗

"What took you so long, Mommy?" Paige demanded when I finally joined them on the beach later that evening. Jasper had gathered some chairs in a semicircle so we could watch the sunset near the water. He and Dody were there, waiting with the kids.

"I was putting things away," I said.

She put her hands on her hips and frowned. "You're always putting things away!"

"Darling, would you and Jordan find me some bird feathers?" Dody interrupted. "If you do, I'll make you each a dream catcher."

Paige nodded and skipped away, pulling Jordan with her.

Jasper gestured to a beach chair. "Have a seat. Want a beer?" He reached into the red cooler sitting next to him in the sand.

I couldn't recall the last time I'd had a beer. The women of Glenville didn't drink beer. They sipped expensive chardonnay from delicately stemmed goblets. Of course, most of them polished off the entire bottle in one sitting to wash down their Prozac. And by them, I mean me.

But I was officially on vacation. Time to kick back and relax. "Sure, I would love a beer. Thanks."

No sooner had I taken the bottle from one cousin's hand when the unmistakable melody of my other cousin rang out.

"Free at last, baby girl! You are free at last!"

Fontaine, Dody's younger son, galloped down the deck steps two at a time, his lime-green shirt unbuttoned and flapping in the breeze. His dark hair was artfully gelled into place and he sported a dashing new goatee. He kissed the air next to my ear. "You look fab, Sades. Broken heart agrees with you."

"Thanks, Fontaine. You don't look too shabby yourself."

He smiled, flashing unnaturally bright teeth, and flexed a slender bicep. "I know, right? I've been doing yoga with Mom."

Jasper choked on his beer. "It's revolting to watch."

Fontaine twitched a dark brow. "You're just jealous because I'm so bendy."

"Right. If I ever need to stick my head up my own ass, maybe I'll join you. Here's a beer." He tossed it to Fontaine, who caught it with a flourish.

"Boys, play nice," Dody said, extending her leg and wiggling her foot. "Fontaine, do you love my new flip-flops? I got them for a steal at the dollar store. They were a dollar."

"What are the odds?" Jasper mumbled, immune to the thrill of finding cute, cheap shoes.

"Sparkly, Mom. Good find." Fontaine plopped down into a beach chair and I did the same.

The sun glowed orange, casting light and shadows across the sand. It was nearly time to tuck my kids into bed, but Paige was giggling, tossing feathers into the air and watching them float downward. Jordan was poking at a dried clump of seaweed with a driftwood stick. Maybe just this once they could stay up late. Tomorrow we could establish our bedtime routine.

"Fontaine, tell Sadie about your magazine interview," Dody said. Then she turned to me. "He was interviewed for a magazine, Sadie. Isn't that exciting? It's all about his new interior design job and how everybody is doing fong shewy."

"It was a blurb, Mom." Fontaine sipped his beer.

"Nonetheless, it was very flattering." She dabbed moisture from her eyes. "You've got your fancy decorating job, and Jasper works at such a nice restaurant and has a beautiful girlfriend. You are both doing so well." Her voice caught with emotion. "Walter and I are so proud of you."

"Have you been talking to Dad again?" Jasper's tone was as dry as the sand.

"Not directly, of course. But my spiritual advisor has. She's very wise." Dody lifted her foot again, admiring how the sun reflected off the sparkles of her one-dollar flip-flop.

"Wise enough to swipe your money and tell you gibberish. If she's so good at communicating with Dad, ask him where he left the good rake."

"He can't be bothered with such trivial, earthbound questions," she answered.

"Why? It's not like he has someplace else to be," Jasper responded.

"Oh, phooey. I'm not discussing this with you anymore. Sadie, ask Fontaine about his magazine article. Oh, and the renovations at his house. That's why he's staying with us for a few weeks, you know."

I spilled beer on the front of my shirt. "You're staying here too?" Damn! How many men was I going to have to put up with during this visit?

"I'm moving a few walls. But the drywall dust is hell on my nasal passages. Besides, you'll have way more fun with me here. You can't just sit around all day with my mom."

Au, contraire! That is exactly what I planned to do. A big, fat nothing! I wanted to lie on the beach for hours, play checkers with my kids, watch mindless television, and give up all personal grooming habits. I was here to escape from men, but my visions of a perfectly estrogen-driven summer vacation were vanishing faster than the polar ice caps. Sure, Fontaine was fun, like cotton candy is fun. But it's also sickeningly sweet and too much gives me a splitting headache. Just like Fontaine.

I forced a smile. "That's great. We'll have a blast."

I looked back over the water and gulped down my beer. This wasn't at all what I had planned. But then again, what in my life was turning out the way I expected?

Fontaine tapped his elbow against mine. "So, sugarplum, aside from the total collapse of your marriage, what else is new?"

He was as blunt as he was fashion conscious, which is to say, very.

"Not much. Richard is still mad I got the house. My mother is still mad I got divorced while my sister is mad I didn't dump him sooner. And I'm thinking about cutting my hair. How about you?"

He nodded. "Yes, I definitely think you should cut your hair."

"That's not what I meant. Hey, wait a minute! You said I looked fabulous."

He was already getting on my nerves.

"You do, mostly. But your hair shows hints of giving up. We'll have to do better since you're back on the market."

I sat forward in my chair so abruptly a flock of nearby seagulls launched into flight. "I am not on the market!"

"Of course you are." He set his empty bottle in the sand.

"That's what I said!" Dody nodded emphatically.

"I am not." I shook my head, equally emphatic.

"Don't even bother, Sadie." Jasper chuckled. "You're their summer project. Didn't you know?"

"Pish-posh, Jasper. Shush yourself," Dody hissed.

"Is that why you invited me here?" A wave of nausea rolled over me and the back of my neck prickled like heat rash. I should have known my aunt's insistent invitation cloaked an ulterior motive. She wasn't president of the Bell Harbor Busybody Association for nothing.

"Don't listen to him, darling," Dody assured me. "We just want to nurture you and mend your broken spirit."

"I don't have a broken spirit!"

Fontaine and his mother exchanged a look. One that said *She's so pathetic she doesn't even realize how pathetic she is.*

"Seriously. I'm fine. I just need a little vacation."

"Don't get your knickers in a twist, kitty cat." Fontaine sighed. "We just want you to have a little fun, you know."

"Yeah, well, fun for me does not involve men."

"But darling," Dody chided gently, "you can't fight against the universal balance. Without the despair of today we can't experience the joy of tomorrow."

"Did Dr. Phil tell you that?" Jasper asked, draining the last of his beer before reaching into the cooler and taking another.

She shook her head. "Not Dr. Phil. Kung Fu Panda. But nonetheless, Sadie can't let one bad apple sour her on romance."

"Romance?" Fontaine snorted, crossing his arms behind his head and stretching. "Who's talking about romance? I'm talking about crazy, rowdy sex. Like…with him." He nodded toward the shoreline.

Jogging along the water's edge was a man. Quite a man, in fact. Tanned, tall, muscular, and sweaty. The type of man who knew how the sun bounced off the waves and flickered over his gleaming muscles. Vain bastard. He was exactly the kind I wanted to avoid, with his long, stupid legs and his dumb, broad shoulders. He might as well have *unfaithful* tattooed right on that bulging bicep I couldn't take my eyes off of. Damn.

"Who's that?" I whispered, sounding significantly breathier than intended. Did I mention he was sweaty?

Fontaine smiled. "I don't know. I just call him *Running Man*."

Running Man continued on, giving an awkward wave as Dody, Fontaine, and I continued to stare and Jasper picked at the label of his beer.

"Hey, Fontaine!" Paige scampered up, breaking our collective trance.

"Hey, sweet stuff! Give me some sugar." He pulled her close for a kiss on the cheek.

My daughter adored Fontaine, thanks in no small part to their shared appreciation of all things glittery.

"It scratches," she said, reaching up and tapping his goatee. "Why is that on your face?"

Fontaine laughed. "That's called style, girlfriend. It's what sets us apart from the animals. And the rednecks."

CHAPTER 2

"COFFEE, SADIE?" DODY EXTENDED HER arm with a full pot tipping dangerously close to pouring even though there was no mug to catch it. This morning she wore a mint-green turban with an abundance of fluffy blonde curls springing forth from the top. She looked like a test tube fizzing over.

"Definitely." I pulled a cup from the cupboard, trying to disregard the stained interior, and handed it to her.

Getting up today had been a challenge. The mattress in my room felt like a bag of oranges, and the sound of the rolling waves hadn't lulled me to sleep at all. They just made me need to pee. When Jordan climbed into my bed at sunrise, bringing the dogs and their slobber with him, I wondered again if coming to Bell Harbor was a mistake. But Dody had badgered me with the tenacity of a Jehovah's Witness until I couldn't think of another reason to say no.

"How did you sleep?" Dody handed back the cup after sprinkling cinnamon on the top.

"Great," I lied, wishing I could inject the coffee straight into my veins. I reached past her to straighten the pot, lining it up with the blender.

"That's wonderful, dear. I was thinking after breakfast we could take a walk. There's a trail that leads right to the playground at the elementary school."

My kids were sitting at the kitchen island, their eyes still a little puffy from sleep but hopeful with expectation. I leaned over and kissed their cheeks. Paige kissed me back while Jordan turned his face into his shoulder. He was getting too old for kisses, and my heart stung a little.

"Please, Mommy? I'd like to see the school." Paige smiled her most beatific smile.

"Did you brush your teeth before you came downstairs?" I asked.

Jordan frowned. "I thought we were on vacation?"

"Not from dental hygiene. Brush them after you eat, then we'll go to the playground."

They fist bumped each other in victory, happy until Dody set steaming bowls in front of them. "Eat your porridge, dears."

Paige frowned at the foreign glop. "What is that?"

I nudged her in the shoulder. "It's oatmeal, Paige. Just eat it."

"It doesn't look like our oatmeal. What are all those specks?"

I peeked down at the sludge. Dody's cooking hadn't improved over the years. As kids, my sister and I sometimes made random bets and whoever lost had to eat one of Dody's peculiar concoctions. Her oatmeal was the worst offender, always gummy and discolored. And sometimes you'd bite into something and couldn't tell what it was or why it was in there. I've long suspected Jasper became a chef purely out of self-defense.

"What *are* the specks?" I couldn't resist asking.

"Flaxseeds. They help you poop."

Jordan's eyes went big and round. "Pooping is funny. One time I pooped a———"

"Jordan!" This was not the time for that story. "Just eat."

"Yes, eat up, darlings. I have to be back here by noon. Harry is taking me skeet shooting." She pressed a hand to her temple and looked at me. "Oh, dear. Is that rude of me? To go out on a date when you haven't had one in *ages?*"

She said the word *ages* as though it caused physical pain. That was harsh, having my sixty-five-year-old auntie feeling sorry for me because her social life was superior to mine. But then again, it always had been. After Uncle Walter died, she'd entertained a constant stream of suitors. It seemed the single gentlemen of Bell Harbor's AARP loved her zany sense of humor and zest for life. Well, that, and the fact that she put out.

"It's fine, Dody. After the playground the kids and I will go to the beach. I want to teach them to swim anyway."

"Hey, toots! Come here," Fontaine called from the deck, doing his best crocodile hunter accent. "Running Man, dead ahead. Crikey, will you look at the sleek hindquarters on that mate."

The runner? Again? What kind of pretentious jerk went running twice in twelve hours? I didn't need to see that. He was nothing to me. Still, I peeked out the kitchen window, where I could see his silhouette fast approaching.

I took a sip from my cup. Well, I guess it was a fresh, sunny morning, perfect for enjoying one's coffee on the deck.

And thus began a lazy morning routine we performed each day for the next two weeks. Mystery porridge for my aunt and the kids in the kitchen and dark, caffeinated nectar of the gods for me and my cousin on the deck. Running Man became an unwitting accomplice to our daily ritual. Fontaine discovered that if we slouched down in the lounge chairs and stared between the railings, we could get a really good look at him. But some days we'd stand tall and boldly wave like tourists on a double-decker bus. It all depended on how my hair looked.

"You should walk the dogs," Fontaine declared one morning, just after the runner had passed. "When Running Man sprints by, the dogs will chase him and then you can introduce yourself."

My stomach flipped, like that moment you see the police car behind you and wonder if you were speeding. "I don't want to introduce myself. These two weeks have given me the best relationship I've ever had. I'm not going to wreck it by actually getting to know him."

Fontaine's dark head dropped. "Baby girl, listen when I tell you this, you have got to get back on that pony. How long has it been?"

I took a slug of coffee. It suddenly tasted old and bitter. Like me. "Since I rode the pony? None of your business." I did not want to have this conversation, not even with Fontaine, who, believe me, held nothing back. I rose from my deck chair and tucked it in snugly under the glass-topped table.

"That long, huh?" Fontaine sipped his own coffee.

"Not that long." I wiped a spot off the tabletop with the edge of my shirt.

"Has there been anybody since Richard?" He put out his foot, making me step over him in my haste to go inside.

I'd gone on a handful of dates since kicking Richard to the curb, but each one had been exponentially worse than the one before. The last had gone so horribly awry I nearly flung myself down an open elevator shaft.

Fontaine pounced like a puma. "Oh, there has been. I can tell. Spill it, cupcake!"

I flipped him the finger and walked inside.

Undeterred, Fontaine followed, fast on my heels. "Oh, come on!"

I knew I'd have to give him something. The man was a pit bull in capris.

"Let's just say that on my last date I made a huge error in judgment, and he never called me again. OK?" I picked up a pair of Jordan's shoes from the middle of the floor and set them down next to the ones I'd lined up by the door yesterday.

"Ah, I see." His nod was all-knowing. He plopped down on the sofa in the living room. "But you shouldn't be so hard on yourself. We've all made that mistake. And it's exactly why you need to get back out there! Don't let *that* guy be the last guy."

I nudged the coffee table over a few inches with my knee. "You are as pushy as your mother. She thinks I should go out with Anita Parker's derelict son! You know, the one who used to throw tent worms in my hair when we were little? No thanks. I am just fine being on my own."

"I don't believe you." He plucked at the fringe of a sofa pillow.

"Why? Don't you think I can take care of myself?"

"Of course you can, but we humans are social creatures and being alone is aberrant behavior. Trust me. I'm an expert on aberrant behavior."

"I'll bet." I tossed a coordinating pillow next to him while dropping Fatso's chew toy into a basket with my other hand. "Anyway, I don't want to talk about this. I'm not interested in meeting new men right now." Or ever, for that matter.

"Oh, fine." Fontaine pouted for a moment, stroking his goatee. I could feel his eyes boring into me as I puttered, trying to bring order to Dody's chaotic collections.

I picked up a speck of fuzz from the carpet and rear-ranged the magazines until his silence became unbearable.

"Stop doing that!" I said at last. "You're starting to freak me out."

His eyes had a mischievous glint, like the time when we were sixteen and he talked me into smoking dope behind the boat shed and I ended up swimming naked in the lake. Then I woke up the next morning covered in beach grass cuts with a half gallon of melted ice cream on my pillow.

"You are giving me an idea," he said.

I scowled. "I don't like your ideas."

"You might like this one. Check it out. I'm an interior designer, right?"

"Yeah?" I hesitated, another dog toy dangling from my hand.

"When I go into people's houses, I see junk. Tons of junk, everywhere."

"So?"

"So, you love to put junk away. You're like one of those robotic vacuum thingies. What are they called? A Roomba!" He snapped his fingers. "That's it. You are a human Roomba. You're a…a humba. It's freakishly mesmerizing, I might add."

"You think I should be a cleaning lady?" I tossed the dog toy into the basket and stacked the coasters on the coffee table.

"No, dumbass. You should be a professional organizer."

My own burst of laughter surprised me. "A professional organizer? Damn it, Fontaine. I thought you were serious. No one would pay me for that."

"Pudding pop, they'll pay huge! There are rich folks out there with piles of loot and way too much stuff. But they're too busy making more money to organize the crap they already own. But you have a gift. Seriously, look what you've done to this place in just two weeks."

I followed the swooping motion of his arms. I had made some improvements at Dody's. It was nearly habitable now, with a clear path from the kitchen to the dining room and on to the sunporch. I'd even convinced her to move the Star Wars figurines to a back bedroom instead of displaying them next to her grandmother's antique crystal vases. Now if I could just get her to move the jackalope.

Fontaine went on talking. "I design gorgeous rooms for my clients and they ruin it with papers lying around and hockey sticks and Wii remotes. They don't know how to put things in order. But to you, organizing comes naturally. Like…sarcasm."

It was true. I spoke fluent sarcasm. And I had always been fastidious. I used to drive my sister, Penny, crazy when we played dolls. All she wanted to do was have Malibu Barbie smooch with Beachcomber Ken, but I always made them fold up all their little clothes first and put away all those tiny shoes.

"A professional organizer, huh?" I sank down onto the couch.

"Yes, girlfriend. Use that personality disorder of yours for good instead of evil. Just think about it." He hoisted himself off the couch and left the room, leaving me to ponder.

Hmm. I did love to categorize. And sort, and fold, and tuck, and stack. In fact, the best gift Richard ever gave me was my own label maker. He bought it as a joke, but I loved it. Of course, if I'd had any brains I'd have put a big, fat label on his forehead that said *married*. But maybe Fontaine was on to something. A job would give me something to focus on, something to move toward, instead of using all my energy to outrun my past. And I liked working. At least I had.

When Richard and I first got married, I was fresh out of college. I had a lovely little job at a bookstore where I met every sort of person. Moms, grandparents, writers, and pseudo-intellectuals. But Richard didn't like that I wasn't home waiting for him. I think he mostly didn't like freethinking individuals out there filling my head with dangerous ideas. Then once Paige was born, I wanted nothing more than to be with her every minute of the day, and staying home seemed like a privilege.

But she and Jordan weren't babies anymore. Soon they'd both be in school all day and I would need something to occupy my time. Maybe having a job would give me some purpose, some direction. Some identity other than Richard Turner's ex-wife. If nothing else, when someone asked, "And what do you do?" it would give me something to answer besides, "I sponge off of my ex-husband's bad judgment."

CHAPTER 3

I CHUCKED MY CELL PHONE into the seat next to me and adjusted the vents, cranking up the car's air-conditioning to let it blow directly on my heated face. I pulled sharply back into traffic after having pulled over to read Richard's text. How could that man make me so angry with just 140 characters?

I was headed into Glenville to drop the kids off for a short visit. Paige and Jordan were in the back discussing whether or not "poop from the potty went to goldfish heaven," and I was in front, sizzling mad at their father.

His text had read, "Running late. Drop kids at office."

Of course he was running late. Of course he thought I could drop his children at the office instead of his apartment. It didn't matter to him that his office was in the thick of downtown Glenville, where traffic was the worst. Or that the red-haired adulteress sat at the front desk.

I hated going into the Channel Seven building. Every time I'd been there, I swear his coworkers smirked at me and whispered into their phones. His charm had brainwashed them. They seemed to think his antics had been harmless. Just boyish bad behavior. Certainly nothing to get divorced over. I'd heard they even renamed the copy room after that infamous party. It was now known as the Copulator Room.

I gripped the steering wheel more tightly and headed into the city. A dozen more harrowing miles and at last I arrived. I parked in the ramp next to the Channel Seven station and called Richard. He could come out to get his children. I was not going in there.

"Hello, beautiful," Richard purred into the phone.

I swallowed my first response. It tasted as nasty as it would have sounded. "You're not supposed to call me that."

"I know, but you are so beautiful I can't help myself."

"Try. We're divorced now, remember?"

His snicker was humorless, like a serial killer plotting. "How could I forget?" Richard asked. "I think of it every time I make another huge-ass mortgage payment on a house I'm not allowed inside of. And you're not living at."

"Maybe you should have thought of that before you banged the weather girl."

He paused as if he had to think about it. "I've never banged a weather girl."

I took a big breath, wishing I could blow away my memory of him with it. "Anyway, we're here. Come out and get the kids."

"You're here? Fantastic! Bring them in." Genuine enthusiasm sounded in his voice, softening my anger.

"No, you come out and get them."

In spite of our history of hostility, Richard could still be very persuasive. If I gave him an inch, he'd convince me to cook us dinner and massage his feet faster than I could say, "Fuck you, you bastard."

"I'm waiting for a phone call. Can't you please just come in?" He whined, which meant he was lying. Actually I knew he was lying because he was talking.

"Nope. Come and get 'em."

His sigh was prom-queen dramatic. "Oh, fine!"

He came out the door in minutes, a broad smile on his face for Paige and Jordan. My breath caught when I saw him. He was tan, and his blond hair was the lightest I've ever seen it. It made his brown eyes seem even darker, deeper. Those eyes always reminded me of chocolate, another thing I once loved but had given up for my own good.

"Hey, guys! Come on! Give your pop a hug!" He threw his arms out wide.

I helped them out of the car and they ran to him like puppies to a biscuit. My heart twisted. Seeing Richard with our kids could still make me melt. It reminded me of all the reasons I'd fallen for him in the first place. But he was my kryptonite. I needed to get away from there, and fast. I pulled the overnight bags from the SUV and all but threw them in Richard's direction.

"Here's their stuff. Where do you want me to pick them up?"

"How about the Waffle Castle at nine o'clock? We can have breakfast together." His voice sounded hopeful, the idiot.

Saturday mornings at the Waffle Castle had been our family ritual. He was too dense to realize his own insensitivity, his stubborn refusal to admit our lives had drastically changed from what they had once been.

"No, this is your time with them." I felt my lips pursing into a prim spinster-quality line.

Richard leaned forward, whispering. "My therapist says we should have friendly family time together. For the kids."

For a split second I felt remorse. Maybe he wasn't dense. Maybe he wanted to recreate that ritual for the kids.

"Your therapist?" I asked.

"Yeah, well, she's not technically my therapist. Just a friend." He shrugged.

My internal fluttering of optimism turned to churning acidic certainty. He was screwing her.

"I'll pass on breakfast."

Richard shook his head and picked up the kids' bags. "Suit yourself. Come on, kids."

I scrambled to kiss Paige on the cheek, already over-whelmed with the heaviness of missing them. Jordan was out of my reach, clinging to Richard's hand and not giving me a second glance. They were so excited to see their father I had become invisible.

"OK, well, have fun," I called after them. No one turned around.

During the drive to Glenville I had worried my kids would miss me too much this weekend.

Now I was terrified they wouldn't miss me at all.

❧   ❧   ❧

I climbed back in my car, knowing the obligatory visit to my mother's house came next. That did not make me feel better. I hadn't told her I was coming to town, but some supernatural ability enabled her to discover everything I didn't want her to know. If I didn't stop by for a visit, I'd be in trouble. Just one more thing for her to add to the list of my shortcomings.

She hadn't forgiven me for divorcing Richard, which made no sense to me at all considering she'd divorced my dad with no regrets when I was eleven. Penny and I had come home from a sleepover at my cousin's house to discover he was gone. No note. No phone call. Just my mom saying she'd told him to leave. No one ever came right out and told us there was another woman, but all the signs were there.

He got remarried a year later, and I only saw him a dozen more times before he died. That was almost fifteen years ago. Eventually the constant ache of missing him became background noise I hardly ever noticed, an ever-present hum, but not so loud it was distracting. Unless I listened for it, as I had when there was no one to walk me down the aisle or on the days my kids were born.

Arriving at my mother's house, I knocked lightly on the screen door even though I could see her standing in the kitchen. "Hi, Mom." I stepped inside and automatically wiped my feet on the doormat.

She wore a crisp white tennis outfit, her sleek black hair pulled into a stylish clip at the base of her neck. The ice in her tea clunked when she set down the glass.

"Sadie, what a surprise." There was no move to embrace. Helene Harper considered physical displays of affection vulgar.

"I just dropped off the kids with Richard. I wondered if you wanted to have dinner or lunch tomorrow or something."

"You should have called first. I've got the museum gala tomorrow. I'm the chairwoman, remember?"

"The gala is tomorrow?" I smoothed back an errant strand of my own dark brown hair. People said I looked like her, but other than the coloring I really couldn't see the similarity.

"I don't suppose you would remember if it's not important to you."

First strike, Mommy.

"Who's the speaker this year?" My feigned interest wouldn't make her forgive my oversight, but we had long been entrenched in this game. I leaned against the counter.

"Some historian," she huffed, dismissing his value. "Without Richard's connections, we had a terrible time finding anyone interesting. Don't slouch, Sadie."

I started to straighten, but caught myself and resisted. "Mother, you play golf with the mayor's wife. Surely Richard is not your only connection."

"Did you come here to be sassy with me?" She sipped her tea and pointedly did not offer me any.

"No, of course not. Sorry." I wasn't really, which was patently obvious. "You're booked all weekend, then?"

"Yes. Unless you want to play tennis with me right now. I'm late for my cardio league." She looked at her watch, pushing aside a dozen gold bracelets to find it.

I didn't bother mentioning her backhand might improve if she took off some of that bling.

"Nope. Still not any good at tennis. What's Penny up to today?"

"You'd have to ask her."

This was ridiculous, two grown women not able to say what was really on our minds.

"How long do you plan to be mad at me?" I blurted out. Damn it. Fontaine's big mouth was contagious.

My mother set the glass down so hard tea splashed out. "What's that supposed to mean?"

"It seems like you're still mad about Richard."

My mother sighed, deep and long. "I'm not mad at you, Sadie. I simply think you rushed into this divorce. Richard made one mistake and you threw eight years of marriage down the drain. And the children will suffer for it."

Heat started in my gut and spread in every direction. My heart pounded as if a gun were pointed at it. "You think I made this decision lightly? You divorced Dad for cheating and Penny and I turned out fine."

Her cheeks flushed carnation red. "What happened with your father and I has no bearing here. Your situation is completely different."

"How?" I had poked the sleeping bear. I may as well let her go full grizzly.

My mother tugged at her Lycra tennis top, smoothing it over her trim torso. "I don't have time for this, Sadie. I told you, I'm already late for tennis."

She picked up her Coach purse and started digging around for her keys. When she looked back up, her eyes were bright with moisture, and I nearly stepped backward from the surprise of it. I'd never seen my mother close to tears. It was jarring. I was suddenly nine years old, telling her about a shattered crystal vase and wanting with all my heart to somehow fix it.

"You're not really going to spend the entire summer with Dody, are you? The novelty will wear off, you know." Her voice had softened. Hot tears stung my own eyes, though I wasn't sure why.

"It might. And when it does, I'll come back." I brushed imaginary crumbs from her spotless counter. "But for now, we're having fun at the beach."

"Fun?" She flicked her wrist, as if fun were an insect to be shooed away. The almost-tears disappeared. Maybe I'd only imagined them. "Well, I'm late for tennis."

And that was that.

❧   ❧   ❧

I arrived at Penny's house minutes later. She and her husband lived in a beige brick ranch that looked exactly like every other beige brick ranch on the street. I always had to count mailboxes from the corner to make sure I was at the right place.

"Hey, Sade! I've missed you! Come see my new kitchen."

Penny tugged at my shirt and pulled me inside with an easy smile. The relationship with my sister was opposite of what I had with my mother. It was open, sometimes too open. In fact, she'd told me things about her husband, Jeff, that would make a sex therapist blush.

Penny's newly decorated kitchen was black and white, with red accents. Everywhere I looked there were ladybugs. A ladybug cookie jar, ladybug seat cushions, and ladybug throw rugs.

Perspiration prickled on my skin. "What the hell?"

"Isn't it darling? I was bored without you in town so I redecorated."

I didn't even want to set my purse down.

Penny bubbled with laughter. "Oh my God, I forgot about your ladybug thing. You're such a freak."

"I'm not a freak. But we had, like, a thousand of them in our garage that one year, remember?" I shivered and flipped over her ladybug placemats before sitting down at the table.

"Whatever. Do you want some wine or tea or something?" She pulled glasses from the cupboard.

"I was just at Mom's."

She met my eyes. "Wine it is, then."

She poured a goblet of white for me, then iced tea for herself and sat down.

"You're not having any?"

My little sister shrugged. "Not right now. So are you going crazy in Podunk? Have they put in a traffic light yet?"

I sipped my wine, but only because gulping it would be tacky.

"Yes, last year. Apparently it was cause for a parade." I filled her in on my time at Dody's, even confessing my voyeuristic observations of Running Man. This was the sort of thing she usually loved, but today she was acting weird, toying with the iced-tea glass and all but avoiding eye contact. Finally I could take no more suspense.

"All right. What the hell's up with you? You're a bigger drunk than I am so why no wine?"

Penny flushed a lovely shade of pink and glanced around the kitchen as if CIA operatives were about to pounce.

I looked over my own shoulder, expecting to see Secret Service agents guarding the door. None appeared.

"Jeff and I are trying to get pregnant." Her whisper was hoarse with excitement.

"It's about time!" I thumped my hand on the table, almost upending my drink. "Thank goodness. Paige and Jordan would be teenagers if you took any longer." I'd been pestering my sister for years to reproduce. My kids needed cousins. Plus I wanted her to understand the unique joys of parenthood so I could give back all the great advice she'd given me over the years. Because no one is more qualified to give a new mother advice than a twenty-two-year-old coed with no children of her own.

"Jeff is so excited. He keeps talking about one of his swimmers making captain of the fallopian swim team. And the other day I was ovulating so I sexted him a filthy message about coming home for a conjugal visit. He's all about the baby making. But don't tell Mom, OK?"

"That you're texting filthy messages to your husband?"

"No. That we're trying to get pregnant. I don't need her nagging me."

"But if she knew about you, maybe she'd get off my back about Richard."

Penny pointed at me. "Seriously, do not rat me out on this one. I'll tell people when I'm ready. OK? Jeff's family will drive us crazy if they hear about this, so he wants to keep it quiet too."

"Of course. I get it. I promise to keep your dirty little secret."

Penny smiled again, lifting her glass for a toast. "Thank you. In that case, I won't tell Mom you're fantasizing over some shirtless jogger from the beach. Deal?"

"Deal."

"Good. And since your kids are with Richard for the next two days, you can stay here and help me plan the nursery."

I shook my head. "I still have my own house here, you know. And there are a couple friends I should connect with, but I will certainly help you."

I hadn't heard much from my neighbors over the last few weeks and I had lots of catching up to do. So often socializing plans were hatched while we were all out in our yards—impromptu barbeques, trips to the community pool, things like that. So it wasn't terribly odd none of them had called. But I kind of wished they had.

CHAPTER 4

"SEE THIS TEAPOT?" DODY ASKED, waving it at me from her seat at the kitchen island. "It belonged to a member of the French Resistance during World War II. Walter and I bought it from this darling little shop in Paris."

I looked over from my precarious perch on a wobbly stepstool. Actually it was the teapot I'd given her for her fiftieth birthday. It was from Sears. I didn't have the heart to correct her.

"Pretty." I nodded.

"Isn't it? I love things that have a story to them." She stroked the side of the pot.

Every relic in Dody's house had some story attached, although more often than not one that wasn't true. Our family often joked that Dody remembered everything, whether it happened that way or not.

"Thanks for letting me practice on your kitchen," I said.

The kids and I were back in Bell Harbor and today I was working on Dody's pantry. If I could get this episode of *Hoarders* organized, I could tackle anything.

I was still contemplating my leap into going professional. I'd done some online research and discovered there was a National Association of Professional Organizers. Figures they'd be organized enough to have a national association, right? They even offered training sessions. There was one close to Bell Harbor in a couple of weeks. Dody said that was a sign from the Universe. I was not convinced. Still, this gave me the perfect excuse to clear away thirty-plus years of Dody-debris.

So far I'd found eleven jars of uniquely colored homemade jellies, potatoes that had nearly taken root into the shelf boards, a variety of ground, milled, pressed, and whole flaxseeds, a thirty-pound bag of brown rice, and a box of crackers that would require carbon dating to establish an age. All of that was stashed amid dried finger paints, glittery pine cones, tarantula food, a tambourine signed by Elton John, an Obama bobblehead, three sock puppets, and a variety of board-game pieces.

I plucked at something high on a shelf. "Why are there peacock feathers in here?"

"Careful with those!" Dody hopped from her chair and took them. "Jasper gave those to me for Mother's Day one year. I wondered where they'd gotten off to." She looked at them lovingly for half a second then jabbed them into a potted houseplant.

I pulled out another chess pawn. "What's with all the chess pieces?"

"Oh, those are to remind me I don't know how to play."

"Naturally."

I lifted the lid off a shoebox. "Pictures."

"Really? Let me see those."

I handed them over.

Dody pushed back the oversized sleeves of her Red Wings jersey and started flipping through the box.

"Look, here's one of Walter riding an elephant in India. Or was that at the zoo?"

I sneezed from the dust and then peeked at the picture. It was definitely not taken at the Bell Harbor zoo. "I'm guessing India."

She nodded. "I didn't go on that trip. Jasper was a baby. Here's one of Fontaine's Mohawk. I'm glad that look didn't last. Oh, goodness, here's one of your mother and me. When was that?" She tapped the picture against her head as if to prod the memory. "I think it was the day our pop took me to get my driver's permit." She looked back at the photo. "Oh, yes! See how I'm holding it up? That was right before I drove his Ford into the side of the garage."

"You drove his car into a wall?"

She rolled her eyes. "Not on purpose!"

Tales of my aunt's mishaps were so woven into our family lore, the expression "Totally Dody" now applied to anyone who did something unexpected and ridiculous.

"I'd only had my permit for an hour before Dad took it away. But I'm glad he did. Why, if he hadn't, I might not have been walking home the next day in the rain. And then Walter never would've offered me a ride in his car and I might never have met him."

"You got into his car when you didn't even know him?" I threw another chess piece into the pile.

"Oh, I knew who he was! He just didn't know me yet. We went to the same school but he was older." She sighed like a bobby-soxer dreaming over an Elvis poster. "My, he was handsome. All the girls thought so."

I pictured Uncle Walter with his freckled bald head, soft belly, and thick-framed reading glasses. Dody's Mona Lisa smirk told me she remembered him differently.

"We used to skinny-dip, you know. Every year at midnight on my birthday. Walter called it 'celebrating under a full moon.'" Her cheeks went pink.

I shook my head in wonder. Imagine, forty years with the same man and still the thought of him made her blush. If true love ever existed, that was it.

*   *   *

"Wow! The kitchen looks amazing! I could actually cook in here now."

Jasper's effusive compliment almost made me forget I was grimy, sweaty, and exhausted from my mammoth endeavor. The sheer volume of random paraphernalia that erupted from Dody's kitchen had trapped me for hours. I'd spent the entire day clawing my way out. But now I was finished, and Jasper was correct. The kitchen did indeed look amazing, functional, and clean.

My kids had even helped, though not without grumbling. Now Paige was coloring and Jordan sat on the floor playing with some trucks.

"Looky, Jasper. I have labels on my shelves!" Dody grinned from the pantry doorway, twirling her wrist like a game show sidekick.

He stepped past her and cocked his head. "How'd you make those labels?"

"With a label maker," I answered.

"You own a label maker?"

My hands went to my hips. "Everyone should own a label maker."

Dody stepped out as Jasper laughed. "I must admit, you've got some mad skills."

"Thank you. Now will you make me some dinner? I'm starv—"

My words were cut off by a whoosh, a whoop, and a sickening *smack*! Dody tripped as she walked from the kitchen, catapulted forward, and whacked her head against a sharp-cornered table. Her body collapsed to the floor with a thud.

"Dody!"

"Mom!"

We reached her simultaneously, just as blood began to seep from her temple. I felt woozy. Blood was so not my thing. I nicked myself shaving in the shower once and nearly had to dial 911.

"Oh, my," said Dody wanly, pressing her hand against the wound.

"Are you OK, Aunt Dody?" Paige asked. "Mommy, we were just playing here and she tripped over Jordan's truck."

I turned to see my son holding up the two halves.

"Aunt Dody broke my truck." His lip trembled.

Blood dripped faster now, dribbling down Dody's cheek. My stomach heaved. I swallowed hard.

"Paige, grab a towel from the kitchen. Hurry!"

"I'm fine," Dody said faintly, slumping toward Jasper.

"Let me see it, Mom." He nudged her hand away and grimaced.

She had an inch-long gash right along her hairline. The skin puckered open. Please tell me that's not *brain matter* oozing out. I felt the room spin and struggled to maintain my bearings. I'd never live it down if Dody got hurt but I was the one who fainted.

Paige handed me the towel, which I passed to Jasper. He patted it gently against Dody's head.

"Stop fussing, you two," she said. "I just bumped my head. It'll stop bleeding in a minute."

"I'm so sorry, Dody! This is my fault," I murmured.

"Of course it's not your fault. You didn't push me." Her gaze rolled my way. "Did you?"

"No, but I shouldn't let the kids leave their toys around."

Jordan's lip trembled faster and a tear popped from one eye. "I'm sorry, Aunt Dody."

She pulled him close. "Oh, nonsense, darling. It's not your fault. It was just an accident." Jasper continued patting at her head with the towel. "Mom, I think you might need stitches. This is kind of deep."

Stitches? Now I felt even worse! Here she had invited us into her home, welcomed us like prodigal children, and all because of that, she'd split her fool head open.

"Let's take you to the med center." Jasper moved to pull her upright, but she resisted.

"Absolutely not. It's Friday night. I have a poker date with the girls, and I have to win my six dollars back from Anita Parker, so you're not dragging me to some crowded emergency room."

"Stop being stubborn," Jasper said. "I've cut myself enough times to know when somebody needs stitches. We are going to the med center."

She shook her head, flinging a droplet of blood onto the carpet.

I looked away. I would make a terrible vampire.

"No, we're not," she said. "But you can get Dr. Pullman, if you want."

Dr. Pullman lived a few houses away. Dody consulted him whenever someone in her family ran a high fever, had a mysterious rash, or accidentally stuck something up their nose.

"What's his phone number?" Jasper asked.

Dody's head lolled back, her eyes clouding over. "My goodness, would you look at those cobwebs on this ceiling? Sadie, I'm surprised you missed those."

Jasper looked at me. "Would you run down there and get him? We may end up in the med center anyway, but maybe he can at least take a look at her."

I nodded, hopping up on shaky legs. I'd gladly go for Dr. Pullman, if only to escape this moment. Dody was white as a ghost and I was getting queasier by the second.

I ran down the street and a few minutes later found myself standing on Dr. Pullman's expensively bricked front porch. Ornate ceramic pots sat on either side of the wide wooden door, but in contrast to the elaborate landscaping, the flowers in them were shriveled and dead. I rang the bell, noticing then the flecks of blood on my shirt. Hopefully Dr. Pullman would remember me from summers past and not think I was some homicidal maniac. I smoothed out my wrinkled shorts and quickly redid my ponytail, as if that minor primping would make a difference.

A fluffy gray cat sauntered up, giving me an imperious once-over.

"Hi, kitty."

She was disdainful in the way only a cat can be. I was beneath her contempt.

"Bitch," I muttered, attempting to exert my human superiority.

As the word left my mouth and hung suspended in the air, the door opened and there, standing before me, was none other than Running Man!

My eyes widened. I suspect my mouth dropped open too. I must have looked like a skeptical eight-year-old finding Santa unloading presents under my Christmas tree. Wow, ogling this guy from Dody's deck had not done him justice. He was much taller up close, and his hair wasn't nearly as dark as I thought. But I'd been right about the muscles. They were everywhere.

My cheeks went hot and I just stood there.

He looked at me expectantly, pleasantly, until he noticed my bloodstained shirt.

"Are you all right? May I help you?"

I started giggling hysterically. I couldn't help it. I was exhausted and stressed out. And an idiot. I wiped my hand across my shirt. "Um, I'm fine. I'm looking for Dr. Pullman's house." I leaned back to check the number posted above the door.

The cat sashayed inside like a saloon girl, pointing her ass right at me as if to say, "Who is superior now?"

Running Man squinted. "Uh, this is Dr. Pullman's house, but I'm afraid he's not in residence."

"What?"

Wait a second.

Seriously?

Did he have an accent?

Unfair!

And dimples? When he wasn't even smiling? An accent and dimples? That put him straight into Panty Melting territory. (Panty Melter: an exceedingly rare species of man blessed with so many desirable attributes he effortlessly gains access into a girl's panties.) *God, Sadie! Get ahold of yourself. Dody's life is at stake here.*

"Um, do you know when he'll be back? My aunt fell over a truck and I think she might need stitches."

His beautiful green eyes widened. "She fell over a truck? You mean, out of a truck?"

I shook my head. "No, over a truck. A toy truck. She tripped and hit a table."

He smiled now, visibly relaxing. "Oh. All right then. In that case, Dr. Pullman won't be back for a few months, but I'm here while he's gone. I could help your aunt."

A haze of irresponsible lust began seeping into my brain, pushing concern for Dody's life far from my mind. She wasn't hurt *that* badly anyway. Pheromones permeated my flushed skin, and I began sputtering information faster than an auctioneer. "Could you? Really? But we need a doctor because she won't go to the med center. It's her poker night and she wants to win her six dollars back from Anita Parker. But it's kind of a deep cut, and Jasper thinks she might need stitches. Dody is so stubborn, though, and now Jordan is upset because it was his truck. But really it was all my fault."

His smile froze. I sounded like an overzealous contestant on some practical-joke show. He must be expecting TV cameras to pop up at any moment.

His head tilted. "Did you say Dody is your aunt? Dody Baker?"

"Yes!" I nodded at his uncanny insight. "She's my aunt." I tapped my collarbone. "I'm her niece."

He nodded, "That's usually how it works."

Was he teasing me? Was that banter? I loved banter!

But this was not how we were supposed to meet. Even though I wanted absolutely nothing to do with him, I had orchestrated an elaborate fantasy meeting. I'd be lounging on the beach at sunset. Due to the fading light, I would look quite attractive. He'd stroll along, looking handsome and debonair with his strategically tousled hair. He'd say, "Why, hello there," and I'd respond with something witty and clever and subversively sexual. Then he'd laugh devilishly and we'd realize we were destined to be together.

It was not supposed to be like this, with me frazzled and covered in blood.

He tilted his head in the other direction. "Stan mentioned her. I'll come have a look."

"Stan?"

Who the hell was Stan?

"Dr. Pullman," he explained at my expression. "I'm his temporary replacement while he's on holiday, and he asked me to stay here to water the plants and such. He told me about your aunt, though."

"He did? Did he warn you she's a little nuts?" I blurted out. Damn it. Apparently I'd left my stupidity filter back at home, soaking in the pool of Dody's blood.

But Running Man chuckled, a velvety, enchanting sound, and said, "I believe the word he used was peculiar. Anyway, let me grab a couple things. Come on in."

He pushed open the door, stepping inside. I followed, like Dorothy entering Oz. The front door bumped against a decorative table in the entryway.

This was getting very strange. I mean, he was smokin' hot and all that, but I couldn't let some stranger poke and prod at my aunt just because he had really nice arms. Could I?

"Um, are you a doctor too?" I asked. "And you're here to water the plants?"

I looked out the still open door at the seriously dead geraniums in the porch pots. He followed my gaze and frowned.

"Hmm. Guess I forgot about those. You said you think she needs stitches?" He started rummaging around in a cardboard box. There were several stacked around the room as if someone was either moving in, or out.

"Yes, my cousin is sure she does."

I perused the decor, noting the Pullmans' expensive if somewhat geriatric tastes. Lots of pale hues that my kids could stain without even touching. I watched Running Man's back flex as he tore open another box. I swallowed a sudden rush of saliva, like Pavlov's horny dog. *What the hell was the matter with me?*

"Where did she cut herself?" The cat jumped up on the box beside him, and he pushed her away with his elbow. She landed on the floor with a thud and glared at me.

"In our living room."

His burst of laughter startled me. Caught up as I was in the grips of my own little hormone storm, it took me a minute to realize that wasn't the kind of *where* he meant.

"Oh! Oh, on her head. She fell and bumped her head."

Ding! Something chimed, and I jumped about a foot. "What was that?"

"Just the microwave. Dinner."

Microwaved dinner? For one? Where was Mrs. Running Man?

Tossing one last item into a nearby backpack, he reached out to take some keys off of a brass, kitten-shaped hook by the door. With my astute skills of observation—added to the fact that his hand was directly in front of my face—I noticed a distinct lack of wedding band. Interesting. But my heart sank as fast as it rose. Maybe he was gay. Shoot. He was probably gay. He had to be. His fingernails were trimmed and clean. His cuticles didn't go halfway to his knuckles. Yep, definitely gay. Oh, well. At least Fontaine would be happy.

We stepped back outside, and he pulled the door shut, sliding the keys into a pocket with his unadorned hand. I suddenly realized I didn't know his name.

I held out my equally unadorned hand. "By the way, I'm Sadie Turner."

"I'm Des."

"Des?" I think I might have squinted. Or possibly scrunched my whole face. Either way, I'm sure it wasn't pretty.

"Desmond. McKnight."

His name was Desmond? Oh, yeah. This guy was totally gay. But then he smiled, triggering maximum dimple wattage, and my belly did a flip that went straight south.

*   *   *

Dody's injury required several stitches, but Dr. McKnight, who had apparently been a boy scout as well, came fully prepared. His backpack held a virtual storeroom of medical supplies. He even had suckers for Paige and Jordan.

Paige, already smitten with this handsome newcomer, ate hers immediately while batting her thick, dark lashes. Jordan, on the other hand, was characteristically suspicious. No random interloper could buy his trust with one lousy piece of candy. His sucker still sat on the table, and every once in a while Jordan would flick it with his finger, just to prove how much he didn't care about it.

"It's a superficial laceration, Mrs. Baker, but head wounds tend to bleed like this. You needn't be too alarmed."

Dody reclined on the wicker love seat on the sunporch, her head resting on a bright yellow pillow. She had wrapped a lace shawl around her shoulders to cover all the brownish bloodstains on her jersey.

"I wasn't alarmed at all. It was these two." She waved a wrist at Jasper and me, her bangle bracelets jingling. "Sadie tends to be a little high-strung. She's a professional organizer, you know. Very fussy. But I suppose I did need some medical attention, and weren't we lucky to find you! Imagine what would've become of me if you hadn't been nearby."

She fluttered the plastic fan in her hand, a gift to her from Walter for their thirty-second wedding anniversary. Allegedly from the *Gone with the Wind* collection.

"I'm sure you would've been just fine, but without stitches you would've had quite a scar." He began putting things back in his bag.

"Oh, I've already got a scar. See?" She pointed at a tiny mark high on her cheek. "Walter gave me this one when his suspender popped off. He was doing a little striptease for me but—"

"Dody!" I gripped her shoulder.

Des smiled. "If you start to feel dizzy or nauseous or have a headache, you should let me know, or call your own doctor. You could have a mild concussion."

"I feel fine. And now that we've got you here, you simply must stay for supper. Sadie spent the whole day labeling the pantry, and Jasper's a chef. At Arno's, you know."

His face remained politely interested, but I sensed Dody had put on her scheming hat. She was starting to worry he might leave too soon.

"Sadie, get the good doctor some lemonade. He must be parched. You're staying at the Pullmans' house, you say? What does Joanna Pullman fertilize her azalea bushes with, do you suppose? They are lush with flowers every spring. Is your wife there too? Did you say you were married?"

Dr. McKnight peered up at me from his seat near Dody. "Did she suffer any loss of consciousness when she fell?"

I bit my lip and shook my head. "She's always like this."

Dody tapped his forearm with her fan. "So? What about your wife? Is she waiting for you?"

He blushed. "No one's waiting. It's just me at the Pullmans'."

"Oh, dear." Her voice was drenched in sympathy, as if he'd just announced his entire family had been recently wiped out by cholera. Or were Republicans. "Then you must stay. It's all settled, Doctor."

"I wouldn't want to impose. And please, call me Des."

"Dody, I'm sure he's busy," I said. I knew he had some preservative-laden, freeze-dried food nuked warm back at his house. And he knew that I knew. I looked over at Jasper, hoping for help, but he shrugged with indifference.

Dody flipped open her fan and fluttered it with practiced skill. "Heavens to Betsy, that's just silly. It's no imposition at all after you pulled me from the jaws of death, Des, dear."

He smiled. "I am kind of hungry."

"Excellent!" She snapped the fan shut. "Jasper, make us some dinner."

The front door banged open, and seconds later Fontaine burst onto the sunporch in his typical mad dash. Catching sight of Running Man, he stopped short, his mouth popping open like that of a blow-up doll. Then he gasped.

"Holy Mother of God! What did I miss?"

CHAPTER 5

STANDING AT THE KITCHEN ISLAND, I tried hard not to think about the phallic implications of the big, thick carrot I was peeling. I strained to hear Dody and Des's conversation over the standard dinner-making ruckus. The two of them sat across from me, on the other side of the island.

"Des. Is that short for anything? Like Desi?" Dody asked.

"It's short for Desmond, but only my grandmother is allowed to call me that. Please, just call me Des."

"I knew a Desmond once. Desmond Arnaz. I think he used to do our taxes." She picked up a handful of pistachios from a bowl in front of her.

"You're thinking of Desi Arnaz, Mom," Fontaine said from his spot next to me. He wasn't really helping with dinner. He just liked the view. Jasper was at the counter behind us whisking up some kind of sauce, and the kids were coloring at the dining table.

"Desi Arnaz did our taxes? Oh, wait, that was Lucy's husband," Dody said. "She didn't really have red hair, you know. But yours has a little red, Des."

"Does it?" He touched it absently, as if red had a texture.

His hair wasn't red. It was brown. Thick and chocolaty brown. And kind of wavy. I nicked myself with the peeler.

"Desi Arnaz was Cuban, you know. Are you Cuban?" Dody batted her lashes in much the same fashion as Paige had, only on my aunt it looked like she had something in her eye.

"Um, no."

"I thought you said you were." She popped a pistachio into her mouth and cracked the shell with her teeth. Then she spit the shell back into the bowl.

I watched his eyebrows rise and fall. "I don't think I said that."

To the uninitiated, a conversation with Dody was very much like playing whack-a-mole. You just never knew what would pop up next.

"What are you then?" She pushed the bowl of nuts toward him. He declined.

"Scottish. I was born in Glasgow, but we moved to the States when I was seventeen."

"Ah, that explains the red."

"And that delicious accent," Fontaine added.

I looked at Des and smiled weakly.

He winked, and I nicked my finger again.

Dody and Des continued talking, but Fontaine turned his back and closed his eyes.

"What are you doing?" I whispered.

"If I listen to his voice, he sounds just like Gerard Butler," Fontaine whispered back.

"Who's Gerard Butler?"

Fontaine's eyes popped open. "Who's Gerard Butler? I thought every straight woman had a thing for Gerard Butler."

"I don't know who that is. Now would you be quiet? I can't hear them."

Fontaine made a girly sound in his throat.

"Don't make me stab you with this peeler," I hissed under my breath.

Paige appeared behind us. "Mommy, may I have a carrot? I'm dying I'm so hungry."

Fontaine handed her a carrot and nudged her back toward the table. "Go sit over there, Paige. Mommy's got a knife and she's itching to use it."

"Shush. I'm trying to listen."

I needed to hear what unappetizing morsels Dody was pulling from her basketful of crazy to share with our guest, not that it really mattered. Even if he wasn't gay, which I had yet to rule out, he was too good-looking and too smooth and undoubtedly too certain of his lady-killing prowess for me to have any interest. I'd already shopped at that store. Besides, I couldn't imagine what lack of judgment, or element of starvation, had made him agree to eat with us.

Whatever. He'd be gone soon, taking his big, sexy hands and his thick forearms, and that damn delicious accent. And once he was out of here, I could curl up with my bottle of wine and watch Stephen Colbert and put this day behind me.

"Glasgow? Isn't that in Sweden?" Dody was asking.

He shook his head. "Scotland."

"Oh, yes, Scotland. Why, you must know Sean Connery then? He's Scottish. Or is he German?"

Des bit back a smile. "He is Scottish, but no, I never had the pleasure."

"Really? That's surprising. Sweden is such a small country."

"Scotland."

"What? Oh, yes. Scotland. Why did you move from there, dear? Was it because of the potatoes?" She patted his hand sympathetically.

"The potatoes?"

"Potato famine was in Ireland, Mom," Jasper said, banging the oven door shut.

"In the 1840s," I added, wanting to show off a little of my vast wealth of useless, esoteric facts. Things like what year the first woman graduated from medical school, how yak milk is collected to make yak cheese (you don't want to know), and the definition of words like *reticule* and *pusillanimous*.

"My dad was in the military," Des said, beginning to go with the flow of Dody's random questioning.

"Really? A soldier?"

"Corps of engineers."

"Fascinating!" Dody turned to Fontaine, who was once again facing them. "Fontaine, when were we invaded by Scotland?"

Des laughed. "It wasn't much of an invasion, Mrs. Baker. It was just our family. My dad left the service and took a job over here."

"Oh, thank goodness. I thought I'd missed something. My mind is a steel trap when it comes to history." Actually her mind was more like a booby trap.

"So he worked on a train?" She spit out another nutshell.

"A train?"

"Yes, you said he was an engineer."

"That's a conductor, Mom," Jasper corrected automatically. He dropped a few spices into a pot of something that already smelled heavenly.

"Oh, yes. So did he drive trains?" Dody nodded at her own question.

"No, Mrs. Baker," Des said. "He designed bridges."

"For trains?"

He smiled. "No, mostly for cars."

"You should call me Dody. When was that?"

"Pardon me?"

"How long have you lived in the States?"

He shook his head. "Oh, um, let's see…about twenty, um…nineteen years."

I tried to tabulate his age in my head. Seventeen plus nineteen is…twenty…wait, nine plus seven is…fifteen, then carry the one is twenty, no…

The strain of computation must have shown on my face.

"Thirty-six, you moron," Fontaine whispered.

"And have you always lived in Michigan?" Dody asked.

Des shook his head. "No, we lived all over the place at first. But we settled in Illinois about twelve years ago. My mum and sisters still live near Chicago. That's where I was before I came here."

"And what brought you to Bell Harbor, then? Your job?"

Dody's questioning was so persistent I thought she might pull out a little clipboard and start jotting notes. But our guest seemed unfazed. Maybe his time in the emergency room had taught him how to deal with loony little old ladies.

"Yes, but I'm only here for a few months, then I'm back to Chicago or somewhere else," he answered.

"Why is that?"

"Right now I'm doing something called locum tenens. It's like temp work for physicians."

"How fascinating. And your father? Is he in Chicago?"

Des shook his head. "No, he died when I was in med school."

"Oh, dear. That's so sad." She nodded knowingly and patted his hand again. "I suppose he was an alcoholic?"

"Dody!" I gasped.

She looked at me with indignation. "What? You know what they say about the Scots!"

Des laughed, causing an unfamiliar sensation to swirl around my insides. That was just the kind of comment that would make Richard angry. But this guy seemed to think she was funny.

"I'm sure my father drank more than his share, but technically it was the tobacco that got him."

"I'm sorry, Dr. McKnight," I said, as much for his loss as for my aunt's lack of social graces.

"That's OK. And please, call me Des." Then he winked at me again.

Damn it. If he didn't stop doing that, I was going to peel all the skin right off my hand.

◦   ◦   ◦

Dinner proceeded without incident, and the dreamy Dr. Des McKnight appeared to take it all in stride. He rolled along with our story fragments and Dody's gross mispronunciations. The conversation blended into a sort of anecdotal jambalaya, with bits of our history woven in with pop culture trivia. Ours was the kind of dinner conversation one might expect to find in an English-as-a-second-language course or in the babble of a Pentecostal church.

During the meal, Des praised Jasper's cooking and laughed at Fontaine's jokes. He answered each of Dody's progressively impertinent questions, such as what size pants did he wear (thirty-four), had he ever been to a nude beach (no, but it sounded fun), and had he ever performed breast implant surgery (yes, during residency). He hardly even batted an eye when she asked, "And do you have any children?"

"No, I don't."

"Not even any bastards?" she persisted.

He just shrugged and took a bite of asparagus. "Nope. None that I know of."

He also talked to me. Not at me, the way Richard used to. Des actually asked me questions and then let me answer without telling me why my answer was wrong.

"Sadie, did you say you're just visiting Bell Harbor too?"

I nodded, hoping there wasn't chicken wedged between my front teeth. "Yes, for the summer. But we'll go back to Glenville in the fall when the kids start school."

"I can't wait for school," Paige said, waving around a whole chicken breast on her fork.

"What grade will you be in?" Des asked her.

She sat up straighter. "First grade. I want Mrs. Lewis for my teacher."

"Is she the nicest?"

Paige nodded and took a bite before adding, "And the prettiest and smartest."

Des laughed. "Those are all very important. You know, my mum was a teacher, and now so is one of my sisters, which is kind of funny to me because my sister used to be a real troublemaker."

Paige's eyes went round, and even Jordan slowed his chewing to listen.

"Why? What did she do?" Paige's voice was solemn.

Des leaned toward her. "When we were little, she'd sneak up behind me, just before we left for school, and spray me with her perfume."

He sat back in his chair and looked to the rest of us. "She'd do it at the very last second, so I wouldn't have time to change my clothes. So I'd spend the entire day smelling like a little girl." His cheeks went pink. "And let me tell you, my pals back then teased me like you wouldn't believe."

He turned to me. "My nickname all through primary school was Posey-boy."

I pressed a hand to my mouth, not sure if we were supposed to laugh. It was hard to imagine him smelling like my daughter's Tinker Bell toiletries. Because I'd gotten close enough to him to know he smelled delicious, like cinnamon and moonlight. And not very gay at all.

"Did you get even with her?" Jasper asked.

Revenge lust ran deep in our family.

Des's smile broadened. "You bet I did. One night I snuck into her room when she was asleep and cut off big chunks of her hair, right in the front. The next day she looked ridiculous. It was awesome!"

Now everybody laughed. A zing and a pop burst somewhere deep in my chest.

"It sort of backfired, though," he added. He turned back to my kids. "My mum was so furious she took me straight to the barber and he shaved me bald. I was the only twelve-year-old in town with a shiny head. It was not a good look for me."

∗　∗　∗

After dinner, Des helped clear the table while talking with Jasper about properly matching wine to the entrée. Dody, having decided this new stranger in town trumped a night playing poker with her friends, lounged on a cushioned chaise like Cleopatra.

Paige sat next to her, playing with a doll. "This is how you did it, Aunt Dody," she said, providing a dramatic reenactment of the fall. "You went, step, step, step, wahhhhhhh!"

Then Paige whacked the Barbie's head against the arm of Dody's chair.

"Oh, that's lovely, dear."

"Can I see your snitches again?"

"Stitches, Paige. And Dody needs to keep her bandage on. Stop pestering her," I said.

Des looked over from the kitchen. "I'll stop back tomorrow to change the bandage, Paige. Then you can see the snitches."

Fontaine gave me a discreet thumbs-up. I turned away. What difference did it make if Dr. Delicious came back? He was only coming to check on Dody. It didn't have anything to do with me. And I didn't care anyway. I wasn't interested. Nonetheless, the elastic in my underpants suddenly got very itchy.

CHAPTER 6

I WOKE UP THE NEXT morning filled with a buoyancy I hadn't felt in years. The sun was shining, the birds were singing, and a handsome man who was in no way related to me had stayed for dinner. Oh, I knew it didn't *mean* anything. But the flirting was fun and having him there had been exciting, like watching a storm roll in from over the lake and wondering where the lightning might strike.

I zipped through my morning grooming routine so I could call Penny. She'd get a kick out of this.

"Hello?" She sounded grumpy. I must have woken her up.

"Hi. Go pee and call me back."

As a sign of respect, we had agreed to never use the toilet while talking to each other on the phone. Well, it was partly out of respect and partly because of the time Penny dropped her brand new cell phone in the toilet.

"I already peed. And I'm not pregnant." She sighed.

"Oh, Penn. I'm sorry. Sometimes it takes a while."

"Yeah, I know. I just thought it would be fun if it happened right away. It's been three months already. We tried for a couple months before I even told you."

"It'll happen. Didn't Jeff tell you he has bionic sperm?"

Penny sighed again. "No, he says he's got a bionic penis."

"Oh. That's different."

"Yeah. If only it were true. Anyway, what's up with you? How's life in Dody's world?" Penny never wallowed in self-pity for long. That was my department.

"Guess who ate dinner with us last night?" I fell back onto the bed and put my feet up on the wall like I used to do as a teenager.

"I don't know. Richard?"

"Ugh! God, no. Why would you even think that?"

I heard her huff. "I'm still in a bad mood. Just tell me."

This should cheer her up. "Running Man!"

"The good-looking guy who runs on the beach every day?"

"That's the one." I provided her with my abbreviated version of last night's events, including the fact that he had an adorable cowlick right in the front.

"He's staying at the Pullmans'?" she asked.

"Yes, while they're on vacation. He said they're traveling around Europe for two months and then going to visit their daughter in Arizona. Des is Dr. Pullman's temporary replacement at the hospital."

"What happens when they come back?"

I readjusted the pillows behind my head. "I don't know. I guess he goes back to Chicago. Does it matter?"

"Hmm."

That was not an ordinary, run-of-the-mill *hmm*. It was fraught with meaning.

I sat up on the bed. "What, hmm?"

"He sounds like a perfect transitional man. You know, get a little wet in the dating pool, as it were."

I fell back on the covers. "Great, you sound like Dody and Fontaine. Just because I think he's cute, don't go making something out of it."

"Hey, I'm not the one who called at the butt crack of dawn to chat about him," she teased.

"Hardly the butt crack of dawn, you lazy ass. It's nine o'clock. Once you have that baby you'll be getting up before the sun. Speaking of that, I should see if my kids are poking forks into the toaster. And I'm determined to get them in the lake today. They're still too chicken to swim. I'll call you later, OK?"

"OK, I'll be around. Probably doing yoga and thinking fertile thoughts. Oh, and before I forget, I happened to be over by your place the other day and your grass looks terrible. It's turning brown."

"It is? It looked fine to me last week. I wonder if the sprinkler system is messed up again. Can you check on that?"

"I can try, but you guys have that hi-tech system. I'd have an easier time defusing a bomb. Can't you ask Richard?"

My stomach churned. "If I do, he's going to tell me I'm the one who messed it up, whether I did or not. I hate to give him the ammunition."

It was so easy now, being annoyed with Richard even when he wasn't there. It hadn't always been that way. I fell in love with him the day we met, but I'd been slowly trying to claw my way out of that hole ever since. Still, maybe he'd surprise me and be gracious and helpful.

Yeah, and maybe I was a D cup. I looked down at my barely Bs and sighed. Nope. Some things would never change.

⚜ ⚜ ⚜

"Mommy, it's too cold!" Paige screeched. "The waves are ginormous."

"Stop it. They're, like, ankle deep. Come on! Just get your feet wet. Mommy is right here."

We'd been down at the lake for an hour, and my brave little soldiers still refused to dip so much as a pinky toe into Lake Michigan.

Fontaine sat on a lounge chair while wearing one of Dody's sun hats. The effect was quite spectacular.

"The water is too big, Mommy!" Jordan shouted from his safe spot behind Fontaine's back. "I don't like it."

"Seriously, you guys! If you're not going to play in the water, we may as well go back to Glenville."

Paige gasped. "You can't take us back yet, Mommy! Aunt Dody promised to teach me how to bejewel!"

"I'm not going home," Jordan pouted. "And I'm not swimming either. I'll swim when I'm big as Jasper."

This battle was lost. It was too beautiful a day to argue with them. "Fine, fine, fine. You guys win. But sooner or later you're going to have to get in this lake."

I walked from the shore and slumped down in the sand next to Fontaine. Paige gave Jordan a fist bump of victory before they took off for drier ground.

Fontaine ruffled my hair. "You wouldn't swim when you were little either. Don't you remember?"

"Yes, that's why I'm so anxious to get them in the water, so they'll realize there's nothing to be afraid of."

That was a lie, actually. I knew there were tons of things to be afraid of in that lake. Slimy, sinister creatures lurking just beneath the surface, waiting to grab your ankle and pull you under. Like gargantuan electric eels or water-logged corpses from the *Edmund Fitzgerald*. OK, so that sank in Lake Erie, but still…

Fontaine adjusted his Dolce & Gabbana sunglasses. "Right. So anyway, I talked to my boss, Kyle, and he agrees this organizing thing could be a massive hit with our clientele. He wants to meet you."

I sat up straight.

"Are you crazy? I'm not ready for that. I'm not sure I want to do it at all. I'm here on vacation, remember?"

"Oh, relax, spazmotron. Just talk to him and hear what he has to say. He's a dreamboat to work with and you'll love him." He brushed sand from one foot with the other.

"I'm sure he's marvelous if he can stand working with you, but that's still not the point. I don't know what I'm doing. I haven't had any special training. I mean, cleaning Dody's closets is one thing, but organizing for somebody else would be too scary." I shook my head.

"Too scary?" He pulled those same sunglasses down his nose and peered at me over the rim. "Too scary, like swimming in a lake just because you can't see the bottom? Honestly, woman, have some cojones. Take a risk once in a while."

A hot wind swirled around us, stirring up sand and stinging me like Fontaine's words.

"That's not fair. I take risks. Didn't I let you talk me into this new haircut? And color? Am I not wearing blue fingernail polish? If that's not a risk, I don't know what is."

Fontaine pushed the sunglasses back up. "Look, you finally divorced the Big Dick. And that is a major step in the right direction. But what have you done to get your life rolling again? And you know I'm not talking about nail polish."

I didn't like this conversation. It was hard enough to ignore Fontaine's suggestions when he was being silly, but when he was being earnest, it was twice as bad. Once he sank his teeth into something, he was relentless. "It's only been a few weeks, you know."

"Liar. It's been over a year since you broke up with Richard. What are you waiting for?"

I kicked sand over his feet, pretending it was an accident. I wanted to defend myself and say I'd been doing all kinds of bold and risky stuff, but I couldn't think of one thing. After catching Richard with that redhead, my life had been occupied with divorce proceedings and trying to get through each day without doing permanent psychological damage to my children. I'd had a garage sale, bought new bed linens, burned the old ones, and changed all my lamps over to energy-saving bulbs. Other than that, I was pretty much on autopilot.

"It's not that easy, Fontaine," I whispered.

He put his arm around me. "I know, sugarplum. But it's time. And organizing is something you're really good at. So you should make the most of it. Plus it's something you can do once you're back in Glenville. Just think about it. I told Kyle we'd have lunch with him tomorrow."

I jumped up, scattering sand everywhere. "Fontaine! Why did you do that? I'm not ready."

"Fake it till you make it, baby girl. Just trust me on this." He stood up and patted my shoulder. "You'll be fabulous. I'll take the kids up to the house now, and you think about it."

He gestured to the kids, and they skipped after him up the steps, leaving me to stare out over the water and ponder.

I bit my lip. It was ridiculous, me trying to be a professional anything. Sure, I was great at figuring out which cupboard should hold baking supplies and which should hold the coffee cups. And maybe Dody's efficient new pantry did sparkle with crisp, color-coded labels. But that didn't mean I was some kind of expert.

Still, what was the worst thing that could go wrong? Somebody wouldn't like the font I used for their labels? Or they'd think alphabetized spice racks were overkill?

Maybe Fontaine was right. I was good at putting things in order. Maybe, just maybe, it was time to start doing that with my own life. Maybe I could do this. Hadn't I already organized kitchens and closets for my friends back home? I could do the same for complete strangers, right?

I sat back down in the sand and let my mind wander over the wonderful possibilities. And there were loads of them. Then I mentally categorized those possibilities. Because that's what I do. As I soaked up the sun, I came up with a plan. Sure, it might be a little risky. But hey, I was a gal wearing blue nail polish. I could take on anything.

*   *   *

By late afternoon, my euphoria, like a tan heading into September, was patchy and fading fast. Back at the house, the brief blip of enthusiasm I'd felt over Fontaine's idea had turned to pure dread. I didn't know the first thing about being professional at anything. And the flirty joy Des had stirred up in me at dinner last night was as dead as a fish rotting on the sand. It stank like that too.

The good doctor had been charming, yes. But that had nothing to do with me. He was a nice guy doing a neighborly house call for a crazy old lady, and that's all there was to that. He must have swarms of women buzzing around. I was nothing more than another drone in his ear. Not that I cared, because I wasn't interested in a relationship. And Penny's stupid notion of a transitional man? What was that all about?

Anyway, he probably had a girlfriend. No doubt some Argentinean supermodel currently on a *Sports Illustrated* photo shoot. After he'd left our house last night, they'd probably had scandalously wicked phone sex while I, on the other hand, had put on my rattiest pajamas and watched *Animal Planet* with Fontaine.

What the hell was I thinking, getting all fluttery and jittery over some sweet-talking, muscle-bound iron man? Had Richard taught me nothing?

"What is your problem?" Jasper snapped as I slammed the dishwasher door.

"Nothing!"

Being unmarried, Jasper naively thought I meant it.

"Then be careful. You'll break the dishes."

"Mommy, did Daddy call today?" Paige wandered into the kitchen. Jordan was sitting at the island, eating ice cream from a dog bowl, because Dody thought serving food in a dog bowl was the funniest thing in the world. I could only pray she had washed it first.

"No, baby, he hasn't. I'm sure he'll call soon." I looked at my watch. Classic Richard. He'd promised to call at lunch, but it was much closer to dinner.

When Dody's phone rang fifteen minutes later, I let Paige answer.

She chatted on the line for a minute, so I knew it must be him. Better late than never, I guess. Then she handed the phone to me. "He wants to talk to you."

Ugh! Talking to the sperm-donor-formerly-known-as-my-husband was just the garlic frosting I needed on this total piece of shit day.

"What do you want, Richard?" I grumbled into the phone.

A moment of silence ensued.

"Richard?" I barked, my voice unpleasantly loud.

"Uh, no, it's Des."

My throat went dry, like a wooly mitten was stuck inside. Shit. Shit.

"Sorry. I thought you were somebody else," I choked out.

His laugh was shallow. "Yeah, I get that a lot. Women wishing I was somebody else."

My own chuckle sounded equally false. My temples suddenly throbbed as if an alien were scratching his way out. I bit my lip and pressed my hand to my head.

"I wondered how Dody was feeling," he added after another awkward pause. "I can stop over if you want me to."

Dody was fine. She'd beaten me at five games of back-gammon that afternoon and only skipped her tai chi class because Harry took her for a ride on his Harley.

I didn't want Des coming over. Seeing him again would just prolong the torment for me. I wanted to go back to watching him anonymously on the beach and not knowing his name or that he had a fluffy gray cat and no wife.

"No, don't bother. Thanks, but Dody's fine."

"I'm not fine!" Dody shouted, trotting in from the sunporch. "Is that Des? Tell him it hurts! Tell him I'm dizzy. I'm seeing spots. Give me the phone, Sadie! Give me that phone." She tried to wrestle it from my hand.

I covered the receiver and twisted away from her. "God, Dody! Be quiet. Don't be silly."

"It's really no bother," I heard Des saying on the line. "I'm on my way home anyway."

Dody snatched the phone. She was certainly agile and strong for somebody needing a doctor.

"Please do stop by, Des, dear. I'd feel so much better if you did. I've been feeling the teensiest bit light-headed this evening."

I rolled my eyes. She was using her breathy, Elizabeth Taylor voice. And she was light-headed because Fontaine had given her a quadruple martini. What a faker. The only reason she wanted him over here was to try and get me laid.

Oh, fine then. Let the Patron Saint of Desperate Housewives bestow upon us the blessings of his company. I still wasn't on the market. I didn't need a transitional man. I didn't need any man. I was fine.

I stomped upstairs and threw myself on the bed, wondering if every divorced woman felt this way or if I was just that special. I never should have let myself get worked up over him in the first place. Or this job business. It was all too ridiculous.

Minutes later, Fontaine's well-coiffed head appeared around the door frame.

"What the hell are you doing? The McKnight in Shining Armor is on his way."

"So?"

"So, primp. Do some fluffing and some poufing. Time's a-wasting." He grabbed me by the ankle to pull me from the bed.

I tried to kick him with my other leg. "Fontaine, he's coming to see Dody, not me. I'm not interested. And even if I was, which again, I'm not, I refuse to make a fool of myself."

He dropped my foot. "Are you really that dense? Did you not catch him checking you out last night?"

I sat up. "He was not checking me out."

"He was! Even though you looked like hell. So let's glam you up a little and get this party started." He flung open the closet door and began rummaging.

Ego tapped me on the shoulder. Fontaine's compliment was taking effect.

"Did he really check me out, or are you just saying that?"

Fontaine avoided eye contact. "Baby girl, would I lie to you?"

"Yes."

"That's true. I would. But I'm not lying to you now, so get your butt in that bathroom and put on some mascara already!"

By the time Dr. McRunning Man arrived, I had brushed, flossed, moisturized, blotted, and put on a sundress. Fontaine peeked out the bathroom window when we heard a car in the driveway.

"BMW convertible," he said.

Of course. What better way to showcase his Argentinean supermodel? I looked in the mirror, hoping to see a miraculous transformation, but I was as average as ever.

"I love your new 'do," Fontaine said, fluffing my hair. "I was right about going with the darker brown. You should never argue with me again."

"Brown hair and brown eyes. It's kind of boring, isn't it?" I asked.

"No, it makes you exotic and mysterious."

I snorted with laughter at my own expense. I was about as exotic as vanilla yogurt.

"Well, the snorting isn't very sexy. You might want to work on that." Fontaine left the bathroom and trotted downstairs to open the door. I hesitated another minute. I didn't want us all pouncing on Des the moment he arrived. I should let him get in and settled so I could make an entrance. Even though I cared nothing about him. This was just for practice.

I heard the door open and shut, and voices wafted up the stairs. Oh, God. The accent was killing me.

"Hello, Fontaine. Mrs. Baker. How are you feeling today?"

"Fine, now that you're here. I'm sure I asked you to call me Dody."

"Yes, ma'am," he answered.

I moved to the top of the stairs, counting to one hundred, and then I strolled down like I just happened to be passing through the family room on my way to somewhere intriguing.

I caught sight of Dody swooning on the chaise again, wearing a red-and-gold silk robe. It was gift from Uncle

Walter for their sixteenth wedding anniversary, allegedly purchased at the Great Wall of China gift shop.

Des was sitting by her side, her wrist in his hand. He looked up, and my breath caught. Was that a hint of positive appraisal in his expression?

I sucked in my stomach, just in case, and smiled. "Oh, hello."

Fontaine shook his head and turned his back, pretending to cough.

"Hi, Sadie. You look nice," Des said.

Dody nearly clapped her hands with glee.

"Oh, thanks," I said again, plucking at the top of my sundress in the universal gesture of "you mean this old thing?"

Jordan ran over, wrapping arms tightly around my waist. "Why are you so pretty, Mommy?"

I smoothed his hair and whispered, "It's just a sundress, honey. Mommy wears them all the time."

"No, you don't." Jordan frowned.

"Would you like some candy, J-man?" Fontaine asked, nipping this conversation in the bud. Thank you, Fontaine.

Des turned back to Dody. "Shall we have a look?" He took off the bandage, and Paige leaned in close against his arm, resting her hand on his shoulder.

"Wow, those snitches are weird," she said.

He smiled. "You think so?"

Paige nodded. "Definitely. Like Frankenstein, only not so green."

"Paige, back up. Give him some room." I tugged on the back of her shirt.

"She's all right," he said. "Paige, hand me that white square thing."

She reached into his backpack and pulled out some gauze.

We watched while he applied some ointment and a fresh bandage.

"Des?" Paige whispered, leaning toward his neck.

"What?"

"I like your perfume."

His head went up for a second then dropped to his chest. I remembered the story of his sister spraying him with her flowery perfume. "It's cologne, Paige," I corrected. "When a boy wears it, it's called cologne."

Dody piped in, "I can't smell anything. Lean over here, dear. Give me a whiff."

"Oh my God, Dody!" I gasped. "You can't ask to smell somebody. It's rude!"

Des's face flushed.

"No, it isn't. It's rude to *say* they smell. Not to *ask* to smell them. Besides, I know he smells good. You told me so last night."

Des's head lifted, his smile instant as he looked at me. Now it was my turn to blush.

*   *   *

"He only stayed about twenty minutes," I told Penny over the phone, taking a sip of merlot. I needed to decompress and debrief over the recent visit from the man I cared nothing about. From my vantage point on the deck I could keep a judicious eye on my kids, who were playing on the beach. Not that I worried they'd go in the water. Still no chance of that.

"It's Saturday. Do you think he had a date?" she asked.

"He said he had work to do. Sounds suspicious to me."

"Everything sounds suspicious to you."

"With good reason. If he's not at the hospital, what could he be doing?"

Her chuckle was loud in my ear. "Maybe he's a vampire. Or a male escort."

"Or both," I mused. "Paige told him she liked his perfume. And Dody asked if he was wearing shoulder pads."

Dody had yet to give up on the eighties shoulder pad craze, certain it was making a comeback. She heard somewhere, probably during the eighties, that shoulder pads made your hips look slimmer. So she'd tuck in three or four at a time inside her blouse, only she wouldn't pin them, so inevitably they'd fall down, creating migratory lumps all over her torso. Eventually they'd fall out of her sleeves, leaving a trail like Hansel and Gretel.

"I assume he wasn't wearing shoulder pads," Penny said.

"No," I sighed. "The shoulders were all his own."

"Did you invite him for dinner?"

"No, because Jasper wasn't home and I've forgotten how to cook. Besides, it would've seemed desperate. Anyway, it's not like I wanted him to stay." I drained my glass in a final gulp.

"Uh-huh."

"You know what's kind of weird, though?"

"Richard's inordinately huge nostrils?"

"Besides that." (They weren't *that* huge, by the way.) "Jordan is starting to trust him. You know how shy and clingy he's been since Richard left. But after Des changed Dody's bandage, Jordan started showing him his trucks."

"Weird," Penny agreed. "Maybe it's like how dogs can sense a dog person."

"You think my kids are like dogs?"

"No. Well, a little. But I mean, maybe he likes kids and they can sense that. He's an ER doctor, right? He's probably had lots of practice putting kids at ease."

Disappointment flicked me in the forehead for not thinking of that on my own. Any connection he had with my kids wasn't some grand sign from the universe. Once again, it was just his good bedside manner.

CHAPTER 7

"KYLE, THIS IS SADIE. SADIE, this is Kyle." Fontaine made introductions as we gathered for lunch at an artsy little bistro on Marigold Lane. Bell Harbor was locked in a time warp, but trendy pockets of style could be found amid the tourist traps and antique shops.

Kyle's thick blond hair was short, and his dark tan set off eyes so brilliantly blue it was impossible to look away. We shook hands, and I expected little sparks to go off he was so supercharged with sexy.

"Sadie, it's great to meet you. Fontaine has told me so much about you."

"Only the good stuff," Fontaine joked.

"There's only good stuff to tell," I assured him.

"Please, sit down." He pulled out my chair.

What a gentleman! I tried to keep my thoughts on business, while silently reprimanding Fontaine. He should have warned me his boss was smokin'! Then it hit me. Maybe that was the whole point. Maybe this whole *professional organizing* thing had been a grand scheme to introduce us! I felt a flush of annoyance. How dare Fontaine manipulate me that way? And yet, this guy was yummy with a capital *yuh*.

I wasn't interested in anything romantic, but he was so pretty to look at I could hardly stay mad at Fontaine.

The waitress came, and the men ordered merlot. I ordered a cosmopolitan, hoping to seem, well...cosmopolitan. Plus I didn't want my teeth to turn purple.

"Tell me about yourself, Sadie." Kyle leaned forward and touched my arm. I was pinned beneath his piercing gaze and felt a flood of primordial need. I had never been so instantly attracted to anyone in my life. Not even Richard. Kyle was dazzling. Suddenly Penny's advice to land myself a transitional man bumped up against my sense of restraint. This guy might be Bachelor Number One.

While we waited for drinks, Kyle asked me assorted questions, only half of which pertained to organizing. He was obviously flirting. He'd felt the instant connection too. I felt tingly right to my toes.

He leaned forward as we looked at the menus.

"The lobster ravioli here is to die for."

He was so close, his breath tickled my neck. His crisp, button-down shirt gapped, and I caught sight of a small tattoo on his chest. In that instant, disregarding all sense of reason, I added *Screw a Hot Guy with a Tattoo* to my Bucket List.

Throughout lunch, I did my best to dazzle him with wit and charm. Whenever Fontaine pinched me under the table, I'd dial down the flirtation a little. Along with favorite movies and dream places to travel, we talked about organizing and how Kyle thought my talents might benefit his design firm.

"We'll need to give this a trial run, of course. But I have a project in mind," Kyle said. "Some great friends of mine have recently moved in together. They don't need decorating, but they definitely need help blending their stuff." He turned to Fontaine. "You know Owen and Patrick, don't you?"

Fontaine nodded, quirking one dark brow. "Patrick who you used to live with?"

Kyle laughed. "Yes, but that was in college. He's got ten times more stuff now. When we shared an apartment, we had one twin bed and one blanket."

I laughed with them. "That must have been awkward. Did you take turns sleeping in the bed or what?"

Fontaine burst out laughing and choked on his water.

Kyle's smile went supernova bright. He caressed my forearm again. "Take turns? You're hilarious, Sadie. Fontaine was right."

Why was that funny? I didn't get the joke.

And then I did.

Oh. My. God. *This* guy was gay. I had just spent two hours of my life, not to mention risking a potential job offer, flirting outrageously with a gay man. No wonder Fontaine kept making faces at me. I was such a dolt. How had I missed it? All those innuendos weren't for me. He was just being colorful.

I downed my cosmo in three fast gulps and tried to pretend I'd known all along. If Kyle noticed a change in my attitude, he didn't let on. The rest of lunch passed in a blur, and at the end he promised to introduce me to his old lover and his old lover's new lover.

So I didn't get the guy, but at least I got my first paid organizing job.

*   *   *

"Now let me get this straight," Jasper asked as we sat on the beach. "You were hitting on Fontaine's gay boss while he interviewed you for a job?"

I nodded, and Jasper fell back into the sand, laughing uproariously. "You idiot," he sputtered.

I wanted to defend myself, but could hardly blame Jasper. Fontaine's retelling of the lunch fiasco had painted me in the worst possible way. Accurate, but unflattering nonetheless.

"Mommy, look, it's flying," Jordan called to me, pointing at his kite whipping around in the sky.

"Good job, baby. Hold on tight to the string," I shouted back.

Paige had given up on her kite and played with dolls in the sand. Still no swimming.

I noticed someone, someone who looked very much like Des, jogging down the beach. Didn't that guy ever just walk? I ignored the quiver in my nethers. After what happened at lunch yesterday, I was off men again, for sure. And this time I meant it.

Jasper looked over. "Is that Des?"

"I can't tell." But I could.

Jasper waved. Des waved back and then stopped to talk to Jordan, who promptly handed over his kite string.

"Let's hear about this girlfriend of yours, Jas. How come I haven't met her yet?" I said.

"She's been traveling for work. But you'll meet her as soon as she gets back. Man, I can't wait until she's home. This is the longest we've ever been apart." Jasper hung his head down.

"How long have you been dating?"

"A year this August." He twisted a beach towel in his hands and glanced over at Des and the kids. He turned back to me. "Can I tell you a secret? But you have to promise not to tell anybody."

I leaned close. "I won't tell anyone."

"I'm going to ask Beth to marry me."

The joy I should have felt at such an announcement failed to materialize. They were too young! Too naive! Too stupid to know how love wouldn't last. I forced a smile to my lips.

"That's great, Jas. Really. But are you sure? I mean, what about buying a restaurant?"

He tipped his head and frowned. "What's one thing got to do with another?"

"Nothing, I guess. It's just that weddings are expensive. And rings, and houses. Where will you live?"

He leaned away. "Geez, Sadie. I thought you'd be happy for me."

"I am, really. Don't misunderstand me. I'm sure she's great and all that, but marriage is hard work."

"Not if you find the right person instead of some cheating schmuck. You think because it didn't work for you, it won't work for me?" He twisted the towel harder.

I've never kicked a puppy, but I imagine this must be how a puppy kicker felt. Try as I might, I could not conjure up a memory of when Richard and I were in the hazy flush of newly wedded bliss. It must have been delicious once, before we got to the gristle and the greasy aftermath.

"I'm sorry, Jasper. I didn't mean that like it sounded. Of course I'm happy for you."

"Yeah, well. Thanks. Anyway, I'm late for work." He jumped up, brushing off the ever-present beach sand. He sprinted to the deck steps without another word.

Dody liked to say "You can't un-rip paper." If I could, I'd take back the last five minutes. I didn't mean to make Jasper feel bad, but marriage was not unicorns and rainbows. He needed to know that.

The sun was high in the blue sky. Heat rose from the sand in shimmery waves and made the flush of my regret warmer still. Even the wind didn't cool things down.

I watched as Des showed Jordan tricks with the kite. It strained against the string, twisting and spinning. I felt like that kite. Hanging on by a slender thread, with no certainty or control over which direction life would turn me next.

Jordan squealed, excited over Des's kite prowess. Paige had joined them too, hopping on the sand and trying to mimic the movements of the kite in an awkward dance.

Des turned then, his smile bright as a breath-mint commercial. I had no choice but to go and say hello.

"Hi."

"Hi. You're quite handy with that thing," I said.

"I'm quite handy with all sorts of things," he answered. Was he flirting? He sounded like he was flirting. But so had Kyle. My signal reader definitely needed calibrating.

Des's chest was sweaty again from his jog. It was quite distracting. Only the presence of my offspring prevented me from blurting out something totally Dody like, "Did you know the Romans made aphrodisiacs from the perspiration of gladiators?" (It's true. I learned it on the History Channel.)

"Mommy, Des says we can go in the water if you say we can," Jordan squeaked.

My eyes snapped from Des's torso to Jordan's face.

"You want to go in the water?"

My son's white-blond head bobbed.

Who was this changeling and what had he done with my child?

"I thought you were afraid of the waves."

Jordan straightened his shoulders with mini-machismo. "Am not!"

"I want to go too!" Paige added.

"You do?"

"Sorry," Des said. "I told them I was going to swim, so they asked."

What kind of pied piper was this guy? I'd been trying to get them in the lake for almost a month.

"They don't know how to swim."

"It's really shallow right here." He gestured toward the stretch of water right in front of us. "If you come with us, we'll be fine."

"Come on, Mommy." Paige grabbed my hand and pulled.

Was it his accent that made every suggestion so impossible to resist? He could've asked me to drive a getaway car and I would've agreed.

Before my faint agreement had scattered on the wind, Jordan was running toward the lake with Paige and Des, leaving me to wonder over the drastic change of heart in my children's attitudes.

They halted at the shoreline until I joined them.

"Ready?" Des asked Jordan, offering his hand.

Jordan hesitated now, curling his toes as second thoughts and a six-inch wave nearly overtook him. He held up his arms without taking his eyes off the water.

Des didn't miss a beat. He scooped up my son and walked into the lake. *I'm surprised he didn't just walk over the top of it. Who was this guy anyway?*

I picked up Paige, who giggled and wiggled and squealed. Following a step behind the boys, I watched Jordan. His eyes were as wide as the smile breaking across his face.

A wave splashed up against Paige's foot. She tried to climb higher on my body, but there was no place for her to go. At least concern for the safety of my children made me momentarily forget about all those corpses and eels and God knows what else was floating around in the water. Well, not entirely forget...

Ten minutes later, my children were bobbing around like baby ducks, all fear of getting splashed or dunked gone. For weeks I had cajoled, bargained, threatened, and bribed, trying to get them to this spot. And now, thanks to this man from Atlantis, they were frolicking like little Nemos.

The water was calm. I didn't need to worry about a riptide suddenly pulling them out into the depths, but I reminded them to stay close. Not that they were paying me the least bit of attention since Des the Superhero was there. They were magnets to the Man of Steel.

"Come on, guys, give Des some space. You're like car-buncles," I pleaded.

"What's a carbuncle?" asked Paige.

"It's that stuff that grows on the bottom of ships," I replied.

Des choked back laughter. "I think you mean barnacles."

"Do I? What's a carbuncle then?"

"It's a skin abscess. Like a boil."

"Are you sure?"

He nodded definitively. "Pretty sure."

Well, shit. Dody was rubbing off on me. I'd always thought those were carbuncles. I wondered how many times I'd used the wrong word.

"By the way," he asked, "is that a waterproof watch?"

I looked at my wrist. My watch was full of hazy lake water, the second hand tick, tick, ticking over the same spot. Drat.

"Is yours?" I asked, trying to deflect my embarrassment.

He nodded and glanced at his own. "Oh, shoot!" he exclaimed. "I'm going to be late for work. I have to go. See you later!"

He waved a hand back over his shoulder as he started to move toward the shoreline. Then he stopped and turned, pointing to Jordan. "Are you OK out here in the water with them?"

Was I OK keeping an eye on my own children? Of course I was, and yet the offer was so genuine I nearly laughed. How many times had Richard asked if I needed help with the children? Um, exactly never.

CHAPTER 8

"SADIE, I HAVE THE MOST delightful surprise for you!" Dody waggled ring-bedecked fingers as she floated into the family room. Since Dody's surprises typically involved herbal concoctions that smelled of decaying yard waste and tasted slightly worse, I was not excited.

"I'm reading to the kids right now, Dody. Can it wait?" Jordan was next to me, half listening, half playing with his trucks, while Paige paid rapt attention. Reading was her favorite pastime, a byproduct of being named Paige Turner, I guess.

"It can't wait. I've arranged a reading for you with my psychic advisor, Madame Margaret." She beamed like I'd won Powerball. "She's wonderful. You'll love her." She shoved a stack of picture books to the floor and sat down on the sofa with a whoosh of fabric.

"Dody, I don't need a psychic. I need an accountant."

"Oh, pish-posh. All they do is account. But Margaret can light the pathway to your higher purpose."

I wasn't certain I had a higher purpose. I couldn't even get through the self-actualization exercises in my *Oprah* magazine.

"Do you really believe in that stuff?" I asked.

"I believe in whatever helps a person clear away their negative energy and focus on the positive. And you, young lady, are chock-full of negative energy. Margaret can give you just the push you need. She's expecting us in an hour."

"What about the kids?"

"We can drop them off at Anita Parker's. I've already asked her."

I was not on board with this. I didn't need some kooky Gypsy making up a bunch of crap about me taking a long journey or meeting a tall, dark stranger. Or worse yet, she'd be a *real* psychic who told me my future held nothing but heartache and loneliness. I already knew that. I'd get better advice from a bartender, along with a gin and tonic. But Dody had made up her mind, and that meant I was going.

An hour later I settled into a folding chair at Madame Margaret's Boutique. Mystic baubles and Wiccan whatnots adorned dusty glass shelves. The scent of lavender and kitty litter wafted faintly through the air, and clinky, plinky Eastern music played softly. What the hell was I doing here?

A short, pudgy woman with silver bobbed hair and red-framed bifocals entered the room. She had on a pink running suit. I was surprised and frankly a little disappointed when she sat down across from me. This was the psychic? Where were her veils? And her thick, black eyeliner? Where was the gold hoop earring? This was a rip-off.

She smiled warmly and shook my hand. "Hello, I'm Maggie."

"Hi," I said stiffly, not wanting to give anything away. If she was so psychic, she should guess my name.

"And you are Sadie," she said.

"Yes!" I gasped. Wow, she was good!

She chuckled at my reaction, tapping a piece of paper on the table between us. "Your name is here on my schedule."

"Oh, yeah." I shifted in my chair.

She handed me a deck of ornately decorated cards. "Shuffle these, please. I'm not sure we'll need them, but it will make you less nervous."

"I'm not nervous," I said, too quickly. Should I be nervous just because she was about to tell me my future looked bleak and devoid of joy?

She closed her eyes and breathed slowly.

This was ridiculous.

Then she opened her eyes and took the cards from me, flipping a few over in a deliberate pattern. They had crazy pictures: a tower getting struck by lightning, a couple of toga-clad women holding up golden chalices, a hermit with a lantern. And a black-cloaked dude riding a horse. That card had the word *death* printed right on it! That could not be good.

She stared at the cards for a silent minute and my skin began to itch. Were they so full of doom she'd didn't know what to say? But when she spoke, her voice was very calm.

"You are unbalanced."

Unbalanced as in crazy?

She pointed to the first card. "This is the Tower card. It represents long-held beliefs and ideas being challenged. All aspects of your life are currently in flux and you must be open to change. Certain troubles will end only after you get rid of something or someone, either physically or emotionally. Have you recently ended a relationship? Or are you thinking of ending it?"

Dody must have told her about my divorce. I nodded once, still not wanting to reveal too much.

Madame Margaret nodded back. "It was the right decision. He was flash and little substance. But there is more work to be done with him before you get to a better place. The Hermit card speaks of inner wisdom. You have it, you just don't trust it. You must adjust your attention from your everyday life and look inward. That is where your problems begin and where they will be solved."

Oh, I don't think so. My problems started and ended with Richard.

"Ah, and the Six of Cups," she went on, pointing to another card. "Very significant in this position. It connects one's past with one's future. It makes sense these two would be together in your present circumstances. You may suddenly find yourself thinking about past experiences, maybe even yearning for the beauty of an old relationship."

Wow, not a chance of that happening.

"This is also a period of emotional renewal. You will finally break free and come into your own with a deeper appreciation of your journey."

So far this seemed like standard issue fortune-telling to me. Pretty ambiguous stuff, especially since Dody had obviously prompted her.

She pointed to another card. "This is the Ace of Pentacles. It promotes good health. And the Star next to it is the card of inspiration, insight, and hope. Contact with someone who will change your life dramatically. A new relationship, perhaps."

Oh, yeah. That had Dody-speak all over it. I was being set up.

"I'm not anticipating a new relationship," I said. I needed to nip this right in the bud.

She smiled benignly. "One rarely anticipates this kind of thing. But that's the beauty of tarot. Now you know to watch for it."

I wanted to argue but could see there'd be no point. She seemed like a nice enough little lady, this wacky sidekick of Dody's. I guess I could let her spin her tale.

"The Three of Cups here tells me you are entering a period of fun."

Thus the cups, no doubt. They must be full of vodka.

"Over here we have the Knight of Swords and the King of Swords. These may be men in your life, both past and present. Both have charm and wit and eloquence, but one hurls himself at you like the wind and is gone just as quickly. He is easily bored."

Hmm, that could sure be Richard.

"But the other represents someone in a position of trust and responsibility, a professional advisor. A lawyer or a doctor."

Oh my God. Seriously? Did Dody write a script for this woman?

Margaret frowned and stared at the next card. "This Wheel of Fortune suggests your luck is changing. A new phase is beginning, but destiny and fate will allow you very little control over coming events. And you crave control at all costs. But, dear, the best thing you can do for yourself right now is go with the flow. And trust those who care about you. Many choices confront you, but only one is right. You cannot do everything on your own."

Yes I could. I'd been doing it alone for ages. Richard was no more help than a husband-sized cardboard cutout.

Then she smiled. "But it will all work out for the best. See the Two of Cups here? That is a new love affair. This next man is a much better match for you. But love has a price. This new relationship won't come without sacrifice."

Didn't they all come with sacrifice?

Wait.

What?

Did she say love? No thanks. I'd sacrificed enough for Richard. I was tapped out.

Then she sat back in the chair and regarded me for a minute. "We can't control events in our life, Sadie. Sometimes we can't even control our reactions. But the harder we fight against the waves, the more exhausted we become. Control is an illusion, you know."

No, love is the illusion.

She flipped over a few more cards and smiled again. "Excellent. The Four of Cups. *You* do not let possessions own you. Yes, go with that. Don't be afraid to tap into your natural strengths. You have much more than you realize. You'll find the balance you need as soon as you let go of how you think things should be and accept them as they are. Watch for the big wave. It'll push you in the direction of joy. You will be happy, Sadie. It's all over these cards."

Of course she'd say that. I'd hardly fork over a 20 percent tip for a vision of mayhem. She went on for another fifteen minutes or so, telling me to trust my instincts and let go of the past. Good advice, sure, but most of the stuff she said could have come straight from Dody's mouth.

See, I should have spent that money on gin and tonic. At least then I'd have a nice buzz.

*　　*　　*

"You deliberately avoided telling me Fontaine was living at Dody's, Sadie! Did you think I wouldn't find out?" Richard's voice was raspy with anger.

He and I were standing in the parking lot of The Waffle Castle where I'd gone to pick up Paige and Jordan after their most recent visit. The kids were currently sitting in my car, watching us rant and rave, just like old times.

"Keep your voice down! And I didn't mention it because I don't see why it matters, Richard. So what if Fontaine is staying there?"

"So what? So I don't want my son exposed to God knows what kind of shit Fontaine has going on. Is he bringing guys over there?"

He stuck his finger in my face, and I wanted to bite it off and spit it out.

"No, he isn't. But honestly, you're such a homophobic asshole. You don't care if Jasper is swinging from chandeliers with hookers. You're only worried my cousin will turn your son gay."

He grabbed my arm and pulled me farther from the car. "Keep your voice down. And damn it, Sadie, that's not fair. You're putting words in my mouth."

A couple walked by. The woman's step faltered as she saw us, but the man hustled her past.

"Look," Richard hissed once they were out of sight, "I don't have time to discuss this. I'm late for work. But you need to deal with this, Sadie. I'm not having either of my kids in that kind of environment. So get your fag cousin out of there or scoot your ass back to Glenville. You've got a five-bedroom house sitting empty while you're playing your stupid little summer camp at Dody's. Enough is enough. I want my kids back where I can see them more often."

My temples pounded. I could hardly breathe, and I wanted to punch him in the groin. Or at least think of something vile to say that would hurt him as much. But I was too slow.

Richard jumped into his car without another glance at Paige and Jordan and sped away.

Shaking like I'd touched a live wire, I climbed into my SUV.

"Mommy, why was Daddy yelling?" Paige asked.

I took a breath. "He's just frustrated about a work thing, baby. He'll be fine."

Just as so many times before, I lied to them about their father. I was not going to be the one to turn them against him. When they were older, they could decide for themselves what type of man he was. Until then, I would protect them.

❧   ❧   ❧

Back in Bell Harbor that afternoon, I was still shaken by the argument. I didn't want to leave Bell Harbor. Not yet. And I wasn't going to ask Fontaine to leave either. I had no intention of even telling him what Richard said. But I was going to have to do something.

I took the kids and dogs down to the beach. Maybe a little sunshine would clear away the storm clouds in my head. Dody had passed on my invitation to join us, already committed to a belly-dancing class with Anita Parker.

I dumped a basket of plastic toys onto the sand to occupy Jordan. Paige had her dolls, and for me, a chair, a wine cooler, and a trashy novel. Sunshine, alcohol, and a little pulp fiction. That was a vacation.

Lazyboy barked, tearing around like a mongoose was on his tail, and eventually settled down beside me for a snooze. Fatso sniffed around in the sand, looking for half-buried junk food left behind by other beachgoers.

After a few minutes, I heard a sharp, short whistle. The dogs were instantly at attention, running toward the sound.

It was Des, jogging down the beach. The ubiquitous jolt that occurred every time I saw him buzzed through all my joints, and I once again reminded myself to get over it. Yes, I was attracted to him, much more than I dared admit, but it was pure infatuation. The thrill of emotions he stirred were almost cartoonish, all zing and zip and zoinks. It was fun pretending he was the Bionic Man with the Sensitivity Chip Upgrade. But he wasn't. Not really. He was just a guy, and if I got to know him better, I'd uncover all his lousy flaws. It was fun to flirt and pretend it meant something, but it didn't.

Des picked up a hunk of driftwood and tossed it, sending the dogs on another wild run, then came and sat next to me.

"Hey."

"Hey," I said back, discreetly tucking the trashy novel and cheap booze behind my chair.

The kids were a few feet away, digging a hole to Australia. (Contrary to urban legend about digging a hole to China, if you dig a hole from Michigan, you'll end up in Australia. Just another bit of useless trivia clogging my brain, along with the fact that toilets flush in the opposite direction on either side of the equator.)

"How are you?" he asked.

"Good. How are you?"

"Good. Where's Dody?"

"Belly dancing."

He chuckled and shook his head, probably trying to dispel the mental image.

Paige ran over. "Hi, Des! See my mermaid? Her name is Rosemerelda Abernathy Sparkleberry Turner. Do you like her?"

"Yes, I do."

"Do you like my new bathing suit too? It has yellow flowers on it. See?" She curtsied, tilting her head and putting a hand on her hip.

"I do. It's very pretty."

"I know." She turned and ran back to her trans-Earth Australian tunnel.

Jordan looked up and waved.

Des waved back.

We sat silent for a minute, watching the kids play.

"You're quiet today." Des leaned sideways, bumping his elbow against the arm of my chair.

"Am I? Sorry. Bad mood. Fight with my ex-husband." Damn it. Why had I said that? Hearing about someone else's ex-spouse was like watching slides from a sucky vacation that you didn't even go on. And yet I found myself still talking. "Richard doesn't want me to stay here. He's afraid Fontaine will give Jordan an incurable case of gay fever."

I looked over at my son, who was every inch the stereotypical boy. He'd abandoned the hole digging to punch and kick at the air, engaged in mortal combat with some imaginary foe.

"That's pretty stupid. What are you going to do?" Des asked, leaning back and tilting his face to the sun, eyes closed.

I took the opportunity to let my own eyes travel over him, but at my silence, he looked at me once more.

"I don't know," I said. "It depends how much trouble Richard wants to cause. It just makes me so mad because Fontaine is great with the kids. He's played with them more in a month than Richard did in five years."

Des nodded slowly. "That's too bad."

I nodded too and pulled my wine cooler out from behind the chair. "Have you ever been married?" Dody's take-no-prisoners bluntness was rubbing off.

He nodded and kicked at the sand with his foot. "Yeah. It didn't go very well."

"Sorry." I passed him my drink, which he accepted.

"It seems like a long time ago now."

"So what happened?"

He took another sip from the bottle. His words followed slowly. "Different priorities, I guess. We were pretty young. Pretty selfish." He shook his head again and handed back the drink. His hand grazed mine. For the briefest second our eyes locked. My heart went hot and shimmery, like the last burst of brilliance from a sparkler before it goes out.

Des almost smiled, but then his face changed, as if he had just that second remembered he'd left a pot boiling on the stove or had forgotten to put on his pants. He turned his gaze back to the water. "You know. Shit happens. Marriages end."

Part of me wanted to press. Part of me knew I wouldn't like what I heard. And anyway, he obviously didn't want to talk about it.

"No hospital today?" I asked instead.

He sighed, and it felt like the sun had faded somehow. "Nope, not today. But I still have tons of stuff I have to do. I suppose I should get to it."

He stood up slowly, almost as if he was waiting to say something more. But he just said, "See you later."

He turned and jogged down the beach.

Note to self: Don't ask Des about his marriage because it makes him sad. And then it makes him leave.

*   *   *

I readjusted the new leather work bag on my shoulder and smiled my best professional-organizer smile. Kyle was right. His old lover Patrick, and Patrick's new lover, Owen, had a lot of stuff!

Their new house was a historical behemoth, the oldest in Bell Harbor. That meant beautifully carved woodwork, an expansive veranda wrapping around the entire place, and old-fashioned pull-chain toilets. It also meant dozens of tiny rooms, the most illogically designed kitchen I'd ever seen, and no closets. Literally no closets! My worst nightmare! This job was going to be a bigger challenge than I expected, and since it was my first organizing assignment, I had to get it perfect.

My clients were crazy-happy in love and so excited to be moving in together. They didn't care about the details of setting up their new home; they just wanted the boxes unpacked with some semblance of order.

But if I failed, and the clutter overtook this house, they'd start fighting over golf clubs tipping over in the hallway or important mail getting lost amid stacks of random paperwork. My failure to create order from this chaos could doom their relationship. They might not realize it was my fault, but I would. So I had to get this right.

"This is the master suite," Patrick said, opening yet another door. "Aren't the windows divine? We're thinking sheer, sexy fabrics all over."

"And there's a maid's room right next door," Owen added. "We're thinking of turning that into a walk-in closet."

A closet? Thank God.

"Because half the fun will be coming out of it," Patrick snickered.

Owen sighed. "That one never gets old for you, does it, baby?"

We spent the rest of the day talking about their hopes for various spaces. I took dozens of notes and pictures and promised to get back to them within a week.

At Patrick's request, I also agreed to bring my label maker with me next time to mark their bathroom towel hooks *His* and *His*.

* * *

Strolling through the hospital lobby a few days later, after Dody's doctor's appointment, I heard a familiar accent. As usual, a tingle trickled down my spine and straight to my girlie bits.

"Hey, Sadie!" Des called.

Dody and I turned, and Des missed a step, taken aback, no doubt, by her turquoise boa. It was sparkly with sequined feathers and dangled from her shoulders like a *Muppet Show* cast member. Walter had allegedly bought it from a Romanian housekeeper who'd pilfered it from Diana Ross's dressing room. I had my doubts.

Des, of course, looked dashing in his doctor duds. What is it that makes a generic white lab coat and scrubs look so sexy, I wondered, just before wishing I'd put a little effort into my own appearance that day. I mean, yes, I was on vacation, but would it have killed me to wash my hair? Was that extra ten minutes in bed worth it? At the moment I wasn't even certain if I had brushed my teeth that morning. Damn it!

I smiled with lips together, trying to taste the remnants of toothpaste in my mouth.

"Why, Dody, don't you look stunning today?" His smile was broad.

She fluttered her boa along with her lashes. "Thank you. That's just what Fontaine said."

Des nodded, eyebrows quirked. "Fontaine would know."

He winked at me over her head, causing my bra to try and unclasp itself in sweet surrender.

"What brings you ladies here today?" he asked.

"Oh, it's nothing serious. Just a checkup with my vagi-nacologist," Dody answered.

"Dody!" I gasped.

"What? Oh, you're so squeamish, Sadie. He knows about these things. He's a doctor, after all. Right, Des? You know all about lady parts, don't you?" She gave a coy flutter of her boa.

His face was Vulcan bland. "I am familiar with vaginacology, yes."

I'll bet.

"We were just going to the cafeteria to have lunch," Dody said. "Won't you join us?"

"No, we weren't," I blurted out, rattled by his presence.

"Yes, we were. I'm starving." She turned and stared at me with intense, round eyes.

Des checked his watch. "I've only got a few minutes, but I'll walk with you."

He pointed in the opposite direction, indicating the enormous cafeteria sign we'd blithely passed. We turned and walked together down a short hallway, arriving at the cafeteria a minute later.

It was nearly deserted. Probably because it was only ten thirty in the morning.

"Maybe we should just have coffee," Dody said. "I'm not so hungry after all."

I knew it! That meddling old liar, still trying to force Des into my world.

"I've got time for that," Des said, gesturing to a corner table. "Why don't you go sit in that booth over there? I'll get the coffee," he offered.

"No, let us buy the coffee. We owe you," I said.

He leaned forward, his hand touching the small of my back. "It's OK. I get it for free." He waggled his brows, nodding, as if free coffee was the best perk ever.

Looks like I had no choice. "OK then. Thanks."

He joined us at the table a few minutes later, setting down three cups and sliding into the seat next to me. He pulled some sugar packets out from his coat pocket and handed them to Dody. She was beaming as though he'd just proposed. To her.

"You like it black, right?" he asked me.

I nodded. "That was a lucky guess."

He tapped his temple. "Keen powers of observation. You drank it black the other night when I was there for dinner."

I looked down at my cup abruptly, not wanting him to witness my growing enchantment. Richard wouldn't be able to answer how I took my coffee if he was covered in honey and tortured with fire ants.

"How long did you say you'd be staying here in our lovely Bell Harbor, Des?" Dody asked, sensing I was mute with adoration.

"A few more months, maybe longer. It depends."

"Depends on what?"

He smiled. "On a variety of things."

His answer made me itchy. It was too vague. What was he hiding?

"And what do you do when you're not working?" Dody obviously realized she'd hit a dead end with the last question, but it wasn't about to dissuade her. I sensed her annoyance at my complete inability to market myself.

I sipped my perfectly black coffee, trying to ignore the heat of Des's leg near mine. That was tough to do in a booth so small. It was also hard to not notice the tiny spot near his sideburn that he missed while shaving, or the faintest little scar at the corner of his eyebrow, which I suddenly had an urge to press my lips against.

"I run, bike, travel, I play basketball. I read and watch movies. The typical stuff, I guess."

"What type of movies?"

"All kinds. I'm pretty easy to entertain."

"Do you like romantic movies?" she pressed on, batting her lashes at him. Her boa fluttered from her breath.

I sighed. Subtlety was nowhere on Dody's radar.

Des chuckled. "I do, actually. I grew up with three sisters, remember? So I've seen quite a few."

"Ah, that's delightful. So what was New York like?"

Des leaned back and his arm brushed along mine. I accidently squeezed my Styrofoam cup, nearly spilling what was left of the coffee.

"New York? I've never been there."

"Really? I thought all illegal aliens came through Elvis Island?"

Des laughed out loud, shaking the seat we shared.

"Dody," I sighed, "there is so much wrong with what you said I don't even know where to start."

"Why, what did I say?"

"Never mind."

Des's phone chimed and he pulled it from his pocket, still laughing. "Dr. McKnight."

He cleared his throat and listened, then occasionally responded. "Yes. No. Ten minutes. Tell her she can wait." He paused again. "No, I waited for her all morning and she never showed up. I'll be there in a minute."

He hung up, setting the phone on the table, and took a sip of coffee.

"Was that your girlfriend?" Dody asked.

He coughed as he tried to swallow. Of all her bizarre questions, this seemed to be the first one to trip him up. His face flushed as he tipped the cup back one last time and drank the last of it. Then he crunched the Styrofoam and gave my aunt an enigmatic smile. "Dody, I don't have a girlfriend."

"You don't?" she exclaimed, beaming at us. "Well, that's just a shame! Isn't it, Sadie?"

CHAPTER 9

I STRUGGLED TO GET THE brush through Paige's hair. It was knotted and crusty and smelled suspiciously like raspberries. The kids and I were in the kitchen with Dody while she made her morning cauldron of gloppy oatmeal.

"Ouch," Paige complained.

When the phone rang she jumped away. "My turn! I'll get it." She picked up the receiver. "Hello? Aunt Dody's house." After a minute, she giggled. "No, silly. Princesses don't answer the phone. I'm Paige." She paused again, one hand on her hip, the other holding the phone to her ear. I was struck with a vision of my future teenage daughter.

Paige nodded. "Yes, she's brushing my hair, but she's not being nice about it at all. Just because I dipped it in yogurt."

"Is that what that is?" I said. No wonder it was such a mess.

Paige giggled again. "No, it tasted the same. OK, I will." Then she handed the phone to me. "Des wants to talk to you."

There went that annoying and persistent buzz of anticipation again. That must be what the Highlander feels whenever another immortal shows up.

"Hello?" I tried to sound skinny.

"Sadie? Hi, it's Des."

"Hi."

Dody stopped stirring to blatantly eavesdrop.

"Hey, sorry to bother you, but I'm in a bit of a bind. I wondered if you could help me out."

Dear God, please, please, make him need help taking off his pants.

"What do you need?"

"I'm waiting on a package that's supposed to arrive by ten, but I just got called in early to work. Is there any chance you could come down here and sign for it?"

That sounded easy. And platonic. "Sure. I can do that."

I heard a sigh of relief from his side. "Really? Fantastic! Thank you."

"No problem. Should I come right now?"

"If you could. Sorry to mess up your morning."

"Oh, I think my social obligations can wait. I'll be there in five minutes."

Realistically I needed twenty to sufficiently beautify, but what would be the point of that? We were ships passing in the night anyway.

Dody clapped her hands together as I hung up the phone. "Oh, my!"

I held up my hand to silence her. "Dody, he just needs somebody there to sign for a package. Don't make a big deal out of it. It's just a neighborly favor."

She crossed her arms. "Alberta Schmidt lives right next door to the Pullmans'. Why didn't he ask her to do it? She's closer."

"Probably because we owe him, like, ten favors already. And because she smells like bad cheese."

"She is a little gassy," Dody admitted. "Ukrainian, you know."

I had no idea what that meant, but didn't have time to get into it. I had five minutes to splash water on my face and find an outfit that displayed casual sophistication while hinting at dormant sensuality. Even a ship in the night wants to look good.

Fifteen minutes later, Des greeted me at his front door.

"Thanks so much for doing this," he said. "I really have to run. Just lock the door when you leave. There's coffee, if you want some." He pointed over at the counter with one hand and scooped up his keys with the other. "If the package isn't here by ten and you have to leave, don't worry about it."

"No, I'm good. Dody's got the kids."

We stood at the front door like a little old married couple, with him heading off to work while I stayed home to clean the house and drink vodka from a coffee cup. I half expected him to kiss my cheek. But he only smiled and left, waving from the driver's seat of his sporty convertible and zipping away to his glamorous job saving lives.

I shut the door and leaned back against it.

Wait a second.

I was alone in Dr. Desmond McKnight's house. Well, shit. I had free rein to snoop to my heart's content. He'd never know.

Oh, where to start? The bedroom? The bathroom? The family room?

I stepped into the living room and felt a queasy rush to my stomach. I paused and turned toward the bedroom, feeling another roll of unease. I waited. Technically going through his stuff was a) unethical; b) unwise; c) inevitable; or d) all of the above. This situation required a second opinion.

I pulled the phone from my pocket and called Penny.

"Hey," she answered.

"Hey, guess where I am?" A quiver of adrenaline squeaked in my voice.

"Um, the secretary of state's office?"

I stomped a foot. "No! Why would I call you from the secretary of state's office?"

"I don't know. Why do you always call me from Dody's pantry?"

"Because it's the only place no one ever looks for me." It was also because I loved gazing at the pristine splendor of the newly labeled shelves and alphabetized canned goods. "Anyway, I'm at Des's. He asked me to wait here for a package because he had to go to work."

"Interesting." I waited, knowing Penny's mind would travel the same yellow-brick road as mine. "So, what have you learned, Dorothy?"

"That's why I'm calling. I've had an attack of conscience. Do I look around or mind my own business?"

"Oh, please! You have to look around!"

"But what if I find something awful? Like kiddie porn or a Josh Groban poster."

"Shut up. I love Josh Groban."

I rolled my eyes, even though she couldn't see me. "Focus, Penny. What should I do?"

"At least look in the bedroom to see how messy he is."

That seemed like an acceptable option. The master bedroom was on the first floor, so it wasn't as if I was really snooping. Not if I didn't go upstairs. I peeked in from the doorway, feeling nervous, as if I had Des whispering into my ear instead of Penny.

The bedroom was nondescript, full of the Pullmans' very traditional furniture. The bed itself was half-made, with a champagne-colored spread pulled up but not tucked in at the top. I could see the slight indentation on one pillow where Des's head must have been. I felt an insatiable urge to run my fingers over the spot or maybe slip my hand between the sheets to feel his warmth. I swallowed the sudden lump in my throat.

"Penny, I don't think I should go in his room."

"What's the matter, Colonel Sanders? Chicken?"

"No. It just seems wrong somehow."

"Why? Because it's calculating and invasive?"

"I love that you realize that and yet still encourage me to do it. You are a terrible sister."

She laughed into the phone. "Why do you call me with your own bad ideas and then judge me for supporting you?"

"Sorry. I guess this just bothers me because it's what I used to do to Richard, you know? Go through all his pockets looking for receipts and condom wrappers."

"Yeah, but what difference does it make what you find at that house? Unless you come across some kinky gizmo in the goodie drawer."

"Ick! I am so not looking in Joanna Pullman's goodie drawer. I don't care about their junk. I'm interested in his junk. Wait, that came out wrong."

"Uh, like Freudian wrong." Penny laughed. "Anyway, I still don't see what difference it makes what you find. Unless...are you starting to like this guy?" My sister's voice lifted.

"No," I said, sounding as defiant as Jordan when I tell him it's bedtime.

Penny laughed again. "It's OK to like him, you big coward. Maybe he's one of the good ones. Like Jeff. There are a few of them out there. And you deserve somebody awesome, especially after what The Dick put you through."

"But what if this guy is as much a jerk as Richard was?"

"If he is, then tell him to go fuck himself because you can find somebody better. You really can, Sadie. I'm not making this up to make you feel better. Dick was a cheating shmuck, but you're still acting like the divorce was your failure. It wasn't. And if you like this guy, hell, even if you don't, you should go for it."

"But that's no good. Eventually he'll get assigned someplace else, and I'll be back to Glenville in September. We'd be breaking up as soon as we got started."

"So you're not even going to try? Honestly! Is there a mirror in that house?"

"What?"

"A mirror. Find a mirror and stand in front of it."

God, my sister was pushy. I stepped inside the master bedroom and planted myself near the mirror over the bureau.

"OK, Miss Bossy-Pants. Now what?"

"Now say, 'I am fabulous.'"

I laughed in spite of myself. "You sound like Fontaine. Now *he's* fabulous."

"Stop trying to change the subject, Sadie. I'm doing an intervention here."

Big sigh. I looked into the mirror at my frazzled self. There was a nice, rosy glow to my cheeks. And I had a little tan going on. And come to think of it, my hair was sort of pretty.

"I am fabulous," I murmured into the phone.

"Louder, and less sarcastic."

"I am fabulous."

"Good," Penny said. "Now say this. I deserve a really great guy because I'm good enough, I'm smart enough, and, darn it, people like me."

I burst out laughing. "Isn't that what Al Franken used to say when he was a comedian instead of a politician?"

"Isn't that the same thing? Anyway, say it."

I shook my head, still laughing. "Look, I get where you're going with this, Penn, and I appreciate it. I really do. I hear you, and I'll think about it. OK?"

"Promise?"

"Yes! Geez, I only called so you'd absolve me of guilt for going through his stuff. What a pain you are."

"I'm your sister. That's my job. And speaking of job, I'm really sorry, but I have to get back to work. Call me later and tell me what you find, deal?"

"Deal."

I slipped the phone back in my pocket and stared at myself for another moment. I wasn't half bad looking. OK, if I was totally honest, I was pretty OK looking. I'd held up.

One nice byproduct of Richard's cheating had been my nearly psychotic drive to stay in shape, thinking I could cardio-boot-camp my way into a secure marriage. I couldn't, of course. But I sure as hell could've kicked the redhead's ass in a street fight. Well, not a street fight because I was too ladylike for that. But I bet I could run faster than her.

In the mirror, the reflection of Des's half-made bed caught my eye. That enticing pillow dent was calling. I kind of wanted to smell it. But that would be weird, right?

Bitchy the cat sashayed past me from whereabouts unknown to jump onto the bed. She lay down right in the center, glaring at me. Then just to prove how her derision of me knew no boundaries, she pointed one hind leg at the ceiling and proceeded to lick herself.

I glared at her, hoping to make her bashful, but she was one bold ho. Giving up, I turned to leave the room, and the doorbell rang, startling me. I'd forgotten all about the package.

I ran to the door and yanked it open, accidentally smacking it against the table in the foyer. A chubby, unshaven delivery man in a mustard-colored shirt about three sizes too small greeted me. He was holding a big envelope and a clipboard.

"Hello," he said, squinting at the clipboard and running a thick, stubby finger down the list. "I have a package for…a Mr. Delmondo McNaught?"

"Desmond McKnight?" I asked.

He pushed his glasses against the bridge of his nose. "Close enough." He handed me the board and a sticky pen.

How to sign this? Should I put Des's name or mine? I decided to go with his, partly because I had yet to outgrow that schoolgirl thrill of doodling a cute boy's name. And also because if I inadvertently authorized a delivery for some nefarious mobster named Delmondo McNaught, I didn't want anyone to trace it back to me.

"Thank you, Mrs. McKnight," the delivery man said. He turned and waddled back to his truck.

Mrs. McKnight? My, my, didn't that have a lovely ring to it?

I stepped back, and the door bumped against the table again. I pondered that for a minute, finally deciding to be outrageously presumptuous and move the table to the other wall. Maybe Des wouldn't even notice. Most men didn't pay attention to things like that. Then I set the envelope down on the relocated table. My work here was done. Still, I wasn't quite ready to leave. I liked being inside his space, even though it clamored loudly of the Pullmans' presence.

I wandered through the living room, sitting on the suede L-shaped sofa, reveling in the cush factor. I imagined, for one secret moment, reclining on the sofa with Des next to me.

Bitchy came out from the bedroom, thoroughly washed. I sensed what was going on in her little feline mind. She wanted me out of there. She was going to take kitten chow pellets and spell out a message on the floor for Des. It would say, "Weird neighbor lady stayed all morning. I hate her."

Cats are so vindictive.

*   *   *

"Come on, baby. Let Mommy get your jammies on, please?" I was tired. I wanted to get my kids through with their baths and into bed. Paige was in her nightgown but Jordan was wiggling in front of me while I tried to dry him off. Somehow I always ended up the wettest during their bath time.

Murmured voices floated up from downstairs. Kyle was coming by to pick up Fontaine for some interior-designer event. Dody had a date with a man from her scuba-diving class since Harry was away visiting his grandson, and Jasper had a date with Beth, who had finally returned from her lengthy business trip. It would be a full house for a while, but soon they'd all go on their way, and then I could get the kids to bed and have a little peace and quiet.

The hardest things to tolerate at Dody's place (besides the awful decor, lousy mattresses, and obnoxious dogs) were the complete lack of privacy and the constant noise. Either Dody and her friends were practicing tai chi on the deck or Fontaine was in my face pestering me about something. Or Jasper was clanging pots around in the kitchen. It was always something.

The times I'd taken the kids to visit Richard in Glenville, I stayed at my own house and reveled in the silence. I didn't even mind that none of my neighbors were ever available to get together during those weekends because I craved the solitude. So tonight, I wanted to relax in lovely aloneness.

"Mommy, can we go downstairs and say good night to Aunt Dody?" Paige asked.

I hesitated. The bedtime process with my kids was often long and arduous, with lots of good-night kisses and books to read and pleasant dreams to be wished upon. But Paige turned her big, sweet eyes on me, and I gave in.

"Sure, but let's make it quick."

She and Jordan scampered down the stairs and I followed.

"Hi, Des!" I heard Paige exclaim. "What are you doing here?"

"I came to say thanks to your mum. Did you get the yogurt out of your hair?"

Had I been a half step farther behind I could've turned around and snuck back to my room to change clothes, or at least brush my hair. But destiny, as usual, had other plans. When I heard Des's voice, my wet foot slipped on the step and I tumbled ass over teacup and landed with a thud at the bottom of the staircase.

Birds chirped in little circles around my head, and strong arms helped me upright. I must have been hallucinating.

The fog cleared, and everyone's face came into focus, with Des's the closest to mine.

"Are you OK?" he asked.

"I'm OK. I just slipped."

"I hope you won the contest," said Fontaine.

"What contest?" I was still a bit off balance.

"The wet T-shirt contest."

I looked down. My white tank top, completely soaked with bath water, was virtually transparent. Adding insult to my injury, I was wearing the bra Penny bought me as a joke. The one decorated with little red ladybugs in an attempt to help me overcome my irrational fear of little red ladybugs.

Chuckles rippled around the room.

I plucked the fabric away from my skin, triggering a questionable suction sound.

It's not as if it was the first time I'd made a fool of myself. Not likely the last, either.

"Are you sure you're OK? Can you stand up?" Des's hands were still on my arm, and I let him help me to my feet.

Mustering as much dignity as the occasion allowed, I said, "I just need to change my shirt."

✽　✽　✽

I came back downstairs in the most opaque T-shirt I could find. Everyone had moved outside to have drinks on the deck. Des was leaning against the rail, a beer in his hand. Fontaine and Kyle were next to him. The gorgeous blonde next to Jasper must be Beth. And the stout, flush-faced man next to Dody must be her date.

"I'm back," I announced, mostly to warn them to stop talking about me.

"Here she is," Dody said, clapping her hands. "Bud, this is my niece, Sadie. Sadie, this is my friend, Bud Light."

He flicked a toothpick from one side of his mouth to the other. "Bud Wright," he corrected.

I shook Mr. Wright's meaty hand. "Nice to meet you, Bud."

He looked me over. "You the divorcée?"

I had little choice but to say, "Yes."

He nodded. "Sounds like you did the right thing."

Discussing the failure of my marriage with this complete stranger fell low on my list of desires. I certainly wasn't going to pursue the topic in front of Kyle or Beth. And certainly not in front of Des! I tossed a pleading glance in Fontaine's direction. *Help me, please!*

He picked up on my SOS. "Um, hey, Sade," he said, turning his back, "do these jeans give me a Ken-doll butt?"

Not quite the rescue I was looking for, but good enough.

Jasper stepped in front of him, tugging his girlfriend by the wrist. "Sadie, this is Beth."

Thank goodness! A useful distraction. "Beth! It's great to finally meet you. Jasper has told me so many wonderful things." I hugged her with too much enthusiasm, my voice going dolphin squeaky. Guilt over my less-than-thrilled response to Jasper's talk of marriage was foremost in my mind, with my tumble down the steps pushing hard from second place.

"It's great to meet you too. Your children are adorable."

"Thank you. That's sweet of you to say. And that reminds me, kids, time for bed!" I looked around and saw them scurry from the living room into the kitchen and try to hide behind Dody's row of aprons hanging from the wall.

"Sadie, dear, I'll tuck them in for you. You don't mind waiting a few more minutes, do you, Bud?" Dody asked.

He held up his nearly empty glass. "Not if somebody will freshen this drink. But don't take too long, Do. I'm so hungry I could eat the ass end of a baby."

Dody's Mr. Wright had a colorful way about him.

"Come along, kids," Dody said, herding them from the kitchen to the stairs. She caught my eye and tipped her head in Des's direction. Subtle as a brick to the skull, that old lady was.

"I'll freshen that," Fontaine said to Bud, taking the glass from his hand. "How about you, Des? Need another beer?"

"Sure."

Paige darted away from Dody and ran to Des, flinging her arms around his waist, coming perilously close to boy parts I didn't want her near until she was at least thirty-five.

"Good night, Des."

He ruffled her hair. "Night, Paige. See you soon."

Jordan approached as well, handing Des two action figures. "Here. You can play with these if you want to."

Des looked them over and offered my son a solemn fist bump. "Thanks, man. I'll be careful with them."

Jordan nodded.

My heart went ping. And then pong. Jordan did not trust easily. And he never shared his action figures, not even with me. As glad as I was to see it, I wasn't completely comfortable with it either. What if Des started to mean something to Jordan? I could protect myself from getting hurt, but my son's feelings were another thing entirely.

I needed to be clear to everyone present I was not interested in this man. I must show them all how impervious I was to Des's charm. Because I was, you know, impervious. In fact, I hardly noticed how the blue of his shirt made his eyes turn a mystical shade of grayish green or that his nose was a little sunburned. I hadn't noticed his haircut either. But if I had, I might have thought that shorter hair made his ears seem a bit too big. Yes, it's true. He wasn't so perfect. Those were some damn big ears. But then he caught me staring and smiled, from ear to damn big ear, making me feel as vulnerable and exposed as I had been wearing the wet tank top.

Why was he even here, really? Just to say thank you because I signed for some silly little package? He could have called on the phone for that. If I didn't know better, I would think he was flirting. And I didn't want him to.

So what if Dody, Fontaine, and Penny all thought I should dive into his bed. It didn't cost them anything, tossing me into the treacherous sea of love with the albatross of loneliness strung around my neck. It wouldn't be their heart getting broken when he turned out to be just another jerky guy. Or secretly engaged to some nuclear-physicist brainiac who put herself through brainiac-physicist university by modeling lingerie in Paris.

Fontaine came back to the deck, passing out drinks. He handed me something pink that looked harmless enough, but I knew better. He wanted me tipsy, just to see what might happen next. I was a notorious lightweight when it came to liquor. I could handle gallons of wine, but two shots of vodka and I was down for the count.

Everyone took seats around the deck. Kyle and Fontaine sat with Bud on one side, Jasper and Beth sat on the other. Des settled on the wicker couch and smiled at me. He patted the spot next to him. Like Fontaine's drink, sitting next to Des was sure to be intoxicating.

I was powerless to resist. He was obviously using Jedi mind control. *Help me, Obi-Wan Kenobi!* I took a gulp of Fontaine's love potion and sat down.

"Thanks for handling my package this morning," Des said without guile.

"What!" Fontaine burst out. "Sadie handled your package? Why the hell am I just hearing about this now?"

"Shut up, Fontaine," I mumbled under the laughter.

Des blushed, realizing what he'd said. "Sorry. That's not what I meant."

We both took a drink.

"Hey, just out of curiosity," Des asked a second later, "why did you move that table in the entryway?"

"You noticed that, huh?"

"Did you think I wouldn't?"

Richard wouldn't have noticed if I moved a couch. "It was in the wrong place. The entryway is much more welcoming with the table where I put it. But you can put it back if you want to."

"I don't really care," he shrugged. "I just wondered why you moved it."

The sun sank lower, casting a magical gold coating over everything. A fresh breeze over the water cooled the hot deck, and the sound of waves was hypnotic. Fontaine's cocktails were taking effect, and a lovely, jovial mood enveloped us. Dody came back from putting the kids to bed, and she and Bud went on their way, leaving me with Des, Fontaine, Kyle, Jasper, and Beth.

"We could just get pizza and chill out here," Jasper said to Beth. "Unless you want to go to that movie."

She shook her head. "It's too nice a night to be inside. Let's stay here."

There went my evening of peace and solitude. Des's arm brushed against me, and suddenly a night alone didn't sound that fun anymore anyway.

"What do you think, Kyle? You want to stick around here too?" Fontaine asked.

Kyle looked at his drink. "Will you make some more of these little devils?"

"Sure."

"Then I'm staying."

And so it was. We ordered pizza and kept the drinks flowing. Beth turned out to be warm and funny and a perfect complement to Jasper's snappy commentary. I also began to suspect that Kyle had a crush on Fontaine. But then again, I'd once thought Kyle was hitting on me, so maybe I just couldn't read him very well. Nonetheless, Kyle's sense of humor made me laugh until I snorted, a sound which I had never planned to share with Des.

Someone decided we should take turns telling the worst jokes we knew, and whoever laughed had to take a drink. Trying *not* to laugh can make even the most moronic joke funny, so when Des asked, "What did the Englishman say to the Scotsman?" and then answered, "Would it have kilt you to put on some pants?" every one of us had to drink.

"We should play I Never," Jasper suggested once the joke game got old.

"What's that?" Des asked.

"You've never heard of I Never? Where did you go to college?" Jasper demanded, amazed at this failure of our educational system.

Des shrugged. "Just...Massachusetts."

"Massachusetts? As in Harvard?" Fontaine asked.

Des scratched the back of his head, "Yeah."

Of course he went to Harvard. Where else would a sexy, shmexy, accent-talking doctor go? I heard the question in my head and wondered if it was Fontaine's drink talking. Anyway, what difference did it make if Des went to Harvard? It didn't matter if he went to college on the frickin' moon. I wasn't interested.

"Where'd you go to medical school?" Fontaine prodded. He just couldn't let it go.

"Still Harvard. I managed to not get kicked out. So how do you play this game?" Des rubbed his hands together.

I found myself smiling at him. He looked like a kid, all giddy about some silly game. This was a Harvard man, huh? Des was ever a surprise to me. I mean, in spite of the Ivy League college and his heartthrob good looks and the cool job, he seemed like one of us. He didn't constantly brag as Richard always had. In fact, Des never bragged at all. And he could have if he'd wanted to. He had the goods. He had it all going on.

An idea began to take hold in the base of my slightly tipsy mind. Maybe Des was one of the good ones Penny had told me about?

"It's pretty simple," Jasper explained, interrupting my thoughts. "You say 'I never'…and then you add something. Whoever has done whatever you said has to take a drink."

"It's a drinking game?" Des asked. He sounded optimistic.

"Didn't you have drinking games at Harvard?"

"Oh, we had lots of drinking games."

"Yes," said Fontaine, "but they drank from snifters while wearing their ascots."

Des shook his head. "Hardly. Let's play."

"Let me check on my kids first. I can't have them overhearing this!"

Paige and Jordan were snug in their beds and loudly snoring, although I did have to remove a tiara from Paige's head and turn Jordan around 180 degrees. He liked to sleep with his feet on the pillow.

I arrived back at the deck just as I heard the end of Jasper's joke. "Rectum? Damn near killed him!"

I can only imagine how that one started.

*   *   *

Our game began tamely enough, with Kyle saying, "I've never Googled my own name."

He, Jasper, and Fontaine drank.

"Is there another Fontaine Baker out there?" Beth asked.

"Nope. I'm the one and only," Fontaine answered smugly.

"Yes, you are," Kyle added.

"Why would you Google your own name?" She was still perplexed, or maybe the beverages were making her thickheaded.

"For fun," Kyle said. "I found four other Kyle Tanners just in Michigan."

"But none like you." Fontaine patted his leg, and I started to wonder if there was monkey business going on with their design business.

"I've never given anyone stitches," Jasper said.

"That's not fair," Des complained, but he took his drink anyway.

Beth was next. "I've never stolen anything."

Everyone but Beth took a drink.

"You've never stolen anything? Not even a piece of candy?" Kyle asked.

Beth shook her head. "I don't think so. The guilt would kill me."

Jasper leaned over. "Oh, but you've stolen my heart."

Everyone made retching sounds while Beth blushed and kissed Jasper's cheek.

Then Fontaine said, "I've never ridden a unicycle."

No one had.

We went around the table a few times, saying things such as, "I've never painted myself blue...peed in the shower…gone to the movies alone…worn shoes from two different pairs."

Then it was my turn again. "I've never driven on the opposite side of the road."

Not a great one, but I was distracted by Des's big knees coming out of his shorts. Even his knees were cute, and nobody had cute knees. How did he manage that?

He went next. "I've never…kissed a girl."

Everyone drank except Fontaine.

"Oh, you have too, you cheater," I shouted at him. "Remember Delores DeForrest?"

Des laughed the hardest, leaning forward toward Fontaine. "You knew a girl named Delores DeForrest?"

"Yes," Fontaine giggled. "And she's a florist. Delores DeForrest the florist. Can you imagine?"

The drinks made us decidedly stupid. With each round our laughter grew louder and more obnoxious.

Fontaine said, "I've never been to Scotland."

Des slapped his own leg. "Damn it, why are you picking on me?"

"Because picking on Sadie is too easy," Fontaine answered.

"Thanks," I said. "Just for that, I never manscaped my chest hair."

"Touché," Fontaine responded, picking up his drink. Then he added, "I've never had sex with a Highland sheep."

"Hah! Neither have I!" Des exclaimed, but he got confused and took a drink anyway. Then he tripped himself up by saying, "I've never lived in another country. Oh, shit. That's me."

I would have felt sorry for him except he was such a good sport about everyone making him drink. Plus he was getting completely hammered.

Beth smiled sweetly and said, "I've never worn a kilt."

Des sighed with exaggeration, picking up his glass once more. "What's this game called again? Get the new guy drunk?"

"Have you worn a kilt?" I asked, not quite able to picture it. Sexy and Scottish as he was, I couldn't see him pulling off the whole Braveheart look, even with the cute knees.

"Not often. I wore one in my cousin's wedding. Apparently…" He paused a second, pointing his finger at no one in particular as laughter overtook him. "Apparently you have to be more careful…how you sit…in a kilt."

"Show off a little Loch Ness monster there, aye, Des?" Jasper asked.

Des nodded fast. "Nearly."

We howled with laughter.

Then Fontaine, being his diabolically provocative self, said, "I've never had a sexual fantasy about anyone on this deck!"

A collective snicker went round the table. Jasper and Beth smiled at each other and toasted, clinking their glasses together.

Then suddenly everyone was looking at me!

What the hell?

Curse you, Fontaine! He knew I had tawdry visions of Des tucked away in my mind, but I wasn't about to own up to it. If I didn't drink, would he call me out? Fontaine was a bully that way.

I made a face at him, but he just waggled his eyebrows and nudged the glass closer to my hand. I sat motionless, still as a statue, resisting the urge to cross my arms. I was not confessing to this one.

Then to the left of me, Des let out a little snort. He picked up his glass, drained the whole of it, and thumped it back down on the table with defiance.

The others doubled over with raucous laughter while my mind whirled out of control.

Was he fantasizing about me? He couldn't be. Oh Lord, this was embarrassing! I bit my lip. Seconds passed, until finally I peeked over at Des. He was grinning at me like a kid holding the last ice-cream cone available to mankind. He was daring me, that arrogant bastard. What were we, twelve?

Oh, what the hell.

With pinky raised, I took a genteel sip from my glass, daintily dabbed at the corners of my mouth, and then threw the glass over my shoulder and right off the deck.

By this time, they could hear us laughing in Wisconsin.

CHAPTER 10

I SPREAD OUT MY BEACH blanket, wishing with all my heart that my sunglasses were bigger and darker. The sun was blazing and not helping my dull hangover. Thankfully Paige and Jordan were watching a movie with Dody up at the cottage so I had a few minutes to myself. I settled in with my new book, *The Moron's Manual for Starting Your Own Business*. A gift from Fontaine.

The smell of hot sand and cool water was a tonic, lulling me into a lethargic stupor. I closed my eyes and my mind drifted back to last night. The end part was a little fuzzy. The last thing I remembered was watching Des lumber unsteadily down the beach toward the Pullmans' house.

I opened my eyes sleepily. There he was, lumbering again. I blinked, thinking it might be a mirage. But he was really there, making his way toward me much slower than usual.

"Hey, how are you?" I asked when he finally reached my blanket and sat down with a heavy thud.

"How do you think?" he asked. He took off his sunglasses, making me gasp.

His left eye was swollen and red, with dark bruises all around it. He looked like the final scene from a boxing movie.

"Oh! My! God! What happened to your eye?"

He scowled. "You guys got me drunk last night."

Uh-oh. I think I might be in trouble. I hesitated to ask, "And?"

"And when I got home it was very late and very dark."

I bit my lip. "And?"

"And you know that table you moved in my front hallway to make it look more *welcoming*?"

He said *welcoming* the way most people say *horseshit*.

"Well, I walked in the door, tripped over the goddamned cat, and crashed into the table on my way to the floor."

He was annoyed. And I should feel terrible! This was all my fault, just like Dody tripping over Jordan's truck had been. But the mental picture of him stumbling and bumbling through a dark house and falling flat on his face was too much to bear.

I tried to fight it. I really did. But then I busted out with a full-volume, head-tipped-back guffaw. I couldn't help it! I slapped my hand over my big, loud mouth but the laugh was already out there.

"You think this is funny?" he asked.

I pressed my lips together and shook my head, but the bubbles of laughter were filling up my throat and going into my nose.

"Sadie," he huffed again. "It's not funny!" But one corner of his mouth twitched.

"I know!" I nodded fast then burst out laughing even harder.

He stared at me, until at last, he started laughing too.

"I'm so sorry, Des!" I choked out.

"You don't seem sorry."

"Oh, but I am, really." I tried to appear sincere, attempting to do my Sad Paige impression.

He shook his head slowly.

"Does it hurt?"

"You bet it does. I woke up this morning and thought my head was going to explode. I figured it was just from the drinks, but then I saw myself in the mirror."

I laughed again, imagining the scene.

"Of course, it hardly hurt at all when I did it! The cat kind of broke my fall. Anyway, I'm willing to let you make it up to me." His other eye crinkled in amusement.

"And how would I do that?" I asked.

He put his sunglasses back on. "Go out to dinner with me tomorrow."

All the alcohol still in my system rushed back to my head. I felt dizzy and slightly seasick. He was asking me on a date. I didn't want him to ask me on a date. I had an allergic reaction to dates. I wasn't sure what to say. "I'm only here for the summer, you know."

Des smiled. "Dinner should only take a couple of hours. We should be back in plenty of time for you to pack up for Glenville."

The seasickness swelled. I tingled with hope and panic. A date. He was asking me out on a date. A million reasons I should say no pinballed around inside my skull, colliding and ringing warning bells. Loudly.

"So how about it?" he asked.

"Um, sure," I heard someone answer. Someone who sounded just like me. "That would be nice."

"Great." He fell back against the blanket, flung his arm over his eyes, and promptly went to sleep. Wasn't that just like a man?

*　*　*

Arriving back at the cottage after my afternoon in the sun, I found bags of pretzels, candy wrappers, and soda cans strewn all around as Dody, Fontaine, Jordan, and Paige lounged together on the big brown sofa in the family room. They were watching *Phantom of the Opera*.

"Um, I'm thinking that movie is not so appropriate for my kids, Dody." I bent over and started picking up wrappers.

"Don't be ridiculous. It's a musical. Didn't your mother ever let you watch musicals when you were little?"

"Yeah, like *Chitty Chitty Bang Bang*."

"See?" She drank from her soda then offered it to Jordan.

"That's not quite the same thing."

"Shhhh, shhh!" Fontaine hissed, not taking his eyes off the television. "The Phantom is luring the girl into his dungeon lair."

"I know! That's a little dark and twisted for a six- and four-year-old, don't you think?"

Paige was sitting on Fontaine's lap, enthralled by the movie. "Why is he wearing a mask?" she whispered.

"Because he's a mutant musical genius," Fontaine answered. "Like Lady Gaga."

I looked around the room, conflicting thoughts swirling in my mind. If I went to dinner with Des, I'd have to ask one of these two to watch my kids. Could I really do that?

Jordan's head rested in Dody's lap while she petted him like a dog. Richard would have a conniption if he saw this. Where was my parental guidance? Where was the adult supervision? I bit my lip and thought about Des's hair and the way it was always just a little messy, begging me to run my fingers through it. My hand twitched. I could almost feel his hair against my palm.

Oh, what the hell. My kids would be fine.

I took the plunge. "Dody, can you watch the kids tomorrow night so I can go out?"

Fontaine's head popped up like a prairie dog's. He immediately paused the movie while he and Dody looked at me as if I'd just announced my nomination for the Nobel Peace Prize.

"Who are you going out with?"

I crossed my arms. They didn't need to sound so surprised. "Just dinner with Des."

My aunt and cousin high-fived each other. Very mature.

"Of course I'll watch the children," Dody said.

Fontaine hopped up, oblivious to Paige tumbling onto the floor from his lap. "And I'll go pick out your outfit."

"Fine," I said. "And I will go call Penny."

Penny didn't answer her phone, which was an enormous problem for me. I needed her to talk me down from the ledge onto which I had crawled. What the hell was I thinking, telling Des I'd go out to dinner with him? I could have said I had plans. I should have told him I had to sort Dody's ceramic-unicorn collection or help her tie-dye a tablecloth. Maybe it wasn't too late to cancel. I could wait until tomorrow and then tell him Jordan had a fever. But

Des was a doctor. He'd want to come over and help. Frickin' Hippocratic oath.

Fontaine walked into my bedroom and started strewing my clothes all over.

"What are you doing?" I yelled. "That's sorted and organized."

"Into what categories? Ugly clothes and uglier clothes? I have been dying to do this, girlfriend. We have got to take you shopping. What the hell is this?"

He held up my most prized possession, a sweatshirt from spring break during my senior year of college. It was faded, tattered, and perfect for wearing while eating peanut butter with your fingers and crying about your incredibly shitty marriage. I tried to snatch it from his hands.

"Give me that."

"Not a chance. It's going in the composter with this other pile of crap you call a wardrobe. Like this stuff would ever decompose. No wonder I've had a stuffy nose. It's all these synthetic fabrics you snuck in here."

Fontaine's assault on my meager wardrobe further shredded my nerves. What the hell was I going to wear?

"There is nothing to work with here," he sighed. "Get your shoes on. It's time for a little Extreme Ho Makeover."

"You expect me to go shopping simply because some guy asked me out to dinner?"

"Of course not. But you can go shopping to buy things to make you feel pretty. You deserve it. It's not for him, it's for you."

Fontaine sang a different song two hours later as I stood in the dressing room of a Bell Harbor boutique.

"Des will love that!" he said.

I was stuffed into a tiny red dress with a plunging neckline and not enough fabric. Even my feet felt naked in strappy high-heeled sandals with rhinestone buckles.

"It's skimpy. He'll think I'm trying too hard."

Fontaine shook his head. "The only thing that dress will make him think about is taking it off you."

My stomach recoiled like I'd been kicked in the gut. Taking it off me? I hadn't even thought of that! I mean, I had thought about it, but only in the most movie-version way. The way I imagined the right conditioner could make my hair swirl around like it does in the commercials, or how I daydreamed about doing something fabulous for mankind and being congratulated by Bono.

Fantasies were one thing, but actual physical contact with another human being? Fontaine was talking about skin to skin. There was no way I was ready for that. I suddenly remembered my last horrific blind date. This time I would know better.

"The shoes are too much. I have shoes I can wear."

"Those white sandals I saw in your closet? No fucking way, baby. Those puppies have been donated to the community theatre for their production of *The Golden Girls*. Next stop, Victoria's Secret."

* * *

I didn't feel any better about the dress, or the shoes, or my silky new unmentionables the next day either as I stood in front of the mirror minutes before Des was scheduled to pick me up. I tugged at the neckline, but that only made the dress shorter. No good. And the sandals were cruel, pinching my toes as if I were Cinderella's ugly stepsister who had accidentally scored a date with Prince Charming. What if he showed up and said, "Wait, I didn't mean you. Where's the pretty one?" I started to hyperventilate.

"Fontaine, I have to change. Let me wear the black pants."

"Get a hold of yourself, woman!" he scolded. "You're not going to a craft show with Dody. This is a date. Don't make me slap you, because you know I will."

I knew he would. He'd done it once before, when I used up the last of his strawberry-kiwi-scented exfoliation scrub.

"Anyway, why are you so blasted nervous? It's Des."

I tried to take a deep breath, but the dress wouldn't let me. "I know. That's the problem." I bit my lip. My voice dropped to a whisper. "Fontaine, what if I start to like him? I mean, really like him?"

Fontaine patted my arm. "Then let yourself really like him. The alternative is pure boredom, and you're too fun for that. Now I'm going downstairs to make you a cocktail. You're so jittery, you're making me nervous. Just relax."

Fontaine went downstairs, and I sat in my bedroom to collect myself. I could do this. Of course I could. This wasn't some cheesy blind date like the last guy had been. It was Des. He was a nice guy. This would be OK.

Dody and the kids were in the kitchen and I was coming down the stairs when my date arrived. Fontaine opened the door to let him in, and I was grateful for the distraction they offered. Gracious. Des looked so delicious he took my breath away. I'd only seen him in doctor stuff and scruffy beach clothes, in which he was damn fine. But cleaned up? Yum yum. His hair was combed, and he wore nice slacks and an ironed shirt. The idea of him standing at an ironing board pressing his clothes for a night out with me gave me tingles in all the places tingles tingled most often.

The kids swarmed around him like eager puppies, and he scratched at their heads as if they were. Fortunately Lazyboy and Fatso had been locked out on the porch, or Des would be covered in slobber. Then again, that might happen anyway. My tongue suddenly felt too thick for my mouth.

Finally Des looked at me. His eyes started at my shoes and traveled up slowly, making my nerves so taut I thought I might be audibly crackling. He hesitated ever so slightly at the neckline of my little red dress. Damn. I think Fontaine was right.

I stood up a little straighter, leveling my shoulders like a broken athlete daring to go out onto the field for one last play. Put me in, coach. I'm ready.

I saw his Adam's apple bob as he swallowed. "You look nice."

The words were plain and simple, but the way he said them made me flutter inside.

"Thanks, so do you."

"Oh!" Fontaine uttered softly, pressing a fist to his mouth. He wrapped an arm around a beaming Dody. "You kids go on. We'll be fine here."

CHAPTER 11

DURING THE SHORT DRIVE TO the restaurant I tried
not to think about what the wind was doing to my carefully
styled hair, choosing instead to feel giddy at how Des had
opened my car door back at Dody's. Richard never opened
doors for me, not even when I was in labor. He was too busy
worrying my water might break in his new Lexus. I shook
my head. *No thoughts of Richard tonight.* I was on a date. A
real, honest-to-goodness date with someone who knew me
and asked me out anyway.

Des parked the car on the corner of Chic and
Picturesque, in a section of Bell Harbor so quaint it was
nearly in black and white. Historic buildings lined a tree-
shaded, cobblestoned boulevard.

Des got out, and I tugged at the hem of my dress, wondering if he would open my door again. I pretended to
fuss with the buckle on my shoe, stalling just long enough
to see that he was indeed coming around to my side. Ah,
chivalry! If there was a puddle, would he throw his cloak
over it? Oh, wait. He wasn't wearing a cloak. Never mind.

The thought made me smile nonetheless.

"What's so funny?" he asked.

"Oh, nothing. I'm just happy we got such a great parking spot."

He looked up and down the nearly carless street. "Uh-huh."

His sporty BMW was low to the ground and my new FMPs were like walking on stilts. I struggled to get out of the car without twisting my ankle. What was I thinking, letting a tasseled-loafer-wearing gay man select my footwear?

Then Des reached out and took ahold of my hand, helping me from the car.

God damn! That Fontaine was a genius, making me wear these shoes!

Des's innocent touch sent a wicked chill through me. His grip was gentle but firm, with just the right amount of squeeze. And he didn't let go as we headed toward the restaurant. I bit back a girlish giggle and resisted the urge to swing our arms back and forth. Richard never liked to hold hands. He said he found it constrictive. *Darn it, no more thoughts about Richard.*

Des and I passed an artsy boutique with overflowing flowerpots sitting in front, and the bistro where I'd had lunch with Kyle and Fontaine. Across the street were a kite store, a candy shop, and an old-fashioned ice-cream parlor with red-striped awnings. The brick-paved sidewalks beneath our feet were spotlessly clean, and every few blocks rested a bench made to look like an old wagon wheel. And all the birds in the trees were chirping Beethoven's "Ode to Joy." Well, that might have only been in my imagination.

"How does sushi sound?" Des asked as he pointed to a restaurant on the next block with a stone dragon near the doorway. "A friend at work said that place is good."

"Great," I answered, not wanting to admit I'd never had sushi. Richard's vast array of prejudices extended to any restaurant with foreign words on the menu, sufficiently ruling out Asian, Indian, and even some Italian places.

We crossed the avenue, still hand in hand, and went inside. The restaurant was elegant, with an ornate stone fountain in the center and a wall of tall windows overlooking the lake. It was beautiful and serene, so fancy it didn't even have a drive-through window.

A willowy gazelle with thick, gorgeous hair approached, batting her doe-like lashes at Des.

"Good evening. Welcome to Matsusaka's. I am your hostess, Eliza." She bowed her head.

I simultaneously felt invisible yet Amazonian. I tugged at the neckline of my dress.

"Thank you," Des answered. "We'd like a table near the window, please."

"Of course. My pleasure. Do you have a reservation?" She looked him over in a sensual way, and I heard the hidden message in her sultry voice. She'd said *reservation,* but what she meant was *Lose the gargoyle in the red dress and meet me in the coatroom.*

He nodded. "I do. McKnight, for two."

"Ah, yes, right this way."

Des pressed the small of my back, nudging me to walk ahead of him. But that would put me next to her. And quite frankly I wasn't sure I wanted him to see both her ass and mine at the same time. I would suffer by comparison.

The elegant Eliza led us to a cozy little table in the corner.

He pulled out my chair, scoring another point and helping me almost forget the wafer-thin hostess.

"Enjoy your time with us this evening." Her voice was tranquil and hypnotizing, almost making me forgive her for so blatantly coveting my escort. Our waitress appeared seconds later, handing us leather-bound menus. She was another reedy, black-haired beauty with gravity-defying breasts and a matchstick waist. Where did this restaurant get these girls? A lingerie catalog?

I bit my lip and silently scolded myself. Richard flirted with waitresses in the most obnoxious fashion, insisting it was only to get better service. I never dared ask him which service he was referring to. But Des wasn't paying them any special attention. I mentally clunked myself in the head. If I let my insecurities get the best of me, I would ruin this evening before it ever started. *Get a grip, Sadie.*

Des took off his sunglasses, and I winced at the sight of his bruised eye. The swelling was gone, but a dark purple blotch remained. It was rather dashing, but I still felt bad about it.

"I'm sorry I moved that table in your foyer," I said.

He smiled. "I'll let you make it up to me."

"I thought I was making it up to you by going out to dinner."

"It's a start. Would you like a drink?"

Contemplating his not-so-subtle innuendo, I said "Yes!" with far too much gusto.

Des chuckled and picked up the wine list. "Red or white?"

He was asking me? Richard never—*God damn it!* I was going to purge Richard from my mind tonight if it took an exorcist to do it. "You decide."

I shifted in my chair, trying to cover up a little more leg with my red dress. It was a futile attempt, so I took my napkin and draped it over my thighs like a lap blanket.

Des perused the wine list, mentioning details about different kinds of grapes and eventually choosing something very pricey. I didn't have the heart to tell him that expensive wine was kind of a waste on me because I drank the cheap stuff just as fast. But if he wanted to impress me with his vast knowledge of vineyards in southern France, so be it.

I opened my menu after he ordered our wine. It was cryptically worded, and other than the California roll, I had no idea what any of it meant. Sashimi sounded like the move Dody did when getting on her bathing suit. Tempura was a type of mattress, right? And miso? As in *miso horny?*

"What looks good?" Des asked.

"Gosh," I lied, "all of it."

The wine came and I took a gulp from my glass as Des lifted his to toast.

I swallowed hard. "Oops, sorry." I lightly clinked my glass against his. "To…?"

He paused, as if measuring his words carefully. "To new friends."

The whump in my chest felt strangely like disappointment. *Well, what had I expected him to say? Here's to Sadie and her hot, rockin' baby-mama body?* I forced a smile and clinked his glass again.

"Sure, to new friends."

The rest of my wine went down fast and easy, and I began to relax. Harp music mingled with the bubbling sounds from the fountain. We chatted casually about mundane things, such as how pretty the restaurant was and how nice the weather had been. This wasn't so hard. I could do this.

I picked up the menu again, and my momentary peace of mind fled. This actually wasn't going to work. I'd have to come clean about my Japanese-food ignorance or risk inadvertently ordering octopus and then having to eat it. "I have a confession to make."

Des lowered his own menu warily. "Yes?"

"I've never had sushi."

"You've never had sushi?" His good eye widened.

"No, I've never had sushi."

"How is that even possible? Don't you like it?"

"I'll probably like it." I set down my menu. "Richard hated fish. And rice. And Asians. And Mexicans who looked like they might be Asians."

Des took a sip of his own wine. "He sounds neat."

"He's a one of a kind. I hope."

Des ran a hand through his hair. "Do you want to go someplace else?"

"No, I like fish and rice. I just have no idea what to order." I lowered my voice. "And for the record, I personally have no issue with Asians or Mexicans."

He smiled. "I'm glad to hear that."

Then he explained to me about the intricacies of Asian cuisine. This guy was so smart.

"And we should probably have a little sake too. But be careful. It's very potent stuff," he warned.

"Isn't it, like, rice water?"

He shook his head. "Don't be fooled. It doesn't have much flavor, but it's got a hell of a kick."

"Sounds like my ex."

Des chuckled. "Mine too."

The waitress returned and we ordered. Des was cordial with her, but not the least bit flirty. I relaxed a little more and sipped my second glass of wine. Then, just for fun, I crossed my arms on the table and leaned forward, sort of setting my breasts on them in a maneuver Penny called "displaying your wares." She was a master at this, and every time she did it, some guy would buy her a drink. Of course, her wares were bigger than mine and hadn't gone through two pregnancies. As soon as I thought of that, I sat back up.

The sake was brought to us in a small ceramic bottle along with miniature cups. It reminded me of one of Paige's little play tea sets. Des filled one tiny cup to the brim and handed it to me before pouring one for himself. This time I waited to see if there would be toasting. Sure enough, he lifted his hand.

"To new adventures," he said.

That was more encouraging. "To new adventures." I nodded. Then I courageously tipped back the cup and drank it down in one swallow. The sake was warm, which startled me. And it heated up as it went down. I looked at Des in surprise, only to find him gaping back at me with an equally stunned expression.

"Wow!" I sputtered.

Then he started laughing. "Sadie, you're supposed to sip it. It's not a shot glass."

I looked at the cup in my hand. "It isn't? Are you sure?"

He laughed harder. "I'm positive."

"Oh." The warmth of the sake mingled with burning embarrassment, and I flushed from head to toe.

He shook his head and refilled my cup. "Sip it," he said again.

So I sipped it. But it was very tasty, and I still seemed to be drinking mine much faster than Des.

The tables around us began to fill with other diners as we talked and enjoyed our drinks. Then the food came, and I discovered I loved sushi as much as sake. So far this evening was going quite well. I mentally patted myself on the back. Either I was naturally charming and vivacious or the alcohol was giving me superpowers of seduction.

Des smiled brightly as I told him how Paige cried when she lost her first tooth because she was worried it might be her "sweet tooth." Then I remembered Fontaine's warning not to spend the entire evening talking about my kids, so I changed the subject.

"You have three sisters, right?" I actually remembered him saying a few things about them before, but this seemed like a nice, safe topic. And the more he talked, the more I could listen to that yummy accent.

He nodded. "Yep. Bonnie, my older sister, is a pediatrician. Shannon is the teacher, and Robin is a museum curator. No brothers."

"Two doctors in the house, huh? That's interesting."

He deftly picked up a piece of sushi with his chopsticks. "Bonnie and I were pretty competitive with each other, so once she got into Harvard I couldn't resist the challenge. It turned out to be a good thing for us, though. It forced

us to help each other out since we were there and the rest
of the family was in Illinois."

"Are you close now?"

He finished chewing before speaking. Had I been allow-
ing myself any comparisons between him and Richard, I
would have noted that my ex-husband frequently talked
with his mouth full while Des did not.

"Yeah, we're all close," Des finally answered. "But I've
been moving around a lot these last few years, so I don't
see any of them that often. It's always good to visit home."

"What made you decide to do that local tenant...what's
it called again?" I sipped more sake.

"Locum tenens." He shrugged. "Quite honestly, after
my divorce I wasn't sure where I wanted to be. Chicago was
home, but I kind of needed a break, you know?"

I nodded, and he refilled my cup.

"I had a bunch of job offers at the time, but nothing
felt quite right. I didn't want to move someplace for the
sake of moving. Then a buddy of mine suggested I try this
for a bit until I found a place that clicked."

"And have you? Found a place that clicks, I mean?" I bit
my lip, hoping he might say yes but realizing my question
was totally Dody in caliber.

His smile was enigmatic. He took a sip of wine before
answering. "Some places have more perks than others."

That wasn't quite the glowing endorsement I was going
for, but then he winked at me and my breath escaped in a
soft gasp. Damn, he was delicious.

The conversation veered to other topics. I told him
about my foray into organizing, and he had the polite for-
titude to act as if that was fascinating. While we talked, I

tried to mimic his chopstick skills but wasn't having much luck. Mostly I kept pushing the sushi around on the plate. Every once in a while, when he wasn't looking, I'd pop a piece into my mouth using my fingers. I didn't have trouble with the wineglass, though. That was easy, and so I kept drinking it.

As Des talked and smiled, I marveled at my being on a date. With him. Tall, dark, handsome him.

But he was more than good-looking. He was kind and sweet and funny and bawdy. He laughed at my dumb jokes and told silly stories of his own about medical school and crazy things that happened in the emergency department. He asked me questions about my life back in Glenville and my childhood and family. I drank more wine and noticed he had a subtle crook to his nose, and that the tip of it moved the teensiest bit when he chewed. I looked at the little scar near his eye and wondered how he'd gotten it. Its paleness stood out amid the bruising. These were flaws, technically, but they made him more magnificently real. He wasn't some beautiful, glossy, anonymous creature running past me on the beach anymore. He was Des.

And I was falling for him.

The thought startled me as much as the warm sake had. Because I had no business falling for anybody. It wouldn't be convenient or logical or wise. It wasn't part of my plan. I gulped another shot of sake when he looked down at his plate. I felt the stirrings of a panic attack. I'd had a few since finding Richard with the redhead but thought they were behind me. Apparently not.

The room spun. It was warm in here with all these people. I looked back at my date, in his ironed shirt with his hair all combed, and my anxiety doubled. This was too much. He was too much. Des, with his intense gaze rolling over me like hot lava, making me sizzle right to the bone. I wasn't ready for this.

But I wasn't sure it was up to me anymore.

The buzzy din of the crowd pressed in, and it got harder to hear what he said. But I wasn't listening to his words so much as watching his lips move. They were luscious lips, full but not too full. His dimples deepened when he smiled.

In the candlelight Des glowed bronze like a gleaming fertility statue. He took a drink from his water glass, and suddenly I longed to be that glass in his big, strong hand. Or better yet, to be the water, pouring myself into him.

Wait.

What?

Oh…no…

Oh, shit!

I was wasted.

Damn it! I was completely and totally wasted! Pouring myself into him? What the hell did that even mean? Crap, crap, crap! If I was drunk, how the hell was I supposed to keep on my little red dress? Full-blown panic descended.

I needed to eat more, quickly. Something to soak up the booze. But the chopsticks taunted me, refusing to bring food to my mouth.

I looked at Des helplessly. He smiled back, ignorant of the alarms clanging in my head. He needed to stop looking at me that way, as if I was interesting and desirable, because I was intoxicated enough to believe him. I was woozy and delirious. My head and stomach rolled in opposite directions. I was seriously drunk. And besides that, I was seriously drunk.

He leaned forward to say something, something illicit and persuasive, I was certain. He slid his hand over the table toward mine. He was about to ask me back to his place. And I would say yes.

But before he spoke, something caught his eye. He sat back abruptly and dropped his hand into his lap.

I felt the whoosh of cold air, and then I saw her. She was tall, with white-blonde hair and full, pouty lips curved into a seductive smile. As she sauntered toward our table, her clingy black dress did what clingy black dresses do best.

Des shifted in his chair. I saw his skin flush as he adjusted the collar of his shirt.

"Why, Des. What a surprise. Have you been hiding from me? What happened to your eye?"

He stood up, and she pressed herself against him and kissed the air near his ear.

He leaned away. "Long story. And no, I'm not hiding. I just haven't had time to call."

"That's a shame. You know offers like mine don't last forever."

The cold finger of reality goosed me in a most unpleasant fashion. It was like being out with Richard again. The woman's body language practically screamed they'd been lovers. Or if they weren't, she wanted to be. And she was stunning. I, on the other hand, had two children, a C-section scar, and 230 pounds of ex-husband strapped to my back. Why would Des be interested in a woman like me when he could have a woman like her? The truth was he wouldn't be. I must have made a mistake.

I downed another shot of sake and let it burn all the way to my gut.

Des smiled. "I haven't forgotten. But it's not the time to discuss it." He glanced at me. I crossed my arms and stared back, hoping I looked bored rather than despondent.

"Oh, I see. And who's this?" She reached out a well-manicured hand. "Hello. I'm Reilly Sommers."

I reluctantly shook her claw, but before I could respond, Des said, "This is my neighbor, Reilly. We're finishing up dinner as you can see. Would you excuse us? You and I can talk later."

A neighbor? Did he just call me a neighbor? Not a date or even a friend. God, I wasn't even an acquaintance. I was someone you borrowed sugar from. He had confirmed my fears. He wasn't interested. The sake roiled in my gut and nearly returned itself to the table.

"Of course. Sorry to interrupt. But don't forget to call me, Des. We really need to talk."

He nodded. "I'll call soon. I promise."

She slithered away, and I found myself wondering if she could possibly have anything at all on under that dress.

Des sat back down with a thud.

"Sorry about that. Now where were we?" His bright smile didn't reach all the way to his eyes. I considered blackening the other.

Where were we? We'd just gotten to the part about how I'm your neighbor.

I forced a smile in return. "I think we were about to leave, weren't we?"

His face fell. "Please don't be upset by her. I would've introduced you but—"

"It's OK," I interrupted. "We're only neighbors. It doesn't matter." How many times had Richard said that? "Don't be upset." As if my being angry over his bad behavior was the problem.

But I wouldn't be angry at Des. At least not so he'd see it. He'd done a nice thing, bringing me out to dinner. He probably felt sorry for me, the poor lonely divorcée with the crazy aunt. I bet she put him up to this. Oh God. She probably did! That would be just like Dody. I took another gulp of wine and let its swirling powers overtake me. I was more than halfway to drunk, but I wanted to go all in.

He sighed. "How about some coffee?"

The catwalk-strutting hostess wandered by, and I watched her, wishing I looked like her instead of me.

"Sadie?" Des said.

"What?" My voice was louder than I expected.

"Would you like some coffee?"

Coffee? Hell, no. I wanted to dunk my face into a fishbowl full of sake and drink myself blind. But that might be rude, so I said, "Sure, let's have coffee." I swished my hand as if it held a magic wand that could (*poof!*) bring coffee.

Des signaled for the waiter. That should work as well. He started saying something about being in Bell Harbor, but it didn't make any sense to me. We were already in Bell Harbor. Maybe he was drunk too. Maybe that's why he was so blurry.

What was he talking about now? New assignments? Finally he fell silent. The weight of it crushed me, along with any lingering hope that he had been interested in me. *Just a neighbor?* Fuck him.

How naive could I have been? Of course he wasn't interested in me. Hadn't he already hinted he was on his way out of town as soon as he got a better offer? I had let myself pretend that this night was the start of something. But I was wrong. Again.

"Hey, Des. Hey, Sade." I heard Jasper's voice. It seemed far away, but suddenly he was standing right next to us. Damn. Was everybody at this restaurant tonight?

Des's response was terse. "Jasper, hi. What are you doing here?"

"Just checking out the restaurant competition," he answered. "Beth is in the ladies' room." He looked at me. "Sadie? What's the matter?"

That tipped the scale. I lost it and burst into tears.

"Hey! What the hell? Geez, Des! What did you do?"

I couldn't hear his response because I started crying harder and poured another cup of sake before Des pried it from my fingers. I let him take it and reached for my wine instead. I leaned back in my chair, confused by having the bed spins, which was totally weird because I wasn't in a bed.

Jasper said something, but it was warbled and nonsensical, so I ignored him. What did he know anyway? Stupid, naive Jasper wanting to get married. What a dumb-ass. Someday he'd probably end up living at Dody's with his kids too. Like me. He talked to Des for another minute, frowned at me, and then left.

Des stood up, came around the table, and started pulling out my chair, which was just plain rude because I was not done with my drink.

"Let's go home, Sadie." He pulled me up by the shoulders.

Walking through the restaurant lobby, I felt as if scorpions were attacking my feet. I tried to kick them away before seeing the satin instruments of torture Fontaine had made me wear. It was those fucking shoes. I took them off and walked barefoot to the car. I heard the woof of expensive leather upholstery compressing in my seat. I wasn't crying anymore but felt the cold trail of leftover tears as Des put the car in motion. All I wanted to do was take off that stupid dress and get into my lumpy bed.

Sometime later we pulled into Dody's driveway and Des stopped the car. He turned as if he wanted to say something, but I opened my door and climbed out, tugging at my hemline. God, I hated this dress.

His car door opened and shut.

"Sadie," he called after me.

I turned around reluctantly.

He held out his arm, and I saw my shoes dangling from his fingers.

Damn, I must've left them in the car. I could go in without them. It's not as if I'd ever wear them again. But Dody might want them for salsa dancing class.

I stepped gingerly toward him, realizing now how rough the gravel was under my bare feet.

He smiled, the rotten prick.

When I reached for my shoes, he moved his hand back so I had to step closer. I hesitantly took another step and reached for them again. Every time I grabbed, he moved his hand. Didn't he know it was pure meanness to taunt a drunk girl with pretty shoes? I stomped one foot in frustration and winced as the gravel dug into my sole. And soul.

"Ouch." My voice was petulant.

He chuckled and finally handed me my shoes. He turned me around by my shoulders and steered me to the front door.

"Are you going to be all right?" he asked.

"Peachy keen, jelly bean."

"OK. Go put yourself to bed, Sadie." Then he got in the car and drove away.

CHAPTER 12

RELENTLESS KAMIKAZE PILOTS FIRED WEAPONS inside my brain. I woke to an excruciating headache, as if someone were operating on my skull with rusty knitting needles. When I rolled over, it took a full eleven seconds for my stomach to catch up. Then memories of my disgraceful behavior flooded over me. I had cried. I had sat at that lovely restaurant in my sultry red dress and my strappy sandals and let some stupid boy make me cry. No, even worse. I'd let some skanky ho make me cry. I'd made a complete fool of myself. A YouTube video of me dancing the hokeypokey naked with a weasel on my head would have been less humiliating.

Des must think I'm psychotic. But then again, so what? We were only neighbors, right? It's not like I gave a flying rat's ass what he thought of me anyway. And now I didn't have to wonder if he was attracted to me. I'd ruined any chance of that and saved myself a lot of time and trouble.

So why did I feel like my body was rejecting an organ transplant?

Outside my window the gorgeous blue sky and beaming sunshine mocked me. It was a beautiful new day. Against my will, I started to cry again. I didn't want a new day full of the same shit as yesterday. I didn't want to be alone. But I didn't have the courage not to be.

"Mommy?" Paige opened my bedroom door and peeked inside.

I swiped away my hot tears. Oh, that's right! I wasn't alone! I had my children. They would comfort me in my dotage when I started wearing orthopedic shoes and a bra on the outside of my blouse. Jordan would pick me up from the Golden Years old folks' home every Sunday for church, and then we'd go to the park to feed the ducks. On Wednesdays, I'd wear my ratty gray cardigan and Paige would take me grocery shopping. It wasn't a very exciting future, but it was good enough for me.

"Come in, sweetie," I said listlessly.

She scampered over, her exuberance widening the chasm between her vitality and my imminent spiral into miserable old age. She climbed up and over, bumping her knee into my stomach, making it churn again.

"Did you have fun on your playdate with Des?" she asked.

"Yes, honey." No sense in telling her the truth until it was absolutely necessary. Let her be the fairy princess a little longer.

"What did you do?"

"We had supper at a restaurant."

"Did you have macaroni and cheese?" She picked at the fringe on one of the bed pillows.

"No, I had fish."

She wrinkled her nose. "Yuck. I don't like fish. Did you have ice cream for dessert?"

"No."

"Hmm." She looked down at my face. "Why are your eyes all fat?"

I rubbed them with both hands. "I'm just tired."

"Why are you tired? It's morning."

Should I tell her I was tired because her father is a deplorable excuse for a man who ruined my outlook on life? Or that I was boarding the Solitaire Express with a one-way ticket to Lonely-ville? And most of all, should I warn her that no matter how much a man might pretend to like her, he'd always have his eye on other women?

"Oh, no reason," I said. "Where's Jordan?"

"He's downstairs watching Fontaine do Yoda."

"What?" Please tell me she meant something else.

Paige swayed her arms up, clasping her hands over her head then bringing them down slowly in front of her tummy. "The bendy exercise. Yoda."

"Oh. Yoga. OK. Well, anyway, Mommy has to get dressed now. Why don't you go downstairs and I'll be there in a minute." I pushed off the covers and took a very deep breath.

"Can we go swimming?"

"We'll have to see, honey. Mommy doesn't feel very good right now."

"Des says it looks like a good day for swimming."

My churning stomach nearly dumped into my mouth. "When did he say that?"

"This morning."

"You talked to him this morning?" Neurons fired in every direction in my brain, with not one making a logical connection.

Paige nodded, her little curls bobbing in her face.

"When this morning?"

She wiggled off the bed. "When we were having breakfast on the deck and he was jogging."

Only my maternal instinct prevented me from grabbing my precious child and shaking her by the shoulders. "What else did he say?"

Taking me literally, she replied, "He said, 'Hi, Paige. Hey, Jordan.' I think he said, 'What's up, Fontaine?' Then he told a grown-up joke and I couldn't hear them."

"How do you know it was a grown-up joke?"

"Because when I asked what was funny they said it was a grown-up joke."

And there it was. Word was out. At least I'd be spared the indignity of having to share it myself. "Is he still here?"

Paige shook her head and walked to the door. "Nope. See you later, alligator."

She left with a flip of her curls. I sat up, with effort, and tried to come to grips with the last twenty-four hours, dreading the knowledge that the next twenty-four could be even worse.

I pulled on some loose pants and a huge T-shirt and tried to brush my teeth. Working up a lather with the toothpaste was tougher than usual. Maybe because my mouth was as dry as if I'd slept with a Shop-Vac in it all night.

I tiptoed downstairs, hearing murmured voices on the sunporch. If I could get to the coffee and ibuprofen before anyone saw me, maybe I could grab it and sneak back to my room. But the minute my big toe hit the hardwood, Fontaine pounced like paparazzi on the latest teen sensation.

"Hold up, kitten chow! There you are!"

I crouched, my reaction time so slow my body still thought it could hide. I'd never noticed how shrill Fontaine's voice was. Was it always like that? He could frighten bats with a screech like that.

He walked into the kitchen wearing bicycle shorts and a nylon shirt the color of circus peanuts. "How was your date last night?"

"Very funny," I said, reaching toward the coffee mugs with a trembling hand.

His dark brows furrowed. "What does that mean?"

"You already know I made a fool of myself."

Furrowed brows rose up. "What are you talking about? What happened?"

I set the coffee pot back in the holder and took a gulp. It burned all the way down my throat yet somehow managed to not leave any moisture behind. I looked at Fontaine through bloodshot eyes. "Des didn't tell you?"

Fontaine shook his head, his bangs flopping from side to side. He pulled out a chair and sat down. "No, he didn't, but you'd better!"

Was it possible Des had not revealed my humiliation? Richard would have made a huge production of such an occasion. He loved to repeat stories of my misadventures. Like the time I accidentally ripped an incredibly loud fart during a funeral at precisely the moment the priest asked if anyone had something they'd like to share. Or the time we were out to dinner with Richard's boss and I discovered I had Jordan's baby poo all over my sleeve.

"Des didn't tell you anything?"

Fontaine smacked his hand on the table with impatience. "All he said was you had a nice time. So what's your story?"

"I cried."

"You what?"

"Yep. Bawled like a little girl." I might as well tell it straight up.

Fontaine smacked both palms against his cheeks, sufficiently aghast. "Why? Why did you do that?"

My next slug of coffee didn't burn nearly so badly now that my throat was scarred over from the last swallow.

"Oh…I'd say it was thirty percent sake and seventy percent because he introduced me to some gorgeous whore as '*just a neighbor*.'"

Fontaine sucked air in through clenched teeth. "That bastard."

I nodded. "I know, right?"

Dody breezed into the kitchen wearing a silky yellow caftan. "Good morning, sunshine. How was your evening?"

"We were just getting to that," Fontaine said. "Apparently our Sadie here had a bit of a meltdown."

"It wasn't that little," I said.

"She's not kidding. I was there," Jasper called out, thumping down the stairs two at a time.

Wonderful. Now we could all share the postmortem details of my evening together.

Jasper kissed Dody on the cheek, flicked Fontaine in the ear, and made a face at me. Then he poured himself a cup of coffee.

Fontaine put his elbows on the table and laced his fingers together.

"All right, let's have it. What's the real four-one-one?"

I shrugged and shook my head. "I drank too much. He called me his neighbor. I cried. He's never going to ask me out again. What else is there to say?"

Fontaine frowned. "When you say you cried, do you mean you had a delicate little tear on your cheek or did you do the whole gasping for breath, hiccupping, scary face thing?"

"I'd say it was somewhere in the middle," Jasper answered.

"It was not! It wasn't that bad."

"Sadie, you wiped your nose with the tablecloth."

"I did not! It was my napkin!"

"No, trust me. You pulled up the tablecloth. Des had to grab the glasses so they didn't tip over."

Oh God. It *was* possible to feel even worse. I didn't remember any of that!

Dody hugged me tightly, patting my back. "Don't worry, darling. These things happen. Des will understand. Did you at least remember to stroke his eagle?"

"What?" I gasped.

"His eagle. You know how much men like to talk about themselves."

"Ego," Fontaine said, interpreting.

"Oh, um, yeah, I guess."

"It couldn't have been that bad. Des was here this morning," Fontaine noted.

"Maybe he wanted to view the body," Jasper teased.

I pinched his arm. "You are not helping!"

"I'm not trying to."

"Clearly!"

Jasper laughed and twisted away from my reach. "OK, OK. I'll be nice. You weren't *so* bad last night."

"I wasn't? Then I didn't wipe my nose on the tablecloth?"

"Oh, yeah. You totally did that. But I think Des thought it was kind of funny."

"He did?" Fontaine was disbelieving. "But that's disgusting."

"Oh, like you haven't done worse?" I challenged.

"Hey, what two consenting adults choose to do in the privacy of their own room, or an elevator, is not in question here. And I have never blown my nose on a restaurant tablecloth."

"I didn't blow it. I dabbed it." The memory was starting to come back to me.

Jasper tipped his head, conceding, "It was more of a dab than a blow."

"See!"

"I'm confused," Dody said. "Why did you cry?"

"Because he introduced me as his neighbor."

Jasper snorted. "You are his neighbor, dumb-ass. How is that an insult?"

"You wouldn't understand," I sniffed.

"You got that right."

"I'm afraid I don't understand either, dear. Why did that upset you?" Dody asked.

Geez, what was wrong with these people?

"Never mind. It doesn't matter now. It's because Des is so..." I flapped my hands as if the words were dangling invisibly around me but I couldn't grasp them. "And

I'm so…well, it's better this way," I said with finality. I looked around to see if they understood all that I was not saying.

Dody scowled. "Humph! Young lady, do you think that rainy day when I got into Walter's car for the first time I wasn't nervous? He was mature and debonair and I was a skinny bit of a girl, soaking wet in a hand-me-down dress with freckles from here till next Sunday. I wasn't always this put together, you know!" She patted her hair, pulling out a pink foam curler. "But I set my cap for him, and nothing was going to stop me."

Fontaine and Jasper smiled at each other. They'd heard this story before.

"He drove me home that day, and I tell you what, he came back the next day and the next day and the day after that. And do you know why?"

I was tempted to answer, "Because Uncle Walter was a boob man?"

Dody went on, "Because he said I was the sunshiniest girl he'd ever met. Being around me made him happy, because I was happy. He said I could find the silver lining in a mushroom cloud, whatever that means. So maybe I wasn't the prettiest back then, or the smartest, or the richest, but I made him happy. So he married me."

"That's great for you, Dody. But I'm not that kind of person. And none of this matters anyway. I'm leaving at the end of the summer, so even if I did like him, and he liked me, what good would it do?"

She poked her finger at my nose. "Glenville is not that far away, young lady. You are using that as an excuse. You have an excuse for everything, but not one good reason."

"So you think I should pretend to be happy so Des will like me? That's a little Stepford Wife, don't you think?"

"No, silly. Don't pretend to be happy. *Choose* to be happy."

She wasn't making any sense at all. You didn't choose happiness. It was pure dumb luck. Either it came your way or it didn't.

"Dody, it's not that simple."

"Yes, it is. You're the one making it complicated."

I looked to my cousins for backup. Jasper shook his head and walked away but Fontaine nodded, his lips pursed in agreement.

Dody patted me again. "You know what they say, darling. When life gives you oranges, have some juice."

⟡   ⟡   ⟡

Maybe my sister would know what I was talking about. Penny was pretty good about this kind of stuff.

"Oh for God's sake," she groaned into the phone, "screw somebody already, will you?"

"That's your advice?" I flopped back on my bed with my feet up on the wall, my standard phone call to Penny position.

"Yes. Honestly, Sade! This whole woe-is-me, my husband cheated on me thing is so last year. Richard was an asshole. *Get over it!* I mean, seriously, so what if this Des guy went out with the blonde from the restaurant? He wasn't with her last night. He asked you out instead, so clearly he wanted to be with you."

"But she was totally coming on to him and he let her. Right in front of me."

"What was he supposed to do? Punch her in the face?"

"He could have at least introduced me by name. But whatever. I gave it a shot. There's no point in dating him anyway."

"Why? Because you don't want to get married again? If you don't, that's fine. But does that mean you're never going out with a man again for the rest of your life? That's stupid."

I tapped my feet against the wall. "You're stupid."

Penny chuckled at last. "No, you're stupid, because you're acting like every date should be a job interview for your next baby daddy. Why must you overthink everything? Go out and have some fun and stop worrying all the time. You exhaust me."

It was unanimous. Everyone in my family, including me, thought I was an idiot.

CHAPTER 13

SINCE INSTITUTING MY EXPERT ORGANIZA-
TIONAL design in Dody's kitchen, putting away the
dishes was a snap. Now if only I could get them to adhere
to my refrigerator-shelf-labeling system, life would be
even easier. But it almost seemed as if they didn't care.
I scolded Fontaine as he set a jar of Dijon mustard next
to a carton of free-range, grain-fed, self-actualized
chicken eggs.

"Hey! Look!" I tapped hard on the correctly label shelf.
"It says right here: *condiments*. Mustard is a condiment."

He scratched the side of his nose with his middle finger.
"Do the words OCD mean anything to you?"

"Those are letters, not words. And you're the one who
told me to organize."

"I had no idea what a field of land mines that would
create."

"Just put the mustard where it belongs and nobody
gets hurt, OK?"

"On one condition. You have to call Des."

"That's extortion."

"Extortion. Persuasion. Whatever. He probably thinks you're mad at him." Fontaine set a jar of pickles next to the soy milk just to piss me off.

I moved the pickles to the pickle shelf. "I am mad. It was humiliating. God, Fontaine. It was like he couldn't remember my name."

"Maybe he was protecting you. Like, maybe she's some crazy stalker who'd come after you with a machete."

"Spaghetti? Who's having spaghetti? We just ate," Dody asked, wandering in from the dining room with Paige and Jordan.

"I want cake for dessert. Not masghetti," Jordan pouted.

"See what you started?" I said to Fontaine.

"Call him."

I covered both my ears. "La la la. I can't hear you."

"Are you calling Daddy, Mommy? Are we going to see him tomorrow?" Paige asked.

They were supposed to, yes. But he hadn't called to confirm, so I couldn't be certain. Richard didn't like to be tied down with tiny details, such as keeping promises to his kids. Plus he was still mad at me for staying here with Fontaine.

"I'll check with him, Paige. I'll go call him right now."

"Hello?" Richard drawled into the phone.

"Richard, hi. It's Sadie. I wanted to check with you about bringing the kids." If I could make this conversation short and to the point, maybe we wouldn't end up fighting.

"Oh, yeah, I was just about to call you."

I braced myself. Here came the cancellation and some lame-ass excuse, like he had to donate a kidney that day or his boss was sending him to Barbados.

"Listen, I want to apologize for being upset with you last time. I guess Fontaine has a right to stay wherever he wants. And if the kids aren't freaked out by him or anything, I guess I shouldn't make you cut your vacation short."

I pulled the phone away and examined it. This must be a toy, with my wishful imagination creating words in Richard's voice. He thought apologizing was for pussies. (His expression, not mine.) But the phone was real. I put it back to my ear.

"Richard, are the terrorists making you say this? Do they have a gun to your head?"

He chuckled. "No, but I've done a lot of soul-searching lately. I'm tired of fighting with you all the time and I guess I haven't been fair—about you staying at Dody's, I mean. It's only for a couple months, right? And you promised me Fontaine is behaving himself, so I'm OK with it."

I sank down to the floor in a heap. Could he mean it? This was 180 degrees from normal.

"Richard, this is so...so open-minded of you."

"Yeah, maybe an old dog can learn a few new tricks, huh? You know, I've been seeing this therapist, and she's taught me a lot. You should be proud of me."

I bit my tongue. So what if he was sleeping with his therapist? If she could turn him into a nicer man, then so be it. It wasn't any of my business.

Richard continued. "And listen, just to prove I really mean it, why not let me come pick them up this time? I can be in Bell Harbor by noon and take them up to my brother Chet's place for a couple days. You know, maybe keep them a little longer this time, if that's OK with you.

I've got a few vacation days saved up and I've been missing my P and J something terrible."

I put my head in my hand. This was unbefuckingbeliev-able. Aliens had taken over my ex-husband's body and somehow turned him human in the process. My insides liquefied. I felt whooshy and soft. Dody kept telling me to forgive and forget. If he was finally coming around, maybe now was the time to give that a test run.

"The kids are anxious to see you too, Richard. I'm sure they'd love to have some extra time. Are you sure you don't mind picking them up?"

"No, it's no problem. It's sort of on the way. Just make sure you pack their life preservers in case we go on Chet's boat."

"Sure, OK." Was he actually becoming safety conscious too? I looked out the window for a flying pig.

"Great. Thanks, Sadie. I really appreciate you being so understanding. Chet and his kids will be there. We're going to fish and camp out, just like we used to do as a family. I'm really looking forward to it."

After our good-byes, I hung up the phone and sat cross-legged on the floor until Jordan found me. "Mommy, what are you doing? Are we going to see Daddy?"

"Yes, baby, you are. And I think you're going to have a very fun time."

CHAPTER 14

RICHARD WAS IN AND OUT the next day like a pizza-delivery man. He arrived on time, was gracious and cordial, and loaded the kids into the car without one hint of drama.

"I don't know, Dody. Do you suppose he's up to something?" I asked after Richard drove away.

Dody shook her head slowly. "You should always give people the benefit of the doubt, darling. But I have to admit, that's one rat I never thought would change his spots."

I bit my lip, pondering a dozen sinister possibilities as we walked into the family room. Maybe he'd kidnap them and drive over the border? No, he couldn't troll for chicks with two kids in the backseat. Plus he hated Canadians. Maybe he'd drop them off at Jesus Camp and bring them back to me as little evangelicals? No, Richard and church didn't mix. Too many rules about monogamy. So try as I might, I couldn't come up with anything. Except that maybe, just maybe, he was being sincere.

"Is the spawn of Satan gone?" Fontaine asked, coming in from the deck.

"I hope you're referring to my ex-husband and not my adorable children."

"Uh, sure. Whatever. So you're childless now, huh? In the mood for some good news?"

I nodded, grabbing a feather duster from the pantry and swooshing it over a shelf.

"I just talked to Kyle on the phone. He went to Owen and Patrick's housewarming party, and apparently they were gushing about what a great job you did for them last week. And now a bunch of their friends want to hire you! And guess what else?"

"What?" My arm froze, the duster poised above Dody's porcelain statue of Abraham Lincoln.

"A couple of them want me to do some redecorating too. At the same time. Isn't that stupendous? You and I can work together. Just think of it, pumpkin pie. This could be the start of a bee-yoo-tiful partnership, don't you think? We decorate, we organize. We're decorganizers! We could start our own company, along with Kyle too, of course." Fontaine began pacing, holding his hands up as if to contain all the fabulous ideas about to burst out. "We need a name. Something clever and catchy." He snapped his fingers and spun around to face me again. "By Jove, I've got it. Stash-in-Fashion."

I fluttered the feather duster over President Lincoln's face. "Hold on, Fontaine. That's great news and everything, but don't get all wound up over it. I mean, there's a lot to consider. I'm not ready to commit to anything."

Dody's eyes glistened. She clapped her hands together. "Oh, you two will be so happy together. I hoped and hoped something would come up to make you want to stay here, darling."

I dropped the duster and nearly knocked Honest Abe from his pedestal. "What? Dody, come on. That's not even what we're talking about."

"Not really, but think of it. If you did move here, the children could walk to school. There's that path from the corner of my yard that goes right to the elementary school. I've already talked to the principal. She's in my stained-glass class. And you could live right here. Fontaine will be back in his place soon and Jasper is always at Beth's, so there is plenty of room. Oh, Sadie, I would love for you to come live here."

I would have laughed if it wasn't so ridiculous. "Are you kidding me with this stuff, Dody? I can't move here."

"Why not?" Fontaine and Dody cried in unison.

I stared at them for a full minute, waiting for the "gotcha" to come. It never did.

Dody sat down on the sofa. "I thought you were enjoying yourself here, darling."

I sat down next to her while Fontaine paced again, biting his manicured thumb.

"I just never thought about it, Dody. I mean, I do love it here, but my life is back in Glenville."

"But aren't you happier here than you were there?"

"That's apples and oranges, Dody. Of course I'm happier here. I'm on vacation. But Glenville is home." I stacked the magazines on the coffee table.

"Why? What's there for you except a house that's too big?"

"Well, there's Penny, and my mom, and my friends." It occurred to me just then that none of my friends had called me in weeks, not to see how I was doing or even to share their latest gossip. And every time I was back in town to drop off the kids, none of them was ever available for lunch or coffee. Had I been voted off the island and no one told me?

Dody shook her stubborn head. "Penny travels and your mother is always busy with her committees. You told me that yourself."

Penny did travel, but she'd be getting pregnant soon, and I'd want to be close by for that.

"OK, so what about Richard? We'd have to drive the kids back and forth all the time."

"Stash-In-Fashion, Sadie. Don't you love it?" Fontaine said loudly. "We can still do it, even if you move home."

"Hush, Fontaine. She needs to move here." Dody patted my hand. "Glenville was your past. But I think Bell Harbor is your future. We should go see Madame Margaret. She'll tell you what to do."

I ejected from the couch. "No, Dody. I'm not letting your psychic advisor decide where I live. And Fontaine, as far as a partnership goes, it might be fun to do this one project together, but after that I'm going to have to think about it."

CHAPTER 15

MOVE TO BELL HARBOR? WHAT a ridiculous idea. I needed to clear the thought right from my head. Some solitude on the beach would soothe away my agitation. Too bad I couldn't seem to get any. No sooner had I stretched out my blue-striped towel on the sand before Dody and Fontaine were on me again. They clumped down the deck steps laden with umbrellas, beach chairs, and coolers. Dody was wearing her floppy red sun hat and a daisy-covered swimsuit. Jasper showed up twenty minutes later with three of his lanky friends, each carrying part of a volleyball net. I must have missed the memo about a beach party, but apparently I was the only one.

By midafternoon, a dozen people cluttered our beach. Kyle showed up, looking liked a well-oiled Calvin Klein underwear model. Dody's BFF, Anita Parker, arrived wearing purple sunglasses and carrying a feathered beer koozie. She was scrawny, freckled, and never stopped talking.

"Hello, Anita," I said. "It's so nice to see you again."

"Nice to see you too, Sadie. Dody's been keeping me up to date. Sorry to hear about your lousy husband." She took a loud sip of beer through a straw.

I exchanged a look with Fontaine. "Thanks. Sorry to hear your cat ate your bird."

"Oh, that was awful, let me tell you. Pure carnage! Fur and feathers everywhere, and nothing I could do to stop it. I don't blame the cat, mind you. It was purely self-defense. Birdie always was mean, but I never expected them to go at it like that. One minute I'm sitting on the couch watching my shows and the next thing I know, there's a deranged cockatoo pecking away at my poor old pussy."

Fontaine's eyes went round, but before he could form a response that was sure to be grossly inappropriate, I grabbed him by the shirt and dragged him to the deck steps, where we collapsed into a pile of laughter.

"What's so funny?" I heard Des's voice ask from over my shoulder.

My laughter faded. When the hell did he show up? I hadn't even seen him arrive! I suddenly became acutely aware of needing to suck some stuff in and stick some other stuff out. Even if I was mad at him, I didn't want to look pudgy in my swimsuit.

Fontaine squawked like a bird and started laughing all over again, but the joke was over for me.

I shaded my eyes and looked up at Des. "Oh, hi. It's nothing. Mrs. Parker's cat ate her bird. It was funnier the way she told it."

"Mmm." He scratched his head absently and looked around. He seemed to be avoiding eye contact. "Fontaine, suppose you could give us a minute?"

"Sure thing, cowboy." Fontaine hopped up and was gone before I could grab his shirt again. He was a terrible wingman.

Des sat down on the deck step next to me, clearing his throat. He clasped his hands, tapping his thumbs together rapidly.

I leaned away. "So what's up, neighbor?" I meant to sound indifferent, but there was no disguising the edginess in my voice. I may as well have said, "What's up, asshole?"

He chuckled, dropping his head down for a second. "I think I might owe you an apology."

An apology? I rubbed the spot where my wedding band used to be.

"I warned you about the sake," he said. "But I guess I should've been more insistent. I didn't realize how bad off you were until that recruiter showed up. Well, and then you started crying. That was a dead giveaway."

A buzz began building in my head. "Who?"

"Reilly, the physician recruiter. She's been badgering me for weeks about taking an extended assignment in Bell Harbor. I told her I haven't decided yet, but she won't let up. That's why I didn't introduce you. She would've talked your ear off."

Little whorls of sand twisted around my feet. A white bird flew overhead. Waves continued to caress the shore, and all around, I heard people chatting and laughing. Nothing around me was different than it had been ten seconds before. But somehow, everything had changed. As Des's words sank in, I began feeling light and floaty, like somebody was dialing down gravity. The buzz swelled then receded.

"A recruiter?"

Des nodded. "Yeah. Stan Pullman has decided to retire and move to Arizona, so the hospital wants me to fill in until they hire his replacement." He turned to me, smiling. "I tried to explain that to you at the restaurant, but by then you were already crying. Then Jasper showed up and I was embarrassed."

There went the gravity, down another notch. I nearly lifted off the step.

"You were embarrassed?"

He nodded. "I don't usually make women cry until the third or fourth date. This was a new record for me."

This day was getting better and better. First Richard was polite, then I found out I had a job if I wanted it. And now Des was apologizing to me? And telling me that woman was a job recruiter? Was it possible? I suppose he could be lying, but why would he bother?

"She seemed awfully...friendly."

Des looked out over the water. "I'm not going to lie to you, Sadie. We went out a few times, but she's not really my type."

"Gorgeous isn't your type?"

"Vain isn't my type."

I crossed my arms. No one ever called me vain. At least I had that going for me. And maybe Penny was right. He could've been with that blonde but asked me out instead. For once I was the other woman.

"I made a fool of myself last night," I finally said. "I should be apologizing to you."

He shook his head and chuckled. "No, don't. I know how sake affects me, so I should've realized it would be too strong for you. Plus you drank about a gallon."

I was still hungover, come to think of it. "How does it affect you?"

"Well, let's see. One time it made me decide public urination should be a constitutional right. Nearly got deported for that one. And another time I decided to steal a street sign from right in front of the police station. I think my picture may still be on the wall of a little county jail in northern Illinois."

"Really?" If that was true, maybe my little bout with tears hadn't been so shocking after all. Was it possible I had overreacted? Me?

I smiled, inside and out. Sitting next to Des, warmed by the sun and his understanding, I felt good. Simply delightful, as Dody would say. For the first time in two days, I took a breath that didn't hurt my chest.

Des pushed his sunglasses up on his head. His eyes, even the bruised one, were bright and beautiful, and mesmerizing. I suddenly found myself breathless and mute. I smiled stupidly, lacking the wit to say anything clever. I pressed my knees together tightly.

Des made a funny noise in his throat and turned his head away.

After a minute I said, "Well, either way, I wasn't at my best. I'm sorry I ruined your evening."

"Likewise. So, you know, I was thinking, maybe we should—"

Sand spewed into my face as a volleyball slammed against my feet, bounced up, and smacked me in the cheek.

"Oh, hey, Sadie! Sorry!" Jasper called out, laughing. He collected the ball, nodding at Des. "Careful, man, she's a crybaby."

I tried to wipe the sand away, but it stuck like Fatso's fur on black pants. Des pulled me upright.

"Come on. Let's rinse that off in the water. I hope we don't have matching black eyes."

And so we frolicked in the lake like sixteen-years-olds playing beach blanket bingo. Ariel the mermaid never had it so good. Waves buffeted me against him, and I let them, thoroughly enjoying the sensations. When a particularly robust whitecap rocked me against his torso, Des caught me by the waist and held me there. For a brief, tantalizing second I thought he might kiss me. But he only dipped his head to my ear and whispered, "God, you're killing me."

The water began to steam.

*   *   *

We made it back to the beach eventually, and Des joined Jasper and his friends in a game of football. I grabbed my towel from where it sat near Dody and Anita Parker, who was now on a rant about her latest medical drama.

"The doctor says I need more fiber. Three bowls of bran cereal this week and I still can't poop for shit."

"I've told you, Anita. Try some flaxseed," Dody assured her. Then she lifted the brim of her big floppy red hat to smile at me. "Did you have a nice time swimming, dear?"

"Why yes, Dody. I did."

"Isn't that simply delightful?"

I went to sit by Kyle before Anita could say anything else about her bowel issues.

"Does that woman ever shut up?" Kyle tipped his head in Anita Parker's general vicinity.

"I don't believe so, no. Mind if I join you?"

"Not at all. Here, have a beverage." He adjusted the back of his chair and pulled out a bottle from his cooler. "So what's up with you and the man from Atlantis? Looks new."

I took the bottle. "Thanks. Um, it's, like, pre-new. It hasn't even started yet."

"Oh, it's definitely started. From where I'm sitting it looked like he got to second base."

A girlish giggle escaped. "What is second base for a gay couple?"

Kyle smiled and shook his head. "Uh, uh, uh. No changing the subject. You tell me yours first."

"There's nothing to tell, really. He lives down there." I pointed to the Pullmans' house. "He's here for a couple of months, like me, so I don't know. He's cute, don't you think?"

Kyle tipped his sunglasses to get a better look. Des, Jasper, and a few others were tossing the football directly in front of us. "Not bad at all. So are you in love?"

I choked on the drink. "Oh God! No. That would be a disaster! What a nightmare."

"Methinks the lady doth protest too much."

"What?"

"Shakespeare."

"Hmm." I know my Shakespeare as well as the next college graduate, but I was distracted watching the sun roll over Des's muscles. He practically shimmered. "Anyway, it's nothing major. Just, you know, practicing in case I ever decide to start dating again."

"Isn't a practice date pretty much a date?"

"Well…it's, I don't know. It would be terribly inconvenient to like this guy more than I already do."

Kyle stared out over the water. "Love is a grave mental disease."

"Shakespeare?"

Kyle shook his head. "Plato."

I crossed my arms and studied him for a minute. "OK, your turn. What's up with you and Fontaine?"

He met my gaze over the rim of his sunglasses. "Loving him would be terribly inconvenient for me, wouldn't it? Since he's my employee."

In spite of sharing every gory detail of his dating history, Fontaine had never mentioned Kyle in a romantic way to me. I had my suspicions, but since I couldn't be certain, I decided to keep my thoughts to myself.

The rest of my afternoon passed in a blissful haze. Things felt right with the world. I wasn't thinking about what tomorrow would bring. I was enjoying each moment as it came and went. Just as Madam Margaret had told me to do—not that I put any stock at all in what she said.

When the sun broiled, we swam. When the water cooled us, we lolled on the sand like sea lions. I could not remember when I'd had such a lazy, selfish day. I didn't even fold my towel when I left it behind.

Hours later, as the sun dipped into the horizon, Des plopped down on the beach blanket next to me, handing me a beer.

"These are the last two," he said, popping off the top for me with one hand.

"Thanks."

Kyle walked by on his way up to the house. "Hey, Sadie!" he called.

"What?"

"Plato was an idiot."

I laughed and didn't bother explaining that to Des. Let him wonder.

The rowdiness of the day mellowed. People were gathering up their things to leave or had already left. Soon it was just Des and me.

"You know, I was trying to tell you something before you got that volleyball in the face, and I didn't get to finish."

A flush started deep within me, spreading fast. He was about to ask for a second date.

He took another gulp of beer. "I know you're only here for a little while longer, and I don't know where my next assignment will be. So, all things considered, I think it's probably better if you and I, you know, keep things platonic. We should just be friends. Don't you think?"

Friends.

Friends?

Friends!

Are you frickin' kidding me?

He had spent the entire day strutting around like a peacock, feeling me up in the water, reeling me in like a master angler, only to fling me back? *What the hell?*

I'd been melting all over him for hours, and now, instead of falling into love, I was falling into white-hot despair.

Seriously. What an asshole. I was pissed, and it showed.

He took one look at my scowling face and burst out laughing. What kind of a sadist was this guy? He was laughing at me! This was beyond unbelievable.

Then he put his arm around my waist and turned his face to my neck, whispering, "I'm totally messing with you, Sadie. I absolutely want to get you naked."

That rendered me speechless. Utterly speechless. *Get me naked? Is that what he just said?*

Well!

I should be indignant.

I should be appalled.

A good girl would slap his face. A nice girl would get up and walk away. But I guess I wasn't good or nice because I started laughing too. And why not? Our courtship dance had been clumsy and haphazard from the start, so why should I expect anything different?

"That was mean," I finally responded, a catch of breathlessness still in my voice.

He hugged me tighter. "I'm sorry. But, wow, you should have seen your face."

"Yeah, yeah, OK." I brushed my head against his shoulder. "You're pretty sure of yourself, aren't you?"

His laughter quieted as he answered simply, "No."

I didn't see how that was possible. But I didn't argue, because I could see in his eyes that he was finally going to kiss me.

My very first kiss was with a boy who tasted like bubble gum and smelled of fresh cut grass, a tangy, sweet combination I've never quite forgotten. No kiss since then had ever tasted or smelled or felt quite so good, until this one. It was flawless. Tentative, searching, then blossoming with the perfect intensity. It was better than I had imagined it could be, and I had imagined it pretty thoroughly. Des's arm pressed against my middle as I leaned into his sideways embrace. The kiss ended too soon, and I sighed like Juliet on the balcony longing for her Romeo.

        ❀   ❀   ❀

I skipped up the steps, nearly tripping over Fontaine and Kyle, who were crouched on the deck.

"Well? How was it?" Fontaine was grinning from sideburn to well-coiffed sideburn.

"Were you spying on me, you jerks?"

"Of course."

"It was like watching *National Geographic*," Kyle added. "Like observing monkeys choose their mate."

I stepped around them. "Nice, you guys. And for the record, there was no mating. All he did was kiss me."

"And? Was it wet and sloppy?" Fontaine rubbed his hands together.

I couldn't help but laugh. "No."

"Dry and tight?" Kyle asked.

"No, Papa Bears. It was just right." I walked inside and headed toward the stairs. "And now I'm going to his house for dinner."

I heard the smack of their high five echoing behind me.

I hurried to shower and get ready. If I gave myself time to think, I'd get too nervous. But even rushing around, it was no use. Someone should invent full body antiperspirant for just such emergencies. Even the backs of my knees were sweating.

I put on a sundress and stood staring at my underwear drawer. I wasn't ready for the big deed with Des, of that I was certain. I pulled out a pair of maternity panties that I kept for especially fat days. Nothing would repel a single man quite like tattered beige underwear large enough to shelter a family of six. But I set them aside. Even if he never saw them, he'd sense them.

I wasn't about to go the other route and wear a thong, either. The only reason I even had one was because Richard bought it. I stuffed that back in the drawer, finally settling on some pretty pastel lace that I'd gotten when shopping for my date dress. This pair was neither too obvious nor too demure.

At last I found myself back on the Pullmans' steps, almost as anxious and worked up as I had been the very first time I rang that bell.

Des opened the door, his hair still wet from the shower. He had a navy-blue towel draped around his neck and wore jeans but no shirt. It rattled me and I didn't know why. I'd seen him shirtless a dozen times, including most of today. But something about the combination of pants with no shirt seemed naughty and risqué. I bit my lip.

"Hey, come on in. I'm almost ready."

I noticed the table still in the spot where I had moved it. Bitchy the cat walked by and yawned. If it was possible for cats to roll their eyes, I'm sure she would've done it.

"I went to the store, that's why I'm running late. Just make yourself at home." He went back into the bedroom. I was nervous, so nervous I didn't want to say anything in case I had helium voice. I swallowed and tried to remember what Dody had told me about deep, cleansing breaths.

"You OK?" he asked when he came out from his room only to find me standing in the exact same spot. "You want a drink?"

I nodded.

"No sake tonight. OK?" He waved his hand over the room. "This is a crying-free zone right here."

He was funny. I started to breathe, finally. This was going to be just fine.

He opened a bottle of wine and handed me a glass.

I raised mine up. "To *National Geographic.*" Damn it, Fontaine.

Des's smile was curious, but he toasted anyway. "If you say so."

He put me in charge of chopping vegetables. I considered cutting my finger so he'd have to hold my hand to examine it, but that seemed a little drastic. Maybe I could be captivating without resorting to self-mutilation. He put on some music and we hummed along while he cooked. I should've guessed he could cook. I wasn't too bad at it myself, but Paige and Jordan had very unimaginative palates, so my repertoire of dishes had been reduced to anything with noodles and butter.

"I think there's a steamer in the pantry, Sadie. Would you mind looking?" he asked.

"Sure." I walked into the tiny room off the kitchen, which doubled as a laundry room. Two of Des's lab coats hung on a drying rack. I ran my hand down one sleeve, unable to resist. Then I spotted the steamer on the top shelf. I tapped a foot against a lower shelf, considering the wisdom of using it as a step.

"See it?" he called from the kitchen.

My voice was strained as I reached. I could barely touch the edge. "Yes, but it's a little too high."

Des came in behind me, reaching over my head. He leaned forward, and his fabulous man parts came into full, delicious contact with my girly backside. I gasped in both surprise and delight, like a spinster librarian discovering pornography in the resource section.

I pressed back, a wanton spirit suddenly controlling my actions. Des's body went still, even as he exhaled slowly, his breath warm against my temple. For a moment we were frozen in place, yet exploding internally. Then his arms came down to wrap around me. He nuzzled my neck for the briefest second before placing a heated kiss in the hollow below my ear.

*   *   *

I ran into Dody's cottage and scrambled up the steps to the safe haven of my bedroom. I slammed the door and slumped against it. With trembling fingers I grabbed my phone off the dresser and dialed Penny's number.

She picked up on the third ring. "Hey."

"I am doomed." I collapsed onto the bed and curled into a ball.

"What happened now?" She was blasé, underestimating the shock of what I was about to reveal.

"Getting drunk and crying at the restaurant? Child's play! I have officially humiliated myself beyond repair."

"How?"

There was a hippo of regret loitering on my chest. "I was at Des's for dinner, because it turns out the blonde chick from last night was a recruiter, right? So I'm over at his house and we're cooking and being all flirty and stuff. And then one thing leads to another, and the next thing I know, my panties are on the floor and I'm getting felt up in the laundry room."

"The laundry room? Is that a euphemism?"

"No, dumb-ass. I mean an actual laundry room."

"Why were you in the laundry room?"

God, how could she be so dense! "It's next to the kitchen, Penny. And that's not the important part. We went into the laundry room to get the vegetable steamer. But I reached for it, and he reached for it at the same time, and when his junk bumped up against me I turned into some crazed nymphomaniac porn star!"

Penny snorted with laughter. "No, you didn't!"

"Oh, yes I did. I was all over him. And it gets even worse." I could hardly tell her the rest. But I had to. I couldn't keep this burden to myself. "Penny, I…I…finished."

"Finished?" She could hardly talk through all her snorting and chuckling. "What does that mean, finished?"

"It means I…well, you know!" I had to drop my voice to a whisper. "I had an orgasm. But all he did was touch me with his hand for, like, two minutes!" I clutched the phone tighter, letting Penny's spasm of hysterical laughter run its course.

"So, wait," she sputtered. "Did you have sex with him?"

"No! We did NOT have sex! All we did was kiss and a little bump and grind, you know. And some groping. Actually there was quite a lot of groping." It was all a blur in my memory, driven by testosterone and desperation. His and mine, respectively.

"But it all happened so fast. I never saw it coming."

My poor choice of words sent Penny into another fit of hysteria. "Are you kidding me?"

"Come on, Penny! I'm embarrassed enough already. You're supposed to help me."

"Help you what? Not be a dope? Why is this even a problem?"

"Because we were in the laundry room, for God's sake! That's so not me. It was like something Richard would have done."

Penny paused. "Oh, now I get it. But you listen to me, Sadie Turner, there is nothing wrong with two consenting adults enjoying each other wherever and however they want, as long as they're not married to somebody else. What Richard did was adultery. What you did is good old-fashioned fun."

"Then why do I feel like such an idiot?"

"Because you are an idiot. Not for fooling around with Des, but because you're worried about it. Can't you just relax? You get more like Mom every single day."

"I'm nothing like Mom!"

"Of course you are. You're so worried about what everybody else thinks you can't decide what you want for yourself. Get over that. And tell me, what happened next?"

I didn't have the energy to take issue with her insult. We could postpone arguing about how I was nothing like our mother another time. "Next?"

"Yeah, what happened after you got your freak on?"

I winced. "God, Penny. I never should have told you."

She laughed again. "You're such a prude. OK, fine. What happened after your very unladylike response to his digital stimulation?"

I held the phone close to my mouth. "I ran."

"You…you ran? What do you mean you ran?"

"I mean I was so embarrassed after I…well, you know, that I pushed him away from me and ran out of the house. Then I ran all the way back here and called you."

"Oh. My. God. Sadie! You are an idiot! So what did he do?"

"I don't know!" I cried. "I mean, he wasn't in any condition to run after me, you know. He had a...well, you know! Guys can't run with one of those things, can they?"

Penny's cell phone clattered onto something rock solid as she dropped it, and the sound of her shrieking laughter will be forever imprisoned in the recesses of my mind.

When she finally spoke again, her message was simple.

"Go back there. Tell him you have some medical disorder or something, like orgasmaphobia. And promise him it won't happen again."

"He's a doctor, Penny. He'll know orgasmaphobia isn't a real disease."

"Fine, then tell him the truth. You find him wildly attractive, but you're clueless when it comes to men and too scared to get into a relationship."

"That's supposed to endear me to him?" I sat up on the bed.

"You're already endeared to him. At least you were, until you left him high and dry in his own laundry room. Pun intended," she added.

"Please don't start laughing again." I put my head in my hand.

"Sorry, but you need to go over there right now. The longer you wait, the harder it will get. Ha! No pun intended that time. I am on a roll!" I heard her fingers snapping.

I'd had about as much of her help as I could take. "All right, fine. I'm going. I'll call you tomorrow."

* * *

Des opened the door, his welcome much less enthusiastic than it had been earlier in the evening. He didn't look surprised to see me. Or glad, either.

"Hey," he said.

I fidgeted with the fabric of my sundress. "Hi. May I come in for a minute?"

"Sure." His tone was dry. He stepped aside, shoving the door open wide. "I'll leave this open in case you decide to bolt out of here again."

Ah, so that's how this was going to go, huh?

I felt disgraced, like Fatso being scolded for pulling a sandwich off the counter. I gingerly shut the door behind me. Then I stood there, my mind brilliantly, blindingly blank while Des glowered at me expectantly.

"I'm sorry," I whispered.

He scowled. "Sorry? What the hell, Sadie?"

"I didn't mean to run out like that."

"OK." It seemed he found my apology lacking. "But I'm not quite sure what happened. I mean, one minute, everything's going great, really great, then all of sudden you shove me aside and take off?" He crossed his arms.

I felt red blotches of heat covering my throat and face. "Have you ever heard of orgasmaphobia?"

He made a grunting noise and scowled.

I sighed. "I got flustered, OK?"

"Flustered?"

"Yes." I stared at my fingernails to avoid his eyes.

He tipped his head. "Flustered? What does that mean?"

"It means upset or agitated."

His arms dropped back to his sides, as if he wasn't sure what to do with them. His sigh was loud. "I know what the *word* means, Sadie. But I don't know what *you* mean. Why were *you* flustered?"

I bit my lip.

He clenched his fists. Frustration rippled on every contour of his face. "Look, I'm not trying to be a jerk. I just don't understand what I did to upset you this time."

Surprise skipped through me. Is that what he thought? That it was his fault? "You didn't do anything."

"Then why did you leave?" His voice crackled with annoyance.

"Because I got scared!" I blurted out.

And there it was. That pesky truth I was trying so hard to avoid. My attraction to him threatened to overwhelm. I couldn't give any man so much power over me again. Not after what happened with Richard.

Des rubbed his chin and exhaled slowly. "Sadie, I'm not some big, bad wolf."

"I know." Somewhere deep within my grossly under-used intellect, I did know that. "Only I'm not usually so... spontaneous. And...reactive."

I saw his lips twitch.

"It caught me off guard, I guess," I murmured.

He walked to the sofa and sat down, running both hands through his hair. After a long pause he asked, "How long have you been divorced?"

"About a year." Thirteen months, twenty-three days.

He regarded me another moment, then patted the seat next to him. "It gets easier."

I sat down next to him, amazed again at his patience. Apparently while I was reading *The Complete Idiot's Guide to Dating*, he'd read *The Guide to Dating a Complete Idiot*. "I hope you're right. I do like you, you know. But you sort of discombobulate me."

His face relaxed slightly. "Likewise. So what do we do about it?"

This was my chance for a graceful exit. I could tell him, "Thank you very much but I'm not ready for you." Or I could stay and see what happened next.

"Maybe we could take it a little slower? Like, not so physical, maybe? Could we try that?" I asked.

"OK." He nodded, leaning back against the couch.

"Really?" I was pleasantly surprised. Richard would have...oh, who cares what Richard would have done?

Des gave me the first genuine smile of this visit. "Of course we can take it slow, Sadie. I don't know many people in Bell Harbor, OK? I just want some company. With or without benefits."

Company? Yes, I could do that. And I guess I could decide about benefits later. Or not. It seemed he was willing to leave it up to me.

"OK," I said.

"OK." He nodded.

We sat there, basking briefly in the ironic glow of agreeing to *not* have sex. When it quickly grew awkward, Des rubbed his hands together. "So, you want to watch a movie?"

Is that what other couples not having sex did? I imagined it was. "Sure."

We settled down on a cushy sofa with drinks and snacks and some boy-type movie with lots of blazing guns and gratuitous violence. I wasn't interested in the story, but I was happy snuggling up to Des. He reclined on the chaise side of the big L-shaped sofa with his legs stretched out in front of him. I curled up on the other side, leaning against him. Eventually I got the nerve to rest my head on his shoulder and he put his arm around me. It had been quite a day. I was exhausted.

Suddenly my own snort woke me up. Disoriented, it took a second before I realized we'd both fallen asleep. The movie was over. Des's arm was flung up over his head, his face turned toward the crook of his elbow. My arm draped around his waist and my head rested firmly on his belly, nearly in his lap. I raised myself up a little, noticing a dark, circular stain on his T-shirt from (oh God!) a puddle of my own drool! I had fallen asleep and drooled on his stomach. Darn it! I wiped my mouth with the back of my hand, wondering how Miss Manners would handle this.

I looked up at Des's face, relaxed in sleep, his lips almost pouty. He sniffed a little, sighing in some dream in which I hoped to be the Star Attraction. I took this chance to stare at him. He was gorgeous. And I knew that if he saw the drool spot on his shirt, he'd laugh and make a joke. Because that's the kind of guy he was. No matter what silly thing I did, he rolled with it.

My heart swelled at the lovely realization. Maybe his charm and appeal weren't simply the work of my lonely imagination. Maybe he wasn't another asshole masquerading as a nice guy. Maybe he actually was a nice guy. They did exist! And luck had brought me one. (What was next? Unicorns?)

Then I had another lovely revelation, even more enticing than the first. Even if this was destined to be a brief fling, even if I went back to Glenville at the end of the summer and Des took his next assignment in Outer Mongolia, I still wanted this. I wanted him. We had right here, right now, and that was good enough. Dody kept telling me life was too short to not have any fun. My kids were coming home in T-minus ninety-six hours, so if I was going to make the absolute most of these next couple of days, I'd better get started.

I leaned over and lightly kissed his mouth, startling him awake.

He blinked, trying to focus. "Sadie?"

"I've changed my mind," I whispered, hoping to sound seductive.

"What?" He was still sleepy.

I kissed him again. "I'm not scared. Let's add benefits." I tugged at the hem of his shirt, inching it up his belly and making my intentions clear (and cleverly hiding the drool spot).

He caught my meaning, putting his hand over my wrist.

"We don't have to, Sadie. It's not a deal breaker."

"Don't you want to?"

"Hell, yes." His voice rasped.

My eyes traveled slowly down his body and back up again. "Me too. I'm sure of it."

He stared at me, his eyes darkening, then he sighed as if he'd been holding his breath for a very long time. His hand slid up my arm to cup behind my neck. He tugged me closer, and although I didn't need the extra encouragement, I welcomed it. I kissed him hard, and he chuckled deep in his throat. I smiled against his lips and ran my hand over his stomach, feeling his muscles quiver and bunch. The heat of his skin nearly melted my fingers, so smooth and hot. Farther up under his shirt I explored and caressed, kissing him until he made a noise of delighted frustration and leaned up from the sofa to gather me tightly in his arms.

Urgency replaced reason as I tugged his shirt over his head, and he pushed aside the straps of my sundress. I had only a moment to be thankful I'd worn the laciest of my bras before his thumb grazed along the clasp and it was undone, sailing across the room. I laughed, nervous again and feeling shy, until he tipped my face up to his.

"You're beautiful, Sadie," he whispered.

And in that moment, I believed him.

CHAPTER 16

I SAUNTERED IN THROUGH DODY'S front door sporting a sublime smile and a mad case of whisker burn. Dody and Fontaine were sitting at the kitchen island having their morning coffee.

"Good morning, you saucy minx," Fontaine said. "Did that filthy scoundrel keep you out all night? Why, I do declare, he has sullied your reputation."

I kissed Fontaine's cheek. "I have indeed been sullied."

Dody hugged me. "Darling, that is simply delightful. Nothing puts the pink in a girl's cheeks like a good roll in the straw."

"Hay," I said.

"Hey, what?" She looked at me, waiting.

"Nothing. So did I miss anything over here last night?"

Fontaine shook his head. "Hardly, but I want every creepy hetero detail from your evening."

I poured myself a coffee, gazing up at the ceiling without really seeing it. Last night had been a slice of heaven, but I didn't want to share the details. I wanted to enjoy my lovely thoughts without Fontaine's crass editorial commentary. I wanted to dwell in the bliss of my wanton behavior before my brain kicked in with the inevitable reprimands.

"It was wonderful."

Fontaine held up his hands. "And?"

"And that's all. I'm too sleepy to talk about it right now. Take me shopping later and I'll tell you more."

"Deal," Fontaine answered quickly. "And Penny wants you to call her. She said something about doing the laundry?"

I trotted up to my room, a spring in my step. I fluffed the pillows and plopped down on my bed, noticing that today it did not seem so maddeningly, mockingly empty. Last night had been sensational. And not just the first time either, which was a little urgent. (Hardly his fault considering the way I'd left him earlier that evening.) The second time was pure perfection, like floating on a silky mink raft in a pool of bubbly pink champagne, eating Swiss chocolates while Bradley Cooper massaged my feet. It was that good. By the third time, we were tired, so we had the lazy Sunday morning kind, when you have nothing to do but lie in bed and pass the time. I had forgotten sex could actually be fun. Just fun. I stretched, feeling twinges in muscles that had not been exercised in far too long.

I dialed Penny, and she answered almost immediately. We tumbled excitedly over one another's words.

"Guess what!"

"Guess what!"

"I slept with Des."

"I'm pregnant!"

"You are?"

"You did?"

"Holy shit!"

"Holy shit!"

Penny and I haven't giggled like that since sixth grade, when Scott Nickelson skateboarded right into a mailbox because she flashed him with her training bra.

"Why didn't you tell me last night?" I asked.

"I didn't know last night. I peed on the stick this morning. How did you end up in bed with Des?"

We volleyed questions back and forth in our own brand of sister-speak. I was excited for her—and grateful that I could be. I asked about due dates and baby names and what the future grandparents had said when she told them.

"I haven't told anybody yet. Just you."

"Really?"

"Yeah, I'm kind of scared. It's really early yet. Something could go wrong."

"Dody always tells me that worrying about something doesn't do any good. It only makes you worried."

"You're quoting Dody now? We need to get you out of there."

"Nuh-uh, not now. Ask me again in a week."

"What happens in a week?" she asked.

"By then I'll have discovered some incriminating evidence against Des and have to leave Bell Harbor."

"Like he murdered the Pullmans and has them buried under the deck?"

"Precisely. So are you going to tell Mom?"

"Not yet. I'd like to wait until the end of the first trimester. So don't tell her, OK? Don't tell anybody."

"Listen to you, little mommy, talking about trimesters. I'm so proud of you. And I promise I won't tell anyone, as long as you don't tell Mom about me and Des. I don't need her judgments right now. Deal?"

"Deal."

*　*　*

"Did I hear you guys are going shopping?" Jasper asked. I was sitting in the kitchen putting on my sandals while Fontaine tapped his foot and jangled keys in the doorway. He wore a white polo shirt and mint-colored chinos.

Fontaine nodded. "Yes, after we check on the construction at my house. They're installing the trim, and I need to make sure they're using the right wood. Why?" Fontaine said.

"Is Mom coming?"

"No, she and Anita are painting protest signs for their rally against putting in a second traffic light."

Jasper sat down next to me. "Remember how you told me that weddings and rings and stuff were expensive?"

I reached over and touched his arm. "I never should've said that, Jas. I was in a bad mood that day. I think Beth is wonderful, and you're smart to scoop her up."

Jasper nodded. "I know. But I was wondering if you'd help with the ring part. I mean, help me pick out something that looks nice but isn't going to break my bank."

Sentimentality overtook me. I threw my arms around his neck. "Oh, Jasper! I'd be honored."

He tensed. "Jeez, Sadie. It's not that big a deal. What's up with you?"

He looked over at Fontaine, who answered, "Sadie finally got laid."

Jasper nodded, as if that explained everything.

*   *   *

Tilly Mason, fourth-generation owner of Mason's jewelry store, greeted us at the door.

"Hello, Fontaine. Are you looking for some new cuff links?" They gave each other a double air kiss.

"I wish. But today we're here for something extra special. My brother here thinks it's time to tie the knot. We need something sparkly and fabulous that costs like something shabby and dull."

Tilly nodded. "I'm sure we can find something wonderful." She sat Jasper down in a velvet chair and pulled out a laminated chart, explaining about color, cut, clarity, and carats until he glazed over completely.

"Wait, what's the difference between color and clarity?" Jasper asked for the third time.

"Why don't we browse a little?" I suggested.

Tilly nodded. "Why don't you?"

Jasper peered into one display case. "What about these over here?" he asked hesitantly.

"Those are anniversary bands," Tilly said.

"What's the difference?"

"They're for anniversaries."

Jasper looked at me, silently pleading.

"What kind of ring does Beth want?" Fontaine asked.

"I don't know. I never asked her."

"You mean you haven't talked about this at all?"

"No, I want it to be a surprise."

"A surprise? Then how do you know she's going to say yes?"

I smacked Fontaine in the arm. "Fontaine! Of course she'll say yes. Don't ask him that."

Jasper's face flushed.

"Oh, Fontaine, now look what you've done," I scolded, putting an arm around Jasper. "I'm sure she'll say yes. She's madly in love with you. I can tell."

Fontaine hugged him from the other side. "Of course she will. I didn't mean that. So how are you going to ask her?"

"Ask her?" Jasper went from pouty to confused.

"Yes. How are you going to propose?"

"Oh. I don't know. I figured we'd go out to dinner or something."

"No, no, no!" Fontaine stomped his expensive Italian sandal. "That's so ordinary. It has to be more romantic than that."

Jasper shook his head. "Beth isn't into all that sort of stuff. She doesn't care."

"Every girl cares," Fontaine admonished. "The proposal story is one she'll tell over and over, so you need to make it good. Put some effort into it."

"Damn it, Fontaine. This is why I hate to tell you stuff. You blow it way out of proportion."

"He does," I had to agree. "But he's right about this one, Jas. It should be something memorable."

"Me asking her to spend the rest our lives together isn't memorable enough?"

"Not if you're sitting at some dingy restaurant," Fontaine scoffed. "And don't even think about putting the ring inside a dessert or a glass of champagne. I can't imagine what misguided Neanderthal came up with that idea."

"God, you guys! Come on. Could we stick to one thing at a time here? First I have to find a ring."

Tilly walked around to where we were bickering and set a tray of diamond rings on the counter. "Why don't you look these over? I think you might find something you like. That would at least give us a starting point."

We bent over the tray in a synchronized motion. There were a variety of styles, some beautiful and simple, others garishly large, and a few with diamazoid specks so tiny they looked like smudges on the band. Jasper zeroed in on one right in the center of the tray. It was gorgeous. Not too large, not too small, not too plain, not too elaborate. He picked it up. It sparkled in the light, sending prisms in every direction. We continued to look around the store, but he kept coming back to that one.

"I love this one, Sadie. But it's too expensive," Jasper whispered. "I've been saving up to buy my own restaurant, you know, but if I spend so much on a ring, it'll put me back months."

I thought the price was reasonable, but then again, I had pretty extravagant taste. My own engagement ring had been ostentatious and flashy, like my husband. It was sitting in a drawer back in Glenville. I couldn't possibly wear it, but I also couldn't bear the thought of getting rid of it. Someday, when all the bad karma of my marriage had evaporated, I planned to have the diamonds reset into a necklace.

"Maybe you could save up for it?"

He frowned. "Yeah, I guess I'm going to have to. The pretty ones are expensive and the cheap ones are stupid."

I patted his shoulder. "We can keep looking." But Mason's was the only jewelry store in Bell Harbor, and Jasper went on home, sad and dejected.

*　*　*

In spite of Jasper's blue mood, I floated around for the rest of the day on cloud ten. Richard called to say the kids were doing great and having a wonderful time. He didn't pick a fight or say anything irritating, which was remarkable considering the phone call lasted nearly five minutes. And I had a date to look forward to! At Des's that morning, before he left for work and I did the walk of shame back to Dody's, he had invited me out to dinner again. I had a brand new outfit, chosen by Fontaine, of course, and more frilly new unmentionables, chosen by myself. I had to draw the line at letting my cousin pick out my underwear.

But at precisely four o'clock that afternoon, Des called. I was on the sunporch with Dody where she was knitting a holster for her gun and telling me about the most fascinating e-mail she'd gotten from a Nigerian prince.

"Sadie, hi. I can't really talk right now. I'm swamped at work," Des said. "But I have to cancel our dinner. My cousin Charlie is stranded at the airport and needs to spend the night at my house. The next flight doesn't leave until seven in the morning so I'm kind of obligated to help out. I'm really sorry."

I deflated like a day-old birthday balloon. The unheard-of-relative-stranded-at-the-airport excuse? I wanted to believe him, but I didn't trust myself to ask for details. It could be legitimate. Or not. And I didn't have the courage to find out.

"Oh, that's OK. We can do it another time." I was angry at the tremble in my voice.

"I work the next two nights, but we can do dinner after that. OK?"

"Sure. OK." My tongue felt thick. I swallowed hard.

"Hey, I'm really sorry. I had fun last night, by the way."

Did you? Good for you, you big dumb jerk. "That's great," I mumbled.

"Shoot! Ambulance is here. I have to go."

I hung up, chucking my phone against the table, where it bounced and clattered.

"What's the matter, dear?"

I shook my head. "Nothing. Des is cancelling dinner for tonight."

"Why?" She knit one, purled two.

"His cousin is in town and he has to pick him up from the airport."

"Oh, that's a shame. But Harry and I are going to a curling exhibition tonight. You should come with us."

"Tempting as that is, Dody, I think I'll pass. I've got stuff to do. I bought some organizing books today so I'll just read those tonight."

"Are you sure? Oh, dear. You look so sad."

"No, I'm fine. I just miss the kids." I wanted to cry, the way the kids did when they bumped their heads or scraped a knee. But I was an adult. And big girls don't cry because someone cancels dinner plans. Even if it is someone they had just slept with.

*   *   *

Fontaine refused to let me mope or drown myself in sangria. He wouldn't even let me lie on the sofa in my bathrobe and eat the jar of Marshmallow Fluff I'd found in Dody's pantry.

"You need exercise and fresh air, sugar pie. And you need to stop wallowing. If he says his cousin was stranded at the airport, believe him. Innocent until proven guilty, remember?"

"That's not how it worked with Richard." I slapped away Fontaine's hands as he tried to pull the robe from my shoulders.

"Des is not Richard. There's no comparison."

"How do you know? I mean, what do we really know about this guy?"

"Hah!" He yanked away the robe. "We know enough. Now put on your shoes. You're coming with me to walk the dogs. I can't take them both by myself."

Reluctantly I did as I was told and soon found myself being yanked down the beach by Fatso. It was dark, with a bright full moon lighting our way. We could see into the various cottages as we made our way toward the pier, and Fontaine relished pointing out gross decorating choices made by the neighbors.

"Why do we need the dogs on leashes?" I finally asked.

Fontaine shrugged. "We don't. I figured I couldn't get you out of the house any other way."

I stopped short, the dog nearly jerking my arm from my socket. "Are you serious?"

"Don't you feel better, getting some fresh air?"

I reached over and unhooked Fatso from the leash and he bolted away. "Not really."

Fontaine let Lazyboy loose and we continued walking. The lights from Des's house came into view.

"Do you think you'd feel better if you got a look at this cousin Charlie so you'd know Des wasn't lying?"

I stopped walking again. "Tell me you did not lure me out here so I could peek in Des's windows!"

I saw the translucent glow of Fontaine's teeth as he grinned. "Of course I did. I don't give a shit about the dogs."

I turned around and started walking back to Dody's, but Fontaine grabbed my wrist.

"Come on, girlfriend. You know you want to take a look. And we're already here. Once you see this Charlie guy you're going to feel loads better. Trust me. Have I ever steered you wrong?"

"Yes."

"Puh! Not this time, I promise. And we have the cloak of darkness to hide our deeds. But if we stand here arguing, he'll see us for sure. Come on."

Fontaine grabbed my wrist, pulling twice as hard as Fatso had. We ran up to the edge of Alberta Schmidt's house, right next to the Pullmans', and crouched down in the shadows.

Idiocy-induced nausea gurgled in my gut. "Fontaine! What if he catches us?"

"We'll tell him we were just taking a walk."

"On *his deck*? This is ridiculous!" I hissed.

A woman's laughter floated through the darkness, and I froze. It sounded as if it came from Des's place. The sliding door from his family room to the deck was wide open, with light pouring out. Music was playing too.

From where we hid, we could barely see into the kitchen window. Fontaine shoved me back against the deck post as Des's head appeared. He must have been standing at the sink. He was talking, but we couldn't hear him clearly. Then he laughed at something and turned around. I felt filthy and ludicrous, spying on someone I'd been in bed with less than twenty-four hours before. Is this what I had been reduced to?

Fontaine pointed at Des's deck, indicating we should get closer.

I shook my head frantically.

Fontaine nodded just as frantically, giving me a rough shove and pushing me out into the shaft of light coming from inside Des's house. I nearly squawked with fear and took three giant leaps, bringing me to the edge of his deck.

I couldn't breathe for fear he'd hear me! What the hell was I doing? This was insane! I was insane. *Damn you, Fontaine.*

Fontaine took a look toward the window, then leaped, landing next to me and bumping against the lattice surrounding the base of Des's deck. It gave a horrific crack, and my chest exploded with fear. I punched Fontaine.

We squatted in the shadow, catching our breath. I could hear the woman talking, but not loud enough to make out the words. It didn't really matter what she said anyway.

"Maybe that's Cousin Charlie's wife," Fontaine whispered.

Maybe.

Fontaine pointed up. "Let's look."

I shook my head again. I was not going to pop up like a prairie dog to peek into Des's house! Listening was bad enough.

Fontaine scowled and rose up, his eyes peeping over the edge. I heard him gasp. And I knew I would have to look for myself. I rose up on trembling legs.

She was young and blonde and stood near the doorway with a glass of wine in her hand. Instant jealousy seared through every vein in my body. This was no one's wife. She was a plaything, a human bauble, to be admired and stroked. She must have been all of a size two, wearing a short little skirt and a tank top. Chunky bracelets adorned one wrist, and her hair was in a loose ponytail draped over one shoulder. If I were a man, I'd bring her home too. Skinny bitch.

Des came into view, and the earth dropped beneath me, like that moment a roller coaster begins its plummeting descent. He smiled broadly and poured more into her glass.

She giggled. "Hey, are you trying to get me drunk?"

"Oh, don't pretend it's the first time," he said, tapping her pert little nose with his finger.

I might have puked right then and there if not for the sound of familiar barking. Fontaine ducked and pulled me back down into the shadow. Lazyboy and Fatso bounded toward us, proving once and for all that dogs have no concept of time. We'd been with them ten minutes earlier, but they leaped around in a crazed barking frenzy as though we'd just returned from an intergalactic space mission! If we shushed them, Des would hear. If we ran, they'd chase us, and he'd spot us for sure!

Fontaine clutched my arm, digging his nails into my skin. I heard the screen door slide open. Never in my life have I so wished to spontaneously combust. This was about to become the worst moment of my life, and I've had some mighty horrendous moments. Footsteps fell on the wood of the deck and the railing creaked. Dody's traitorous hounds bounded up the steps. I pressed myself against the lattice.

Please, God.

Please, God.

"Are these your dogs?" The sex kitten's voice had a sultry huskiness to it. She sounded sensual, self-assured, and well-read.

"No, they're my neighbor's," he answered.

Oh, there he goes again! Just the neighbor. That was me. But she was no recruiter. He couldn't try that line on me again. This girl was built for one thing only.

Fontaine's breath was wheezing in and out.

"They're so cute. Look, they're all drooly and hairy. Kind of like you." She giggled again at her own incredibly lame joke while I hyperventilated and fought down the half jar of Marshmallow Fluff trying to spew back up my esophagus.

Des told them to sit. "This one is Lazyboy. This one is Fatso."

Sure, go ahead. Exploit my dogs for the purposes of your insatiable sex drive, you horny bastard!

Fontaine used the distraction to grab my wrist and pull me around to the side of the house. We scuttled toward the road, trampling through Joanna Pullman's carefully culti-vated garden beds. Once at the road we took off running as if werewolves were on our heels. Then we burst into Dody's house and collapsed inside the door.

I couldn't catch my breath. But if I could've, I only would have used it to cry. And I didn't want to cry. Not over this.

"Sadie, I'm sorry," Fontaine began, but I cut him off with a flip of my hand.

"Save it, Fontaine. It doesn't matter."

"Of course it matters. And it's probably not what it looked like."

"It's precisely what it looked like. He stood me up for a better offer. But it's no big deal. He's a free agent. I just wish he hadn't lied."

"There has to be another explanation," Fontaine argued. "Maybe that was his cousin."

I shook my head. "Look, I've been through this before. I know the signs. We had one night together. It's not like he owed me something. He told Dody he didn't have a girlfriend. Maybe that's because he doesn't want one." I stood up, feeling one million years old. "I'm going to bed."

Lying on my lumpy mattress, I marveled at my self-control. I didn't feel that bad. Liking him had been so intense it was almost a relief to know he was no better than any other man. He was another lying sack of shit. Last night had been useful—the way going to the chiropractor was useful. Or getting your car tires rotated. I'd been serviced. Now I was good for another hundred thousand miles.

But as minutes turned to hours, feelings tore away at my emotional paralysis. It grew, a blazing inferno ignited by a simple spark. It's not as if I thought we were exclusive, but he shouldn't have lied! Was he whispering in her ear right now, telling her she was beautiful? Would he toast *her* a bagel for breakfast and try to undo *her* buttons while she got dressed? Probably, that despicable Scottish prick. He should be deported! Where was the number for the INS? I mean, seriously, didn't we have enough shitty, rotten, American guys around without importing foreign assholes from abroad? Our homeland security sucked.

Damn it! She was a baby! He was a pedophile! I bet he lured her into his car with Pop Rocks. I bet he trolled around the high school parking lot in his lab coat saying, "Why, yes, little girl, I am a doctor." Bastard. That rat-fucking bastard. And to think I had actually let my guard down!

This was Dody's fault, and Penny's and Fontaine's. They were all complicit, feeding me bullshit about there being good, honest, loyal men out there. What a crock of shit. He was no better than Richard. Cousin Charlie, my ass. How stupid did he think I was? Did he not realize I could see his house from my deck! God, not only did he treat me shitty, he wasn't even subtle about it!

On the heels of anger came denial. A glorious place to visit, but a dangerous place to live. It couldn't be true. He was sincere and trustworthy and dependable. There must be some sort of explanation. But the only explanation I kept coming back to was that tonight he picked her over me.

By morning, I had reached acceptance. This was really for the best after all. It was bound to happen sooner or later, and honestly, the suspense of waiting for him to cheat would have been a burden. At least I'd seen the man behind the mask early on, before I got too attached. And if nothing else, this experience taught me unequivocally that dating was not for the faint-hearted or the gullible. I was better off without some man cluttering up my life.

CHAPTER 17

I GOT OUT OF BED with steely resolve, determined to prove I was in complete control of my emotions. I went downstairs and started cleaning. Some people eat in times of stress. I scour. By the time Dody and Fontaine were up, I'd cleaned the bathrooms, scrubbed the kitchen floor, and was taking down the family-room curtains for washing.

"Good morning, sunshine," Dody said.

Dust wafted off the drapes, making me sneeze. "When's the last time you washed these?"

"I didn't know you could. Won't the hooks get caught in the machine?"

"The hooks come off. Are you telling me these have never been cleaned?"

"If you can't tell, then why does it matter? You're ornery this morning."

I bit my lip. "Sorry. Just missing the kids, I guess." I had no intention of filling her in about last night's discovery. She'd just say, "Oh, pish-posh. Have some flaxseed."

Fontaine wisely held his tongue, keeping busy with design sketches until he left to meet a client. We didn't even have coffee on the deck, not that I worried about seeing Des jog by. Certainly he was still entangled in the arms of the blonde and too exhausted from his horizontal cardio workout to go running.

I spent the day polishing everything I could get my hands on. And every second of every minute, I reminded myself I didn't care. It didn't matter that he didn't even call to tell me more lies. I could get over this. Broken hearts mend. At least Richard taught me that much.

When my kids came home late the next evening, I was overjoyed. I hugged and kissed them until Jordan said, "No more smooches, Mommy. You're hurting my face." Tucking Paige into bed that night, I read all her favorite stories.

"Can I tell you a story, Mommy?"

I snuggled down under her covers. "Of course."

She showed me the pictures from *Snow White*, adapting it to her own fractured fairy tale. Basically Snow White and the Dorfs owned a very successful cookie company, but when Prince Charming showed up, Snow White had to decide if she'd quit her job and marry him or keep working.

"But can't she keep her job and still get married?" I asked.

"No, silly, because when you get married, your job is taking care of the Prince."

"Who told you that?"

"Daddy."

I got hot all over. "That's Daddy's opinion, honey. But Mommy doesn't agree with him. When you get bigger, then you can decide for yourself if you want to do both. It's your choice."

"I'm going to marry Des," she sighed. My skin burned hotter still. "Or maybe Fontaine. And you. Can I marry you, Mommy?"

I took a deep breath. She was so sweet, so innocent. I would not ruin that for all the money in the world. "Sure you can, baby. I would love to marry you. Now go to sleep."

I turned off her light and went to my own room. I didn't go back downstairs. I was avoiding Dody and her inevitable questions about Des's whereabouts. I hadn't called Penny to fill her in either. It almost felt like if I didn't tell anyone, then it hadn't really happened.

*   *   *

It was gorgeous outside the next morning, which made me grumpy. The kids were dying to go to the beach, but I was stalling, wanting to make sure we'd miss Des's jog. This was getting a little ridiculous, though. If I was going to keep avoiding him, I might as well go back to Glenville right now.

"Could you take them down to the beach, Dody? I had a little too much sun yesterday, and I think I might need to stay in today."

"Of course, darling. You can't be too careful about the sun. Anita Parker has a very suspicious mole on her inner thigh. I keep meaning to ask Des to look at it. When you talk to him, will you mention it?"

Oh, sure. That would be the very first thing.

"I'll try to remember, Dody. But she should talk to her own doctor. We can't bother him with stuff like that."

"Oh, I suppose. All right, kiddos! Shall we go to the beach and look for seahorse shoes?"

"Seahorses don't wear shoes, Aunt Dody," Paige answered.

"Not in the summer. In the summer they wear sandals. Come on. Let's go."

They moseyed on down the deck steps, and I breathed a tiny sigh of relief. Another potential run-in with my one-night stand averted. I settled down on the sunporch with a magazine and my favorite coffee mug, prepared to caffeinate and brood. I derived a perverse joy in my self-pity, perhaps because it was so familiar to me. But my joy was interrupted by footsteps on the deck and that hypnotic accent I had yet to purge from my memory.

"Sadie?"

From the shadow cast on the sunporch floor, I knew Des was standing at the screen door. I didn't look up. Why should I? I had my magazine with Alex O'Loughlin's baby blues to gaze into. I didn't need Des. Stupid old Des with his stupid flat stomach and his stupid awesome hair. Stupid accent too. It probably wasn't even real. Didn't I see somebody who looked like him on *America's Most Wanted*?

"Hey, Sadie?" He knocked lightly, then opened the door.

Damn it. Pretty much had to acknowledge him now.

I let my eyes flicker over him. "Oh, hey."

He stepped inside.

"Hi. Dody said you were up here. Too much sun, huh?"

I shrugged noncommittally. "Yep, I guess." I flipped the page of the magazine.

"Hmm. So are we on for dinner tonight?"

I tsk-tsk-tsked. "Uh, was that tonight? Shoot. I won't be able to make that."

He crossed his arms and frowned. I could almost envision the thought bubble above his head saying, "This woman is pissed. I don't know why. The next thing I choose to say is critically important. Danger! Danger!"

I can read a lot into one little frown.

I kept waiting for some snarky comment or some excuse about the other night. Like his cousin Charlie was a beautiful teenage drag queen. But he was silent, staring and sucking all the oxygen out of my universe. It took every muscle in my body not to squirm. I casually flipped another page. Good-bye, picture of Robert Downey Jr. Hello, millionth depiction of the Jolie-Pitt clan.

"Sadie," he said firmly.

Oh, was he still here? I had forgotten all about him. I looked up.

"I'm sorry I had to cancel the other night. Is that what this is about?"

For the record, it did occur to me that I was being outrageously childish, but I couldn't help myself. I wanted to have a tantrum. I wanted to kick him in the shins and punch his arms. (His thick…muscular…arms…damn it!) But I wouldn't give him the satisfaction.

"No, I just have a lot going on right now."

His eyes dropped to my magazine. "I can see that."

I tossed it aside, lurching up from my chair with the grace of a pregnant rhinoceros. "Look, I don't appreciate being lied to. It wasn't necessary for you to make something up. You could have told me the truth. So let's just skip the whole friend thing, OK? Thanks for your help with Dody, but we don't need you anymore."

Whew! There! I told him. He was a player, but he hadn't tricked me, god damn it, because I was too smart! Any second now a surge of indignant righteousness would course through me! Any second now... Wait for it...

"What are you talking about?"

Oh, he was good. I had to grant him that. He had the look of a man genuinely confused.

"Cousin Charlie? I saw that little blondey-blonde cheerleader at your house, and that was no Cousin Charlie!"

His eyes widened. "That's what this is about? My cousin?"

"Oh, right, your *cousin*." My air quotes added just the right touch.

He expelled a gusty breath and stared at me a moment. Surely he was searching his big, fat head for a plausible excuse. "Wow, Sadie," he finally said. "I don't even know how to respond to that."

"How about 'Hasta la vista, baby?'"

"How about the 'blondey blonde is my cousin. Charlie.'"

"Charlie? Charlie is a girl?" Hmmmmmm.

"Yes! She got stranded at the airport flying home from Marquette."

He was kind of insistent. I felt the stirrings of uncertainty but hammered them down stubbornly. He was using typical man tactics, damn it! First they make you think you're being irrational so you start second-guessing yourself, and then somehow it turns into a fight about how you *accidentally* dumped a big glass of iced tea all over the keyboard when you thought he was surfing for Internet porn.

"I'm supposed to buy that? I saw her, Des."

"When?"

"On your deck. Fontaine and I were walking the dogs."

"Why didn't you come up and say hi?"

"Because I didn't think she was your cousin. Who the hell names a girl like that Charlie?"

He volleyed back defensively. "You have a cousin named Fontaine!"

Ho, ho, hold on! I wasn't tripped up by that!

"Yes, but Fontaine isn't his real name. I mean, it is his real name, but it's not his first name. It's his middle name."

Hah! So there!

Des paused. His face had the same expression Lazyboy gets when perplexed by something squeaky. "Then what's his first name?"

"Tim!"

Hah! Take that!

He rubbed his temples. "His name is Tim, but he goes by Fontaine?"

"Gay! Hello!" *Stop trying to change the subject, dumb-ass.*

"Charlie for Charlotte. Hello!"

That was a dirty trick, using my own sarcasm against me. But I had too much experience fighting with Richard to let Des get away with that.

"So why didn't you tell me that your cousin was a girl?"

"I didn't realize I hadn't. And because it never occurred to me you'd see her and completely flip out. God, Sadie. What is the matter with you?" He ran both hands through his hair, clutching fistfuls at the top. "You thought I cancelled on you so I could be with somebody else?"

I stood my ground, hands on my hips. "You have every right to be with somebody else. We're not exclusive. I just don't like being lied to."

He pushed against his skull. "But I didn't lie to you! And I wasn't with somebody else!"

"But I didn't know that!" I hissed.

"Well, you know it now!" he shouted.

"Then I shouldn't be mad! But I am!"

Des slapped both hands over his face and shook his head.

Have you ever had one of those funky dreams where a super-famous celebrity is madly and passionately in love with you? Then you wake up? You know it's not real, but it still *feels* real. The emotions are so intense, and all those leftover feelings make it seem like maybe it really did happen? Like once I had a wickedly naughty dream about Matt Lauer, which was kind of weird because he's not really my type. But still, I spent the whole next day thinking he might actually call me.

That was the state I was in right now. I *felt* as though something major had happened and I responded accordingly. The fact I had it all terribly wrong was irrelevant. It was too late because I'd already cried.

Des opened his mouth, but it took a full ten seconds for any sound to come out.

"You're unbelievable, Sadie. I have to go." Then he walked out the door and down the steps.

I should've called after him, but I was still mad. Mad about nothing, it seemed. I think I may have screwed up.

Dody trotted up the steps a few minutes later to find me perched on the edge of the chair, staring vacantly. She wagged a finger at me.

"Sadie Turner, I have never been one to mind my own business and I'm not going to start now. What did you say to that young man? He seemed very upset."

"Who's watching the kids, Dody?"

She rolled her eyes. "They're fine. I told them to stay out of the water. What's going on with you and Des?"

I jumped up, rushing out the door and down the steps. "You can't leave them alone on the beach!"

She hurried after me. "Don't go changing the subject, missy!"

We got to the beach and the kids were fine. But Dody made me sit down and tell her what happened. I told her everything, even admitting my mistake. Now we were sitting under an umbrella while the kids built a castle and decorated it with stones and feathers.

"Darling, you know what they say about assumptions and how they make a dummy out of a *U* and a *Y*."

"An ass, Dody. To assume makes an ass of *U* and *me*. It's a play on words."

"Well, whatever it is, smarty-pants English major, you're being foolish. Why do you work so hard at making things harder?"

"I don't." I was getting really tired of her saying that.

"Yes, you do! You should have asked him about that girl instead of jumping to concussions."

"Conclusions!" God!

"You have to give people a chance to explain once in a while. You're just like your mother. She holds a grudge like an elephant."

I wish I smoked, because I could really use a cigarette right about now. "I'm not holding a grudge."

"Oh, really? You don't think you're blaming Des for something he didn't do because Richard cheated on you?"

"Dody, that's not fair!" I wished Anita Parker was here. She must have a pack of smokes in that big beach bag of hers.

"Fair? Whoever told you life was fair?" Dody pulled a tissue from between her breasts and dabbed at her nose.

"You did! You're always talking about karma and telling me what goes around comes around."

"Yes, it does, but that doesn't mean it's always fair. What I mean is that whatever energy you send out into the universe is what you get back."

"Are you saying I deserve whatever rotten shit I get?"

She took off her sunglasses to stare at me. "No. I'm saying that if you expect the worst from people that's what you'll see. You take offense where none is intended, like your mother does. She didn't used to be that way, you know."

"She didn't?"

"No, she used to be happy and sweet and funny. But somewhere along the way someone disappointed her, and she punished every single person that came along after that. And then, of course, there was your father. He was a big disappointment too. And she never got over it. I don't want to see you ending up like she has, darling. Life is to be embraced. It's meant to be lived and enjoyed. Make your mistakes, but make them with gusto and learn from them. Some people will still let you down, like Richard. He's the type with an itch that can't be scratched. But I promise, if you start looking for the best in people, you'll be very surprised at what you find."

My eyes burned, prickling the way they did when I tried not to cry. It was a familiar feeling.

Dody put a soft arm around me. "I think you might owe that boy an apology. Maybe we should make him some cookies."

CHAPTER 18

"DO YOU REALLY THINK THIS is going to work?" I asked, wrist deep in sticky cookie batter.

Jasper was watching from his stool at the kitchen island. "You can't make him plain chocolate chip cookies. That doesn't say, 'I'm spectacular. Don't let me get away.'"

"It doesn't?" Dody adjusted her ruffled apron.

"No. It says, 'Lonely hausfrau bartering cookies for sex.'"

"And that's a bad thing?" Fontaine asked from his spot at the table, where he was perusing fabric samples.

This was hopeless. Des was never going to forgive me. For those keeping score, this was my third strike.

Dody argued, "We start with regular cookies, then add some secret special ingredients."

"Like what?" Jasper, the professional chef, was skeptical.

"Like flaxseed," Dody answered.

"Flaxseed?" Jasper laughed. "Are you trying to make him fall for Sadie or have an impressive bowel movement?"

"Ixnay on the axflay eedsay," Fontaine muttered.

"The cookies aren't going to make any difference," I pouted, my fragile optimism wavering.

"It's not really about the cookies. These give you a reason to go down there. Once you're at his house and he sees how sorry you are, it'll make all the difference. He'll forgive you." Dody snapped her fingers. "Bee pollen. And agave nectar. That'll get him for sure."

"Unless he's allergic to bees, in which case the cookies will kill him," Fontaine added.

Allergic? This was impossible.

"Fontaine, dear, your commentary is not very helpful right now. Look at what you're doing to Sadie."

My mind went into overdrive. What was the penalty for accidentally poisoning the object of one's affection with irresponsibly made cookies? Life behind bars? Community service at a Mrs. Fields?

It was too much to contemplate, all the pooping and the allergies. Maybe I should take him a six-pack and a bag of chips instead. Or bar nuts. Men liked bar nuts, didn't they?

Jasper was right. I was trying to buy affection with confections, and it wasn't going to work.

♪   ♪   ♪

I checked my reflection in the mirror, hoping to look both lovely and contrite. I had to settle for flushed and anxious.

Dody had taken the kids to the park after making me promise to deliver my mea culpa cookies.

I rang Des's doorbell with a basket of goodies on my arm like Little Red Riding Hood. Fontaine had lined the basket and wrapped the cookies with a plaid napkin and a dotted bow. I had serious doubts about my chance of success but was willing to give it a try.

Des opened the door, looking resigned. He had on a white T-shirt with scrub pants and was eating an apple.

I held up the basket, batting my lashes.

He took a bite of apple.

"What's that?" His tone of voice matched his grumpy face.

"An incredibly lame peace offering." I batted again.

He ignored me, staring instead at the basket, noting the tidy little napkin and bow.

"Can I eat it?" He still didn't smile.

"Yes." I wiggled the basket a little to make it more enticing.

"Then come in. I'm starving." He turned around and walked back into the kitchen.

It was not quite the warm welcome I was hoping for, but it also wasn't the cold rebuke I probably deserved. I followed him inside, gingerly setting the basket on the kitchen counter.

He tossed the apple core into the sink, then unceremoniously flicked open the napkin.

"Cookies," he said sullenly. "Did you make them?"

I wanted to be honest. "Mostly. Dody and Jasper helped some."

"Dody?" He frowned, holding up a cookie and examining it in the light. "Did she put any of her crazy shit in here?"

My vow of truth wavered. "I don't think so."

Now I'd be racked with guilt if he ended up spending the night on the toilet. Maybe we should have skipped the flaxseed.

He sighed, dropping the cookie back in the basket and staring at me. He was still mad. That much was obvious.

I fiddled with the edge of my shirt. "So that was your cousin, huh?"

He crossed his arms and leaned back against the counter. "Yep."

"I guess I owe you an apology then."

"That depends."

"On what?"

"On if you're actually sorry, Sadie. Don't say it if you don't mean it. And don't think acting cute and bringing me cookies will distract me. You were way off base. I don't like being called a liar. I don't deserve it."

I hadn't really considered it that way. I was so wrapped up in how he'd hurt my feelings I never stopped to consider I might be hurting his.

"I am sorry. I didn't think it would matter much to you."

His arms fell loose, as if the strength had gone out of them. I don't think I understood the word incredulous before. But that was how he looked. Incredulous. He rubbed a hand across his face.

"Sadie, when I told you I wanted company, I didn't mean some random warm body in my bed. Is that the kind of guy you think I am? Is that your opinion of me?"

A foreign concept began to gel in my mind. I was so used to Richard trampling over my emotions, crushing me with his will, and here I was doing the same thing to Des. It never occurred to me I might have that power, because I had none over Richard. But Des seemed genuinely upset.

"I'm sorry, Des. I overreacted and I was wrong."

"Yeah, you were! What's it going to take to make you trust me? Because if you can't, then whatever this is between us isn't going to get very far. And I'd like it to."

His intensity was unnerving, heating my skin. His words heated everything else.

"I would too," I said, and acknowledged deep down it was true. Of course I wanted something more. I was not a fling kind of gal.

I scuffed my sandal on the floor. "I don't know how many chances you're willing to give me, but how about one more? Dody says I never see the good in people, but I see it in you. I'm just not used to it."

His jaw relaxed the least little bit. "I'm not particularly good at being good. You'll have to look pretty hard. But I don't lie. And I tend to stick with one woman at a time, because otherwise I get confused."

I smiled and my eyes got watery. If he was making jokes, I was halfway there. "Well, you may not have noticed, but I'm kind of high maintenance. Still, you've seen the worst of me so there shouldn't be any more surprises."

Des sniffed. And sighed. And crossed his arms. He wasn't quite finished being annoyed. "Look, I like you, Sadie. But it seems like you're waiting for me to screw up to prove I'm as bad as your ex-husband. I'm not. So you need to stop doing that. OK?"

He was right. I was doing that. And I should stop.

"Yes, I will. I promise."

We stood on opposite sides of the kitchen, staring. Absorbing what had been said.

"OK," he said again, finally stepping forward and closing the distance between us. "So no more running away when you're flustered and half-naked. No more getting pissed without telling me why. And no more crying at restaurants." He smiled at last. "Agreed?"

I nodded. "Agreed."

"Good." He put his hands on my waist, pulling me against him. "Because I've missed you these last few days."

"You have?" I bit my lip.

He nodded. "Especially that."

"What?" I whispered.

His eyes dropped to my mouth. "The way you bite your lip when you get nervous. God, it gets me every time."

Then he kissed me with days' worth of pent-up longing.

Relief and joy intertwined like our bodies. He lifted me up and set my bottom on the counter. I wrapped my legs around his waist, feeling uncharacteristically bold. His touch was addictive. I craved more with every caress.

It's true. I'd wanted Des from the first moment I saw him running down the beach. My desire then had been equal parts curiosity and deprivation. But that longing paled in comparison to this intensity.

We kissed and clung so tightly not a molecule could slide between us. This was how it was supposed to be. Passionate, fearless, fun. He lifted me again as if I were weightless and carried me into his bedroom. We fell with a bounce and a breathless giggle onto the mattress.

Bitchy the cat was there. She hissed and walked out of the room. And it was quite a while before we got to those cookies.

CHAPTER 19

SUMMER DAYS FLOATED BY AND turned into a week, and then one more. Life became idyllic. Insipid love songs seemed profound. Implausible romantic comedies radiated truth. Everything around me took on the wholesome cuteness of fuzzy kitties and sparkly rainbows. Had it always been that way and I hadn't noticed? *Is* love a many-splendored thing? Truth be told, I'm not sure what *splendored* means, but if it means really, *really* good, then yes, love is splendored.

Yes, of course I knew this thrill ride was temporary. I wasn't really in love. My charismatic new friend (with benefits) had slipped a supersonic potion into my Kool-Aid, and I gulped it down before considering the consequences. I was sublimely, mystically drunk with the effects and riding the wave of joy. Soft whispers of common sense warned me this preposterously illogical jubilation would wear off, but for now I wanted to enjoy it. Like that moment you step on the scale after a bad case of the stomach flu and you're down five pounds. You can't help but be excited, even though you know as soon as you eat anything you'll gain it all back. This was like that. Only so much better.

In addition to playing in the lake with my kids, shopping with Dody and Fontaine, eating far too much ice cream, and reveling in naughty blanket time with Des, I'd attended an organizing conference and came back to Bell Harbor full of ideas and enthusiasm. I was determined to make a go of it, and Kyle had found me two more clients.

As I paced around the sunporch one evening waiting for Des to pick me up for a date, I was plotting how to fit two hundred pairs of shoes into one closet.

"God, woman, would you relax? I can feel your estrogen surging from way over here," Fontaine barked.

"What's estrogen?" Jordan asked from his spot on the floor, where he and Paige were playing with beads and pipe cleaners.

"Nothing, baby." I made a face at Fontaine.

Dody joined us on the porch, wearing blue wire-rimmed sunglasses, bell-bottom jeans, and a smock top circa 1960. She had an orange headband tied around her forehead like a ninja.

"Nice duds, Mom."

She shook her booty. "Thank you, dear. Harry and I are going to the Age of Aquarius Festival at the fairgrounds. When does Des get here, Sadie? I have a medical question."

"Please do not pester him with more of Anita Parker's medical quandaries, Dody. She needs to talk to her own doctor."

"It's not for Anita. It's for...for somebody else."

"Then that somebody else needs to find her own doctor too."

I craned my neck, trying to peek out the window to see if that was Des's car I heard.

Dody's phone rang and Paige hopped up to answer it, scattering beads in every direction.

"Hello? Oh, hi, Grandma."

I shivered with the chill of doom. Was that thunder from the underworld I heard?

Paige continued chatting. "We're making bead bracelets. Uh-huh. Yep, she's here, but she's going to the movies with Des."

No! No! Paige don't tell her that! I nearly ripped the phone from her delicate fingers. The less information my mother had, the better.

But Paige added nail after nail to the coffin. "Yes, he's a boy from the beach. He talks kind of funny, but he gave me and Jordan suckers when Aunt Dody's head was bleeding."

OK, that was enough. I pried the phone from her.

"Hi, Mom. What's up?"

"Who is she talking about?"

"Nobody special. Just a friend."

"Does he have a speech impediment?" Mother would have done well during those dark periods of history when imperfect children were left to the wolves.

"He's Scottish, Mother. It's an accent."

"Hmm. Are you seeing him?"

The Spanish Inquisition had nothing on her. Thank God my mother didn't believe in waterboarding.

"He's a doctor from down the street. He gave Dody some stitches when she fell and cut her head. Now he's taking me to the movies, but please don't make a big deal out of it."

She harrumphed into the phone. "Honestly, Sadie, all I do is show a little interest and this is what I get."

I bit my lip. "I'm sorry, Mom. What can I do for you?"

"I was calling to schedule a visit with my grandchildren, if it's not too much to ask."

"They would love that," I lied.

"Richard is seeing someone else too, you know."

I waited for the pollution of sadness to clog my lungs and make it hard to breathe. But it never came. Technically, Richard was always seeing someone else, even when we were married. But this was the first time the idea didn't make my chest ache.

"Good for him. Listen, I have to run. But I'll call you tomorrow and we can figure out a time to visit, OK? Here, talk to Dody."

Dody tried to evade me, but I kept jabbing her with the phone until at last she took it. "Hello, Helene." She stuck out her tongue at me and then walked into the other room.

I checked the window again. "Where is Des? He's late."

"He's not late, cupcake. You set your watch ahead, remember?" Fontaine reminded me.

"Yes, because I don't like to be late. He should do the same thing."

"Tell him that. I'm sure he'll appreciate it."

When at last Des arrived, he kissed me on the cheek and I forgot all about the waiting.

Paige held out her hand. "Here, Des, I made you a bracelet. I used boy colors 'cause you're a boy. But there's a pink bead too so you'll remember it's from me. And a red one to make you think of Mommy."

He tried to fit the tiny bracelet over his man-sized wrist. "Is red Mommy's favorite color?"

Paige nodded, her curls bobbing. "Yes, 'cause it's the love color."

I pretended to be fascinated by my fingernails.

"Thanks. I'm going to put it in my pocket for now so I don't lose it," he told her. "But I'm sure I'll get lots of compliments on it at work."

Paige giggled. "Fontaine is going to read me and Jordan a story after you guys leave."

"Really? What story?"

"The one with the mean troll guy who puts the princess in a tower. And he won't ever let her out until she guesses his name."

Des smiled. "Oh, I've heard that one. Do you know his name?"

She nodded emphatically. "Yep. It's Rumpled Foreskin."

Fontaine and Des erupted with laughter.

I cuffed Fontaine on the side of the head. "Darn it, Fontaine! Did you teach her that? If she says that in front of Richard, I'm the one who gets yelled at." I turned to Paige. "It's RumpleSTILTskin, honey."

Fontaine grinned. "I didn't teach her that, I swear!"

❧   ❧   ❧

"You're not staying for lunch?" my mother asked a few days later when I dropped off the kids in Glenville for their visit.

"Sorry. Wish I could, but Kyle wants me to meet another organizing client. This will be my third." I stood a little taller, proud of my achievement.

"I still don't understand why you want to paw through other people's belongings. It doesn't sound appealing to me at all. If you're short on cash, you know you could ask me rather than becoming a housekeeper."

I slumped back down. "Thank you, but I'm not short on cash. I'm organizing because it's fun."

I didn't tell her I'd signed up for a business seminar and added my name to an online registry of professional organizers. Or that Fontaine had drawn up business cards for our proposed joint venture. I also failed to mention both he and Dody were pressuring me to move to Bell Harbor permanently. No point in telling her about it when it would never happen.

"So you'll keep the kids here for two days and then Richard will pick them up. Does that still work for you?" I asked instead. I wanted to get out of there before she peppered me with questions about Des. Or anything else, for that matter.

"Yes, I suppose that's fine. It'll be nice to see him."

I did not agree. Richard had been pleasant enough the last few times we talked, but I could not shake the feeling he was up to something. I guess old habits die hard.

"OK, well then, I'd better run. I haven't checked on my house in weeks."

I drove across town and into my old neighborhood. The avenues looked different, the colors or dimensions slightly skewed. Kids I didn't recognize were playing in the yard next to mine. They stopped and watched me as I fumbled with the key in my front door. At least the grass looked fine. Richard must have fixed the sprinklers.

The door stuck a little and finally gave way. I stepped inside.

My extravagant Glenville home had a musty, closed-up smell. Dust sparkled in the rays of sunlight coming through the windows. I'd been looking forward to stopping by, anxious for some tranquility after the endless chaos at Dody's. But it was eerily quiet, like a cave deep underground.

I set my purse on the dusty black granite countertop in the kitchen I loved. I had spent hours agonizing over which colors to choose during my most recent redecoration, completed during a period when Richard seemed never to be home. The monochromatic shades of charcoal and gray that had appealed to me for being stylish and classic now seemed unfriendly. Everything here, the cold stone counters, the stainless-steel appliances, the painstakingly placed decorative plates, it all had a lifeless quality to it. You couldn't find a flaw in the design, nor would you find a hint of personality. I'd have to redecorate again when I moved home. Maybe Fontaine would help me.

I kicked off my shoes and walked over the plush carpet to the family room. Above the marble-tiled fireplace was an enormous family portrait. Richard, Paige, Jordan, and I posed in white shirts and khaki pants. I remembered that day. It was awful. Richard had been late so I refused to sit next to him for the photographer. Then Jordan had cried because Richard scolded him. The smile on my face peering down from the picture looked sincere, but I knew the effort that took. I was an expert at masking my irritation from the rest of the world. But I could see the sadness around my own eyes. That picture would have to go. I'd only left it there for the kids' sake. Paige, Jordan, and I would get a new portrait taken soon.

To the left of the fireplace was a mark in the wall from when I'd thrown a shoe at Richard. I couldn't remember now why I'd thrown it, but I'm sure he deserved it. How had we gotten to that place? Hating him had not come upon me all at once. It was gradual, creeping over me slowly, insidiously, like frostbite, until eventually I was frozen solid.

I'd loved him once. I think he'd loved me too—the way an athlete loves a trophy. I was still in college when we met, and he was already a reporter at a tiny local station. Oh, how shiny and new love seemed in those first months of marriage. We'd had fun, and I loved his attention. At first our fights were seldom but loud, then they faded away altogether, along with any kind of communication other than sex. That was Richard's idea of conversation.

"You want to?"

"Yeah, I guess. If you want to."

"OK."

A siren wailed in the distance, bringing me to the present and scattering thoughts of Richard away.

I went upstairs and lingered in the doorway of my bedroom. Like the streets outside, I felt as if I'd never seen this room before, or was gazing at a museum display.

Here we show the habitat of the modern American family. Note how the male and female of the species sleep as far apart as the mattress will allow.

The huge four-poster bed in the center of the room would have to be replaced. I hated it now. Richard had given it to me as a gift for our fifth anniversary, but I'd been paying for it ever since.

I opened the top drawer of my dresser, where I kept my jewelry. I rummaged around until I found the black velvet box holding my engagement ring and wedding band. I flipped it open. Even with the shades drawn, my ring sparkled. It was a rock and a half, another extravagant gift. Richard thought love should show on the outside, and so he was generous with his wallet. Technically, I guess he was generous with all parts of himself. I chuckled to the empty room. Yes, that was Richard's flaw. He was just too generous.

An idea formed in my mind in an instant. I slipped the box into my pocket.

Heading back downstairs, I dialed my phone to call a neighbor. I had still not connected with any of them the entire time I was in Bell Harbor. Sheila from next door didn't answer. Neither did Nora, or Elaine, or Connie. I'd left them all messages earlier this week, saying I'd be in town but had heard nothing back.

Stepping onto my sunporch, I looked across the back-yards. And there they were, sitting on Nora's patio. An odd sensation tingled in my throat and I had another idea. I pulled my phone back out of my pocket and dialed Sheila's cell once more. She was never without it. I watched through the window and saw her pick up her phone from the glass-topped table and check the caller ID. Her head turned toward my house, and she set her phone down without answering.

Oh my God. I was being shunned. Why?

I sat down hard on the seat next to the window and waited for a rush of indignation. But just as I had when hearing Richard was seeing someone, I felt…nothing. Had I missed these women? Not really. And clearly they had not missed me either. Perhaps being out of the neighborhood meant I'd have no juicy gossip for them and therefore served no purpose. Two months ago, I would have stormed across the grass and demanded an explanation. Now I realized how this simplified things. I had purged some useless friendships without a messy breakup or hormonal drama. When I moved back to Glenville, I wouldn't waste my energy trying to reconnect. I'd find new friends. Better friends. What had Madame Margaret said? "Out with the old, in with the new"?

I guess that went for people too.

CHAPTER 20

DES PICKED ME UP FOR our date looking far too yummy for my own good. As he opened the passenger door, he pointed at my cheek. "You have a little something there."

Great, misplaced lipstick? White residue from the blemish cream I was too old to need? I wiped at the spot. "Did I get it?"

He shook his head and leaned close. "Oh, I see. It's a kiss." He pressed his lips against my face, butterfly soft, and we giggled in unison.

"Too cheesy?" he asked.

"A little, but I'll take it."

He kissed me again before I slid into the car. My kids were with Richard for the weekend and so I was free and easy for the next few days. Heavy on the easy.

As I waited for Des to get in on his side, something sparkled on the floor. I reached over and picked it up. It was an earring. A nagging stir of déjà moo passed over me. You know, that feeling of having experienced this bullshit before?

I used to find random stuff in Richard's car all the time, like matchbooks to restaurants I'd never been to, loose strands of long, blonde hair, half-finished fast-food drinks with lipstick on the straw, and once I even found a condom wrapper. Richard told me a prankster-friend had put a Trojan on his stick shift just to be funny. Yeah, ha ha, very funny.

I studied the earring in silence as Des adjusted his seat and flipped down the visor. I stared at it as if it might evaporate if I wished hard enough. It was distinct, with colored glass beads and coiled wire. It wasn't stylish. In fact, it was hideous. And it was most definitely not mine.

He put the keys in the ignition.

I held up the earring. "Whose is this?"

He looked at me in surprise, glancing at the earring, then back at me.

"Um…isn't it yours?"

I held it closer to his face, raising a quizzical brow. "Does this look like one I'd wear?"

He looked bewildered, as if it were a trick question. As if I'd asked, "Does this earring make me look fat?"

"Um…I guess not."

"Then whose is it?"

He fussed with putting the car into gear. "Oh, I picked it up in your driveway the other day and thought it must be Dody's. I kept forgetting to ask her."

I looked back at the earring. Yes, it looked very much like some monstrosity she might wear. His explanation made perfect sense.

"I'll give it to her." I slipped it into my purse.

"Thanks. Hey, how's Penny doing with everything? Is she feeling good?" He backed the car up with a bit of a lurch.

"She feels OK. She's tired." I had told Des about Penny's pregnancy even though she'd sworn me to secrecy. I knew he wouldn't say anything since he'd likely never meet her. I'd also told Fontaine, although completely by accident. He was as tricky as my mother when it came to interrogation techniques.

"Are they going to find out if it's a boy or girl?"

"No, they want to be surprised."

"Uh-huh. That's good. Do they have names yet?"

"Not yet. Why all the questions about Penny's baby?"

Des smiled over at me. "No reason. Just making conversation."

We ate dinner at Arno's, where Jasper worked. Then we strolled along the Bell Harbor boardwalk, holding hands and leaning into one another until we found a divey little patio bar with live music. It overlooked the beach and was the perfect setting for whatever the night had in store. The tables were tiny. Our knees bumped underneath, giving me goose bumps as I anticipated them bumping again later on.

We sipped cocktails and talked about inconsequential things, like who invented daylight savings time and how weird was the musical *Cats*. I mean, seriously? It's a musical. About cats.

I told him how, when we were little, Penny wanted to conserve energy way before it was trendy, so I would sneak around the house turning on random lights to annoy her.

Des replied, "Bonnie and I were keen on blowing things up. Once we blew up a couch."

"You blew up a couch? Why?"

His smile was lazy. "It was there. We were bored. It was this beat-up old couch that somebody was throwing away, so we dragged it up to the top of a hill. And then we blew it up. Robin ratted us out though. She was always the tattler. My mum hit the roof."

I could not imagine what my mother would have done under those circumstances. "What happened?"

Des tapped his lips thoughtfully. "Oh, let's see. I had to clean the garage, wash the car, scrub the kitchen, walk the dog...pretty much all the stuff she'd been bugging me to do anyway. But I also had to confess to my dad. That was the real punishment."

"Why is that?" Again, hard to imagine, since I grew up with virtually no father.

"You did not want to make my father mad, so I was petrified. I dragged my sorry ass into his office like a dead man walking."

"So what did he do?" I stretched out my leg, brushing against his calf oh so accidentally.

His eyes flickered, thrilling me with my ability to distract him.

"He laughed. The engineer in him thought we were very clever, but he still put me under house arrest for about a week, and Mum kept me working like a dog. She always punished us with housework. Maybe that's why I'm kind of a slob now. I subconsciously equate cleaning with getting in trouble."

"I equate cleaning with a sense of world domination, like putting everything in its proper place grants me ultimate control over the universe."

He took a big gulp from his drink. "I think that's scarier than blowing stuff up. Hey, want to dance?" he asked as the band started playing something slow.

Let's think. Would I like to press myself up against him, swaying back and forth while everyone whispered what a beautiful couple we made? That could be fun. "Yes, please."

I was right. It was fun. I don't know if anyone bothered to whisper about us, but I enjoyed it nonetheless. "You're mighty light on your feet, Dr. McKnight."

"Am I?" He sounded pleased. "I have a confession to make. Bonnie and I took some lessons before she got married. Since our dad wasn't there she asked me to fill in. But she thought we should practice so we didn't embarrass ourselves."

"Oh, that is so sweet."

"Not really. Every lesson we fought like cats and dogs. Nearly killed each other. Worst experience ever." His big smile said otherwise.

I pressed against him. "Well, for what it's worth, I'm glad you practiced."

He pulled me even closer, spinning us around and looking smug. "I guess I'm glad now too."

Then he kissed me, right there in front of all the good people of Bell Harbor.

"I have another confession." His voice was low, melting into my ear.

"What's that?" I asked, breathless.

"I thought about you all day."

"You did?" A delicious warmth started in my middle and spread out in every direction.

"Yeah. Let's go to my place and I'll prove it."

*   *   *

Thunder rumbled. Rain pelted. The morning was gray and dismal, but I had sunshine on the inside. A sheer curtain swirled around in a sensual, film-noir way in Des's bedroom. We must have left the sliding door open in our haste to disrobe one another. I slipped from the bed, not wanting to wake him up. I liked to sneak into the bathroom, tidy my hair, and scrape the goop from my eyes, then slip back into bed so he'd think I woke up looking fresh as a daisy. Beauty might be in the eye of the beholder, but a little primping never did any harm.

I spruced up as best as I could, considering my purse and most of my clothes were in the other room. I had no beauty products and no secret techniques. I squirted toothpaste in my mouth and swished it around. My hair was a train wreck, and I was pretty sure that was a hickey on my neck, but there wasn't much to be done about that. I quietly flipped off the bathroom light and eased open the door.

Busted. Des gave me a lazy smile from the bed.

I ducked back behind the door, all except my head.

"Good morning," he said.

"Good morning." I remained still, not about to saunter out there in the broad light of day. Well, in this case it was the murky light of day, but still too bright for me to parade around in my altogether.

"Um, would you…close your eyes?" I asked hesitantly.

"What?" He chuckled.

"I don't have anything on."

"Then why on earth would I close my eyes?"

"Because I'm shy. I'm embarrassed."

Des was beyond amused, folding both arms behind his head. "That's ridiculous."

"No, it isn't. Come on, I feel like an idiot. Close your eyes." He was being annoying.

"You get that I see people all the time without their clothes, right?"

"Then it shouldn't be a hardship to *not* look at me, you pervert."

"You also get that I've seen you naked quite few times and enjoyed it plenty, right?"

"I was lying down most of those times, and it was dark. This is different."

His laughter was deep. "You're seriously not coming out?"

"No, because I'm naked, and you're all covered up."

"Is that the problem?" He flipped off the covers, proving he was as absent of clothing as I was.

Oh, my.

"There, now we're even. Do you feel better?"

I looked away, blushing furiously. I was a good girl deep down, and good girls avert their eyes when men expose themselves. But I wasn't *that* good, so about half a second later I looked again. He was stretched out, shamelessly comfortable, his skin dark against the white sheet. He patted the mattress playfully. "Come on," he said, like he was talking to one of Dody's dogs.

I weighed my options quickly. I couldn't very well spend the rest of the day in the bathroom. Eventually I'd have to come out, and unless I fashioned a toga out of bath towels, I was going to have to do it naked. He'd won this round.

"You, sir, are no gentleman." I straightened my shoulders and stepped from behind the door, watching his expression change from lighthearted teasing to something else entirely.

Hmm, maybe I had won this round.

We spent the next hour in bed, exploring the merits of nudity.

In fact, we spent nearly that entire day in bed, lying around, pillow talking, laughing, having fun not talking. We ate toaster waffles and microwave popcorn. We watched movies, took a bath in the Jacuzzi, fooled around some more, then took a nap. The food was not good, the movies were plotless and pointless, and I had the best day of my life. Doing nothing with Des was more fun than doing almost anything with anybody else.

"I should probably head home," I said reluctantly from the couch as our date neared the twenty-four-hour mark. I was wearing a pair of Des's scrub pants, which were a foot too long, and one of his T-shirts. My hair was an unholy mess, and I craved my toothbrush with the intensity of Scooby longing for his Scooby snacks. Des was opening cupboards in the kitchen.

His head popped into view. "Got plans tonight?"

"No, but I thought you might be getting sick of me."

"I am. I can't stand the way you keep letting me pull off all your clothes."

I blushed. "These are your clothes. Anyway, I thought I'd played hard-to-get long enough."

He shut a cupboard. "Um, when were you playing hard-to-get?"

I stood up. "Oh, now I am leaving."

He came out from the kitchen and pulled me close. "You know I'm just kidding."

"Humph."

"Sadie, don't go home," he murmured against my ear. "Stay and have macaroni and cheese with me."

"You think you can seduce me with carbs?"

"I'd offer you something better, but it's about the only food I have. That and a jar of olives. But if you stay, you can pick out the next movie."

He was a persuasive devil, offering carbs and B-list entertainment.

"I am dying to brush my teeth. I need my toothbrush," I admitted fervently.

He laughed. "Can't you just use mine?"

"Yuck. That is disgusting. I really need to freshen up."

"I go back to work tomorrow for the next five nights. Are you going to send me off to the trenches with no kisses?" He might have been begging me to stay for purely sexual reasons, but honestly, that was OK.

"I've given you a thousand kisses. But tell you what... I'll go home and change my clothes and such and then come back."

He kissed my nose. "Perfect. I'll run to the store and grab a couple things to eat, and we can meet back here. I'll leave the front door unlocked in case you get back before me."

Des dropped me off at Dody's on his way to buy groceries. I strolled in wearing his clothes and carrying my own in a plastic sack. I was pure class. Fontaine was sketching at the kitchen island while Jasper chopped peppers.

"Hey, guys. Where's Dody?" I dropped my baggie of clothes in a chair and plucked an apple from the fruit bowl.

"She's at the Christopher Walken Film Festival with Harry," Jasper answered. "Nice threads, by the way."

"Thanks," I mumbled, my mouth full of apple.

"Where'd you go to dinner last night, hoho?" Fontaine asked.

"Arno's. And tonight we're cooking at Des's."

"Haven't you been there for, like, a day and a half? Way to get back on that pony, cowgirl."

"Thanks. Hey, Jas, I'm glad you're here. There's something I wanted to show you." I ran up to my room, grabbed the little black velvet box I'd brought back from Glenville, and trotted down to the kitchen. I was lightning fast.

I set the box in front of him.

Jasper studied it as if it were a bomb to be diffused.

"What is it?" He picked up a towel and dried his hands.

Fontaine stared at the box just as hard.

"I've been thinking. I know you want that one ring for Beth and you don't have the cash for it. But if you take this one, you can trade it and probably get some cash back too."

Jasper's face looked like I'd told him I was a cyborg.

"Go on. Open it," I urged.

He picked up the box and slowly eased it open. "Sadie, you can't give me this! This ring is huge."

I shrugged. "I know. But I don't need it. I don't want it. And I'll never make a necklace out of it because it will always remind me of Richard."

Fontaine grabbed the ring from Jasper and held it up to the light, making it shimmer and glow.

"Then you trade it in and get something else, but I can't take it." Jasper shook his head.

"But I don't need more jewelry, Jas. And you do. I would love for you to take this thing off my hands. You know I can't stand having stuff lying around that no one is using. It's clutter to me. But if it makes you and Beth happy, then I'll feel good too."

Fontaine handed the ring back to his brother. "That's a pretty good deal."

Jasper looked back and forth between us and the ring. "Do they even do that? Take trade-ins, I mean?"

Fontaine nodded. "I'm sure they would at Mason's jewelry. I've bought vintage stuff from there before."

Dody's Tweety Bird clock chimed in the hallway as I waited for his answer.

"Are you absolutely certain, Sadie?" Jasper asked solemnly.

I was. It was the right thing to do. "Absolutely."

Jasper closed the box and hugged me as if we were about to jump from a plane and I had the only parachute. His voice cracked. "Thanks." Then he strode from the room, muffling a sniffle.

Fontaine smiled at me, shaking his head. "Sugarplum, I had no idea you could be so magnanimous."

I smiled back. "And I had no idea you knew what magnanimous meant."

*   *   *

I arrived back at Des's before him. I puttered around, tidying things up, washing the few dishes in the sink, arranging the sofa pillows, making the bed, and lining up all his shoes, which had been strewn in one big pile by the front door. Stacks of unopened mail were scattered around the kitchen and eating area. I couldn't resist. I sorted it all, putting the magazines in one pile, the junk mail in another, and whatever looked important into a third. I put the tidy stacks on the kitchen counter.

He walked in as I finished. "Hi there." He glanced around, taking in my handiwork.

In that instant, I realized I had been presumptuous again. Maybe he liked his shoes in a pile and his mail littered through every room.

He set the grocery bags on the counter next to the crisply folded dishtowels. "You've been busy."

I bit my lip. "I'm sorry. It's a habit."

"Don't be sorry." He picked up the top magazine. "Hmm, when did I get this?"

"They're in chronological order, oldest to most recent." My compulsion knew no boundaries. Let's put it all out there.

He pressed his fingertips against the counter and smiled. "Let me guess. You have all the clothes in your closet arranged by color, don't you?"

"Doesn't everybody?"

He smiled wider still. "My sister Robin is the same way. She's going to love you."

The moment hung suspended. He had broken the cardinal rule. Everyone knew it was bad luck to mention meeting a family member this early in a relationship. Almost as bad as saying "I love you" too soon. You know, *premature love declaration.*

His smile faded as fast as it came. He turned to fuss with the bags while I restacked the perfectly stacked mail.

"So, what's for—"

"Spaghetti," he answered before I finished the question.

Spooning that night like a little old couple drifting off to sleep, I pondered the state of this union and fought back sadness. The summer was passing by. Des and I had very deliberately not discussed me going back to Glenville or where his next assignment might be. I knew the offer of an extended stay in Bell Harbor was on the table for him, but since he hadn't brought it up, neither had I.

The reality was this lovely affair was a detour, not a destination. Sooner than I wanted, I'd be back to my real life and he'd ride off into the sunset for his next grand adventure. We knew that from the start, so it would be childish to wish it was any other way. Right? There wasn't any way around it. We'd been living in a bubble, pretending there was a future. But there wasn't.

"Des?" I whispered.

"Hmm?"

"It's fun being with you."

He squeezed my middle, mumbling in near sleep, "You too."

In the morning, I woke up before him, wisely grabbing his shirt from the floor and putting it on. Getting caught naked yesterday had turned out well enough, but I was still modest. I flipped on the bathroom light, and my heart gave a hop, a skip, and a flutter. Resting on the counter next to Des's was a brand new toothbrush. It had a little dental floss bow tied around it so I'd know it was for me. That was about the cutest thing ever. He bought me a toothbrush. I picked it up reverently, as if it were Cinderella's glass slipper. This meant a lot to me, and not because of my meticulous attention to dental hygiene. This toothbrush was special because it meant he wanted me to come back.

CHAPTER 21

"IT'S ONLY A TOOTHBRUSH, SADIE. Maybe it's because you have terrible breath."

I was sitting in Penny's garish ladybug kitchen before picking the kids up from Richard's. Des was spending the next few days in Seattle at a medical conference so I had some time to wander. I stirred my lemonade, wondering if she was right. Maybe I was reading too much into it. "I just think it was cute."

She rubbed her still-flat tummy, a habit she'd developed since learning she was pregnant. "It is cute, definitely. But you shouldn't move there for some guy, especially one who may not be staying."

"Dody's the one who keeps saying I'm moving there. I never said that!"

"Not directly, but you've been dropping hints all over the place. All you can talk about is how fun it is and how friendly everybody is and how much better than Glenville it is. Honestly, it's like you don't even care how you'd be totally abandoning me right when my baby gets here!" Penny covered her face with her arms and burst into tears.

Ah, those first-trimester hormones are powerful little bastards. They will kick you in the knees and make you fall flat on your weepy face. I set my lemonade down to hug Penny's heaving shoulders.

"I'm not moving there. I agree it would be stupid."

"But it wouldn't!" she hiccupped. "It would make perfect sense. It is so much better there than here. Where am I supposed to take my kids to play? There are no parks within walking distance of my house. There isn't a beach or fudge shops or kite stores. Bell Harbor has that, plus those cute little houses that all look different from each other." She wiped her face. "Just think of it. You could buy a darling little bungalow and paint it purple if you wanted to. I have to get a frickin' dispensation from the pope to put a birdbath in my yard, stupid neighborhood association."

"Maybe you should move to Bell Harbor," I said.

"Maybe I will, but you go first."

I sat back down, wishing there was some gin in my lemonade. "So now you're saying I should move there?"

"Probably. But don't do it for some guy."

When Dody and Fontaine had suggested I move, it was easy to dismiss the notion. After all, Fontaine had business motives and Dody is a whack job. But Penny adding her name to the petition changed things.

"Wouldn't you miss me?"

She hiccupped again. "Yes, but I'd come to see you all the time. Princess Buttercup loves the water."

"Who is Princess Buttercup?"

"My baby. That's what Jeff calls her."

"But what if it's a boy?"

"Then he's going to get beat up a lot."

*   *   *

The television blared through the door of Richard's apartment. I knocked a second time, and Jordan opened it a minute later.

"Hi, Mommy." He jumped into my arms, squeezing me tight. That would never get old.

"Hello, beautiful," Richard purred. Oh, that was definitely old.

I stepped through the door into his starkly furnished apartment.

"Wow. I love what you've done with the place."

Richard chuckled. "Yeah, well, you kept all the furniture, remember?"

I smiled. "Are the kids all packed?" The sooner I could get out of there the better.

"What's your rush? Would you like a drink?"

"No, thanks. We have to run. And I'm driving."

"Got a hot date back in Mayberry with this Dezzz character the kids keep buzzing about? Who are they talking about?"

"Nobody special. Just a friend." I kicked aside a newspaper on the floor, looking for the kids' shoes.

"A friend, huh?" Richard leaned against the wall. "Friends are good to have. Is it serious?"

I stopped looking for shoes and gave Richard a stern look. "That's not exactly your business, is it?"

He smirked. "Oh, so it is serious? What kind of name is Dezzz? Is he a biker or something?"

I saw Paige's sandal stuffed under a couch cushion and crossed the room to pull it out. "He's a doctor. Come on, kids. Help me get your stuff together."

Paige hopped around on one foot. "Mommy, where's my other shoe?"

"It's here, baby. Let me help you."

We scurried around, gathering their things and stuffing them into a duffel bag. I didn't take extra time to fold anything. It would all go into the wash as soon as I got back to Dody's anyway.

"Daddy, don't drink my juice box, OK? Save it for me," Jordan told him.

"OK, J. I will. Are you sure you have to rush off, Sade? We could order a pizza, open a bottle of wine. You could tell me all about your new friend. Or better yet, we could reminisce." His innuendo was loud and clear. *Let's put on a movie for the kids and sneak into the other room for a quickie.*

I shook my head vehemently. "No, I have stuff to do. I need to stop by the house before we head back to Bell Harbor."

He frowned. "You don't need to check on the house. I could do that for you, you know."

"That's nice of you to offer, Richard, but I have a couple things I'd like to pick up. Kids, give Daddy a smooch. We have to go."

Paige kissed his cheek and he gave her a hug. Jordan tried to do the same.

"Hey, J. Real men shake hands, remember?" Richard chided.

I bit my tongue. Heaven forbid Richard's son show any sensitivity.

Jordan nodded and held out his hand.

"OK, I think that's everything," I said. "See you later, Richard." I started to walk out the door. The kids scampered ahead but Richard gripped my arm and squeezed. "Sadie, tell the truth. Is it serious between you and this guy?"

Was he jealous? After all this time and all he'd put me through?

I wasn't naive enough to think it was serious with Des. I didn't know if it ever would be, but I wasn't about to let Richard know that.

"It's desperately serious, Richard. I've never been so in love."

CHAPTER 22

"YOU'LL LIKE TOM AND TASHA. Don't be nervous," Des said as we drove to the Bell Harbor marina.

"I'm not nervous. What makes you think I'm nervous?"

"You haven't said a word all morning and your lip is bleeding."

I put my hand to my mouth. OK, maybe I was a little nervous, but who wouldn't be? Today we were sailing with two of his friends from medical school. They'd arrived this morning from Chicago on their own boat. I didn't know star*board* from star*fish,* and they'd been sailing together for years. Wasn't that reason enough to panic? And Tasha was still friends with Des's ex-wife. She wouldn't automatically hate me on sight. Would she?

Des said Tasha was a dermatologist. Super. She'd critique my skin and tell me I should be using better sunscreen. Her husband, Tom, was a forensic pathologist. I guess if the conversation got dull, I could ask about untraceable poisons to snuff out Richard.

Fontaine had dressed me in my nautical best, with white capri pants and a navy-and-white-striped top. I'd drawn the line at the jaunty red scarf he tried to tie around my neck. I didn't want to look like the millionaire's wife from *Gilligan's Island*.

Jasper packed a picnic lunch for us to share, loading the basket with classy but exotic items for which I planned to falsely claim credit. And of course Dody, eager to do her part, flicked kosher salt at my face as I walked out the door, believing this would prevent seasickness. It took a village to launch me on this voyage.

Des and I walked down the dock, reading the names of each boat. We passed the *Tipsy-Turvey*, the *Go Daddy*, and the *Blue Velvet*, as well as the *Breaking Wind* and another brazenly named *Blow Me*. We arrived at the last sailboat in the row, one with bold blue letters across the hull. *Boatox*.

Clever.

"Yay Des!" I heard a woman call excitedly. "Hey, Tom, come up. They're here."

I don't know what I expected, but Tom and Tasha were not it. He was fair-skinned with wispy blond hair and distractingly large teeth. Tasha was short and stocky, with dark, curly hair pulled into two pom-pom ponytails on the top of her head, reminding me of stuffed animal ears. She wore a functional but unflattering black swimsuit and gray sweatpants rolled down at the waist and up in the legs. I changed gears from worrying they'd find me too country mouse to worrying they'd find me pretentiously well dressed. Thank God I wasn't wearing the scarf.

We hopped on board, both of us receiving warm hugs.

"Sadie, it's great to meet you," Tasha said. "From what Des has told us, you're much too good for him. Come on; let's get you guys settled so we can get under way."

"This is a beautiful boat," I said.

"She's a beast, but watertight."

I assumed that meant we wouldn't sink. Very reassuring. I wasn't sure what else to say. "It's a lot bigger than I expected."

Tom turned to Des. "Bet she never said that to you."

Oh, yeah. This day was going to be fun after all.

We headed out into open water after stowing our gear in the cabin below. (That's nautical speak for *We threw our crap inside the boat.*) It was fascinating, watching the three of them coiling ropes and rigging sails and jibbing jibs. As the day wore on, I discovered I liked sailing. And I liked Tom and Tasha. They were funny and gracious and relaxed. Des was practically giddy, and it occurred to me this was the first time I'd seen him interact with anyone besides my family. He always seemed to enjoy himself with my people, but today he was clearly in his element. It was a bittersweet realization.

We sat near the back, with Tom and Des taking turns at the wheel. Or the helm? Is that what it's called? I didn't have the nerve to ask. The sun was gorgeous and bright as we cut across the water, and the waves were gentle enough to keep me from puking over the side. Either that or Dody's salt had done its job.

"Can I get you anything?" Tasha asked. The wind whipped my hair into my mouth every time I tried to talk. I now understood her pom-pom hairdo.

"No, I'm fine. Thanks. I brought a basket of snacks, by the way, in case anyone gets hungry."

Tasha smiled. "I already dug through it. Looks delicious."

"Sadie's cousin is a chef," Des told them.

I tapped his arm. "They were supposed to think I packed that myself."

"Sorry. I'm no good at subterfuge."

"I can vouch for that," Tom added. "In medical school, we showed up late for finals one time because of an awesome road trip the night before. I started telling the professor we got mugged on our way to class because that was the only thing that would save our asses. But Mister I-Cannot-Tell-a-Lie starts telling the *truth*! The truth!"

"It is the best policy." Des grinned.

"I was there that day too," Tasha added. "It was hilarious. Tweedledee and Tweedle-stupid here started arguing in front of the professor."

"So what happened?" I asked.

"I got marked down a full grade for lying and George Washington over here didn't."

"Sorry, man."

I listened as they recounted more stories, ones they'd obviously told time and again. It was a glimpse into Des's world that had been blank before. But I almost wished I hadn't heard any of it, because it made me fall a little harder, a little faster. When I hit the ground it was going to hurt.

"Des tells me you're an organizer? I could sure use one at my house. Even with a housekeeper and a nanny."

"You have a nanny? I didn't realize you had children."

Leave it to a man to forget a detail like that. Des hadn't mentioned them.

Tasha rerolled the hem of her sweatpants. "Three boys, ages six, seven, and nine. They're hellions. We come on the boat to escape them. You have two of your own, don't you?"

Apparently Des had filled them in more thoroughly about me. "Yes, Paige is six, and my son, Jordan, is four."

Des interrupted. "Paige is a riot, very expressive and dramatic. And her hair is in perpetual motion. Jordan is like your Sam, very analytical, always building something. He didn't like me at first."

I looked over at Des in surprise. That was interesting, listening to him describe my children. Was that note in his voice affection? Or just familiarity?

Tasha's glance went from me to him and back again. Suddenly it seemed we were all staring at Des, and there was a long, silent pause in the conversation.

"What? They're cute," he said defensively, abruptly becoming very focused on finding something in the picnic basket.

Tasha looked at me again, and for the first time that day, I felt like I was being measured.

Tom cleared his throat. "So, Des, you interested in doing The Mac this year?"

Des stopped rummaging in the basket and sat up. "You got room?"

"Maybe. Hampton's wife is pregnant, and if she doesn't pop it out before the race she's not letting him go. That's women for you, huh?" He smiled at Tasha.

"The Mac? Is that like a boat race or something? I think I've heard of it," I said.

"It's a huge boat race from Navy Pier in Chicago up to Mackinaw Island," Tom answered.

"They've been doing it for a couple years now, haven't they?" I asked.

"About a hundred."

"No, seriously?" Gosh, I love feeling that stupid.

"A hundred and two, actually," Tom explained. "And if you do the race twenty-five times, you become a member of the Island Goat Society."

Hating to feel stupid notwithstanding, I had to ask, "What on earth is the Island Goat Society?"

"Bragging rights, mostly. They call the sailors *goats* because after four or five days on the boat, we're all pretty shaggy and stinky."

Tasha added, "And because they act like animals. The postrace party on the island goes on for days. It's nothing but a bunch of rum-soaked middle-aged men behaving badly. I went once. Never again. I saw a fifty-year-old man peeing on a topiary on the front lawn of the Grand Hotel."

"What the hell is a topiary?" Tom asked.

"It's a shrub pruned to look like an animal or something."

Tom shook his head. "Anyway, Des, if Hampton can't go, should I call you?"

"I probably can't get out of work, but sure, keep me in mind."

＊　＊　＊

Dinner at the Yacht Club rounded out my nautical experience. Des sat next to me on a bench while we waited for our table. His arm was draped around my shoulders as he played absently with the back of my hair.

He kissed my temple lightly. "Would you like a drink while we wait?"

"I would. Thank you."

"What would you like?"

"Surprise me."

Tasha looked at Tom expectantly.

He let his gaze drift over to the moored boats instead.

She cleared her throat.

He pushed himself up with a sigh. "I suppose you'd like me to get you a drink?"

"Yes, dear," she teased. "If it's not too much trouble."

Tom shrugged. "Well, I'm up now. Did you want a martini?"

"I hate martinis, Tom. You know that. Vodka tonic with lemon."

"OK, one gin martini, two olives, coming up."

"Very funny," she said.

The men walked away and Tasha's eyes met mine, hers gleaming once again with that speculative look, as if she were wondering if a spot on my face was food or a precancerous mole. After a moment she smiled and moved closer. "I've never seen Des like this before, you know," she said.

I squirmed. "Like what?"

"Like all lovey-dovey, touchy-feely, 'Baby, can I get you a drink?' And I've known him for a long time."

I tried to smooth a wrinkle from the front of my pants. "So...is that good or bad?"

"It's good. It's cute. I'm just not used to it." She sat forward on the bench and rested her elbows on her knees. "Don't get me wrong. I only mean he's so...playful. He's always been wound pretty tight, but he seems different today."

"Des is wound tight?" I couldn't hide the surprise in my voice. I'd never considered him to be the least bit tense. Compared to me, he was practically anesthetized.

"Yeah, well, he's had a tough couple of years, I guess. First his dad died while we were in med school. And then of course Stephanie put him through the ringer. That rotten bitch."

I blinked. "Stephanie? Is that his ex-wife?"

Tasha nodded, the pom-poms on her head bobbing to and fro. "What a piece of work she turned out to be."

Was she teasing me? "I thought you two were friends."

She crooked an eyebrow. "Me and Stephanie? Hardly. Especially not after what she did to Des."

I was torn between wanting and not wanting to know. I couldn't resist. "And what did she do, exactly?"

Tasha's other brow rose. "Des didn't tell you? That figures. He's too nice for his own good." She slumped back against the bench with a grunt and shook her head.

I waited, morbid curiosity mingling with anticipation and dread. Certainly I wanted The Ex to be a reprehensible shrew, one who could never lure him back into her bed. But on the other hand, I hated the implication that someone had hurt his feelings.

Tasha glanced over her shoulder to see where Tom and Des were. She spotted them still standing at the bar waiting for our drinks. She turned back to me.

"Did he tell you anything about her?"

"Just that they were young and stubborn and got married during med school. He said it didn't work out because they had different priorities."

"Different priorities?" Tasha snorted. "Wow, now there's an understatement. After they'd been married for about four years she had an abortion without telling him."

I felt my jaw slap against my chest and all the air burst from my lungs. "She did? Why?"

"Because she had another year of residency and didn't want to take the time off." Tasha's face was flushed, her jaw set hard. She crossed her arms. "She never even told him she was pregnant because she knew how much he wanted kids. She was afraid he'd try to talk her out of it. And he would have. But he didn't even find out until it was all over. God, he was a mess after that. Then he started doing this stupid nomadic, locum tenens shit. Classic commitment avoidance. It's time he picked a spot to land." She looked me over again without a hint of subtlety. "But I've got a good vibe about you and this place. I haven't seen him this happy in years. You're not going to break his heart, are you?"

I might have laughed at that if I hadn't been in utter shock. Before I could respond, Tasha said, "Uh-oh, here they come."

She made a chopping motion with her hand across her throat. "Des will kill me if he finds out I told you."

This was information overload. My head was reeling. In all the time we'd spent together, Des had never hinted at anything so tumultuous. Suddenly Richard's textbook infidelities seemed almost passé.

Des smiled and handed me a drink.

My responding smile was tremulous. A neon sign of tender emotions must have flashed across my face because he took one look at me and said, "God damn it, Tasha. Can't I leave you alone for two minutes?"

She grabbed her drink from Tom's outstretched hand and took a big gulp, nearly choking. "Darn it, Tom, that's a martini!"

Driving home from the marina later that evening, I leaned back in Des's sporty little car. The wind tonight could hardly do more damage to my hair. The air was moist and warm. I could still feel the rocking of the boat as we sped along under old-fashioned street lights.

"So what did you and Tasha talk about when Tom and I were getting the drinks at the bar?" he asked, the line of his jaw stern.

"Not much. She told me you were awesome and I shouldn't break your heart." I meant to tease, but he didn't smile or say anything. I reached over and put my hand in his, adding, "I won't break yours if you don't break mine, OK?"

He didn't look my way. He only lifted my hand and pressed his lips against the back of it.

CHAPTER 23

I TUCKED MY KIDS INTO bed at Dody's, giving Paige her requisite twenty good-night kisses. Jordan wanted one kiss, and it had to be on his left cheek. I was tired after my day of working with a new organizing client but was also looking forward to seeing Des. It had been days since I'd seen him for more than a few passing minutes. He'd been working nights at the hospital.

Dody offered to keep an eye on the kids since she was staying home tonight. She'd invited Anita Parker over to watch a documentary about Area 51. So once my munchkins were in their beds, I was off, hoping to end up in Des's.

I strolled down the street toward the Pullmans' place, listening to the crickets and smelling a faraway bonfire. What a lovely little street this was. Bell Harbor was a wonderful place to visit. It was a shame my new sweetheart and I didn't live here all the time.

I got to Des's place and walked in without knocking. He was standing in the kitchen, staring out the window toward the lake. He turned, and his annoyed expression gave me a chill. Maybe I should've knocked?

"Sadie, hi." He gave me a nod but no smile, and the chill turned frostier.

I pointed at the door with my thumb. "Um, should I have knocked?"

He frowned. "What? Oh, no. Of course not. Hey, you want a drink?"

I wanted to walk out and come in again to start this moment over. "Ah, sure. What are you having?"

"Scotch." His tone was defiant, as if daring me to contradict him.

"Are you OK?"

He stared at me, but I felt unseen. Then he huffed a big breath and shook his head. "God, sorry. It's been a shit day. Come on in." He set his drink down and came around the counter to hug me. He was tense in my embrace, but he pressed his cheek against my hair, saying, "I'm glad you're here."

I leaned back and looked into his face.

Brows furrowed, lines etched, he didn't look happy at all. "Are you?" I asked.

He nodded, once, with another big sigh. "Yes. You're the best thing that's happened to me all day. Come on, get a drink."

I let him pull me into the kitchen. "No scotch for me," I said. "That stuff is vile. Do you have any wine?"

He opened a bottle and poured me a glass, filling it much higher than was socially acceptable. I tried to make small talk, which he largely ignored, not even laughing at my story about Dody trying to rollerblade with Fontaine. "So tell me about this awful day," I finally said.

"No." He shook his head and took another long pull from his drink. "I know we talked about seeing a movie or something, but would you mind if we hung out here, maybe watched some TV?"

"No, that's fine."

He tugged my hand, leading me over to the couch. We sat down, and he picked up the remote control, flipping rapidly through channels.

He was acting so peculiar I wasn't sure what to do. He obviously didn't want to talk, and he didn't seem to be paying much attention to the channels. I sat in silence, waiting for him to unload whatever was on his mind.

I sipped my wine, he gulped his scotch.

We watched one inane show then another, but I could tell his mind was light-years away.

"Des," I said when he changed the channel again. "I don't know why you're upset. You know I'll help if I can. But it's not very fair for you to keep me wondering if you're mad at me."

He looked over as if surprised I was there. "I'm not mad at you, Sadie. Not at all. It's got nothing to do with you." He got up and poured himself another drink.

His words stung. Even if I wasn't the object of his bad mood, to say it had nothing to do with me wasn't true. I was here. That made me a part of it. I stood up and set my wineglass on the table.

"I think I'll head on home."

He came back out of the kitchen. "No, no. Don't go home." He pulled me loosely into his arms. "Seriously, I want you to stay. I'll cheer up."

I squeezed him around the middle. "You don't need to pretend to cheer up for me, but seeing you all grumpy and sad brings out my maternal instincts."

"Maternal instincts?" His face suffused with color, and I realized it was quite possibly the least sexy thing I ever could've said. He stepped back and turned away, running a hand through his hair.

"Did Tasha tell you why Stephanie and I got divorced?" he asked, facing away from me.

Now it was my turn to turn colors. I hadn't admitted what Tasha and I discussed. It didn't seem necessary, and I thought if he wanted to talk about it, he'd bring it up. Maybe that's what he was doing now.

"Yes."

He pulled his drink from the kitchen counter and returned to his spot on the couch, slumping down against the cushions.

I joined him, sitting gingerly on the edge, and waited for him to talk.

When he did, his voice was flat. "We probably would've gotten divorced sooner or later anyway. If it hadn't been that, it would've been something else. Stephanie wasn't one to consider anyone else's needs." A humorless laugh, another gulp of scotch. "That being the case, I figured she wasn't cut out for motherhood, and maybe that's why she did what she did."

He looked at me, his gaze intense. His voice was nearly a whisper. "I don't love her anymore, Sadie. I haven't in a long time, so I don't know why this is bothering me so much."

I reached over and squeezed his hand. "Why, what is bothering you?"

"I found out today Stephanie just got remarried. And she's having a baby. Due anytime." He drained his glass. "You know how I found out?"

I couldn't imagine. I shook my head.

"The insurance company called to verify her address because she's still got me listed as her emergency contact. Can you fucking beat that? She's got time to find another guy, get married and have a baby, but she can't get around to updating her goddamned insurance policy."

"Are you sure? Maybe the insurance company made a mistake."

He shook his head. "I made a few calls. It's true."

I was without words. What could I possibly say to something like that? I didn't even know how I felt, so I couldn't imagine what was going through his mind. All I knew was I wanted to make him feel better. I moved closer and took his empty glass, setting it on the table. I slid into his lap and wrapped my arms around his shoulders. He leaned into me, burying his head in the curve of my neck. I could feel the tension coursing through him.

"You know the real bitch of it?" he said quietly, not lifting his head.

"What's that?" I kissed his temple.

"She told me after we got married how she never wanted kids. And I tried really hard to be OK with that, for her sake. Now it turns out she just didn't want mine."

My heart shattered into a million aching pieces. How could one person do that to another? Especially someone as wonderful as Des. I hugged him tighter, knowing words were empty and not what he needed. I kissed him instead, and then I kissed him again.

So many times before, he'd led me to his room and shown me I was beautiful. I was desirable and deserving. But tonight I did the leading, the consoling, the reassuring.

Without saying a thing, I proved to him that she was wrong, and he was worthy.

*   *   *

"What do you think of my new painting? I just finished it." Dody stepped away from the easel so Paige, Jordan, Fontaine, and I might admire her creativity. Personally, I couldn't tell a Picasso from a pistachio, but this looked like something spewed from a blender onto the canvas.

"Wow, Mom. Those are some bold strokes," Fontaine said.

"Thank you. I call it *Piranha Eating Ravioli*."

I squinted. I'll be damned. That's what it looked like.

"Mommy, there's a man coming to the door," Jordan said, pointing at the window with his plastic helicopter.

A black car I didn't recognize was parked in the driveway. An instant later came a knock on the door and the inevitable barking frenzy of Lazyboy and Fatso. They galloped around crashing into furniture until Dody shooed them away.

I opened the door to find a mousy little man with thick glasses and a turtleneck sweater, even though it was the middle of summer.

"Hello?"

"Mrs. Turner? Mrs. Sadie Turner?"

I nodded.

He handed me an envelope, then walked back to the car without another word.

I flipped it over and my stomach plummeted. The return address indicated it was from Richard's attorney's office, Kendrew, Graham & Vollstedt. Or as I tended to think of them, Fook, DeWife & Howe. My hands trembled. I wasn't expecting anything from his lawyer so this could not be anything I wanted to read. I walked to the deck to get away from the kids. Dody and Fontaine followed.

I ripped it open, too nervous to sit down, but after reading a few lines, my legs buckled and I sank to the wicker chair.

"What is it, darling?" Dody whispered.

"Richard is taking me back to court," I said in stunned surprise. "It looks like he wants the house back and joint custody of the kids."

"Can he do that?" Fontaine's voice was an octave higher than normal.

I kept reading the document, flattening it against my lap since my hands wouldn't stop shaking. "According to this, if I understand it correctly, he's claiming that I have abandoned the house and exposed the children to an undesirable environment."

"That's ridiculous," Dody hissed. Fontaine flushed and turned away.

Suddenly pieces to a puzzle that had been bumping around in my subconscious for weeks now began to take shape. A picture emerged. That's why Richard had been so friendly, offering to check on the house and to pick up the kids from Bell Harbor. The longer I stayed away from Glenville, the better chance he had of proving I'd abandoned my own house. That must be what he'd told my neighbors. That son of a bitch. That's why he was interested in my relationship with Des. Not because he was jealous. He was looking for ammunition! It must also be why he'd dropped the issue of Fontaine staying at the cottage. I should've known. A lifetime of prejudice wouldn't go away so easily. That vile, despicable piece of shit. Richard wanted to kick me out of my own house and steal my children!

"Dody, I need to make some calls. Could you keep an eye on the kids for a while?"

"Of course, darling. Take all the time you need. I'm sure we can work this out."

I ran upstairs and called my attorney, Jeannette. She was out of her office so I left a detailed message with her assistant. Then I tried Penny but got her answering machine. I considered calling Des next. He'd help me. He'd know what to do. Just the thought of him calmed my nerves. Last week, when he confided in me about his ex-wife, it seemed our relationship turned a corner.

For a month I'd been pretending what we had was casual, but it wasn't. I was in deep, very deep. Des was a part of my life now, and I didn't want to contemplate saying good-bye to him at the end of the summer.

I was sure he felt the same way. Nothing specific had been discussed, of course, but I felt it in his touch, the tenderness in his eyes when he smiled at me. Somewhere between the sake and the sex, he'd fallen in love. And so had I.

I started to dial his cell but disconnected before it could ring. He was working. This wasn't the time to tell him about Richard's scheming.

I texted him instead, asking him to come over for dinner. He responded, sending a message that work was crushing him. He'd try to stop by but couldn't make a promise.

I smiled at his note, disappointed I might not see him but happy he was not the type of man to make promises he could not keep.

Fontaine came tap, tap, tapping on my door. "How are you doing? I've been downstairs plotting. I have some money saved up. It's all yours if you want to hire a hit man."

His words snapped at me like a rubber band on the wrist.

"I'm pissed, Fontaine. I'm so pissed I can't even think straight! How dare he?"

"I know! The custody thing seems nonnegotiable," he said. "I mean, between his work schedule and womanizing, he hardly has time to see them now." Fontaine stepped over to my closet and started sorting through the clothes out of pure habit.

I punched at a pillow on my bed. I knew it was childish, but I didn't care. "Not once! Not once during the entire year of divorce proceedings did he mention joint custody. It doesn't make sense why he wants that now."

"Do you suppose he misses them?" Fontaine leaned against the closet doorframe.

I huffed in disgust. "I don't care if he misses them! He never spent any time with them when we were married, but he wants them now? What the fuck?"

Fontaine looked down at his well-trimmed nails. "I'm sorry I'm a part of this. You've never admitted it, but I know he doesn't like me being here. I'm really sorry."

I hopped off the bed and hugged my cousin tightly. "That's stupid. You don't have to be sorry for anything. You have been fantastic with the kids and they adore you. Not to mention that you're more discreet than Dody. She's the one who wanders around in her underwear. She's probably what he's referring to."

Fontaine's smile was wan. "Maybe. But I can move back to my house, if you think it'll help."

"Don't you dare. I need you more now than ever. Besides, I'll be moving back to Glenville soon. Maybe this is a sign I should go now."

"I think it's a sign you should move here."

I looked the other way. "You sound like Dody and her psychic." And Penny. And my heart.

"Can't help it. I want to pimp your organizational skills to all my clients and make a ton of money off you. Have you talked to Des?"

"No. He's at work."

"I mean about moving here."

Oh. That. I shook my head. "I'm not sure what I'd say. We haven't made any future plans together, you know?"

"But there's a chance he could stay here, right? Isn't that what the recruiter woman was all about?"

I nodded. "I've wondered about that, honestly. But Des hasn't brought it up and I didn't want to be presumptuous. Besides, there's no sense in scaring him out of town before I've decided what I'm going to do."

Fontaine rolled his eyes. "He's a smitten kitten, you big dope. Tell him how you feel before he signs up for some job in Nova Scotia."

"Let me deal with this Richard thing first, OK? Then I'll figure out what to tell Des."

*   *   *

Des texted me later, saying he could come over for dinner but had work stuff to deal with after that and had an early shift in the morning.

When he arrived, Beth was already there, helping Jasper in the kitchen. The kids were playing Monopoly with Fontaine and me, and Dody was gambling online. Des looked scruffy and exhausted. I knew the minute I saw him that tonight was not the time to dump my Richard woes on his shoulders. We could talk tomorrow. After Des rested, he'd be sympathetic and loving and give me all the support I needed.

Paige ran to him as usual. "Hi, Des. Hey, you've got style, just like Fontaine."

"What?"

She reached up toward his chin. "Whiskers."

"Oh, yeah," he said absently.

Jordan brought him a freshly colored picture.

"Thanks. Is that a…cow?" Des asked.

Jordan shook his head. "It's a rocket."

Des turned the picture, looking at it from another angle.

"It's very modern." I tried to lean in for a kiss, but he held up his hand.

"You don't want to get too close to these clothes. I didn't dare go home to change or I'd fall asleep."

A twinge of tension radiated between us. Something was off balance, and it wasn't just my anxiety over Richard's letter. I wondered if Des had gotten more news of his ex-wife. Maybe her baby had been born? I couldn't read him and didn't dare make any guesses. I'd been so off-kilter all afternoon I couldn't be sure of anything, except I was glad he was there.

"Come and eat!" Jasper called from the dining room.

Like a herd of noisy buffalo, we gathered around the table. Dody sat at one end, sassy in a red leather vest that Uncle Walter had bought at a Liza Minnelli charity auction. Paige and Jordan flanked Des, leaving me to sit across from him. Fontaine and Beth sat on either side of Jasper at the other end.

"I want to move up my birthday party," Dody announced once everyone had loaded their plates and started eating.

"Why? These carrots have ginger butter, by the way," Jasper said, passing the bowl to his left.

"I'd like Harry to be there, and he'll be out of town for my actual birthday."

"I thought you weren't that interested in Harry since you found out he's afraid of heights," Fontaine said, popping a piece of broccoli in his mouth.

Dody shook her head, her jewel-encrusted headband catching the light. "I can't hold that against him. I was surprised is all. I'd made arrangements for us to go sky diving and then he wouldn't do it."

"Remind me to thank him for that! Honestly, Mom. Can't you slow down?" Jasper said.

"Why should I? I don't have much time left."

Des dropped his fork with a loud clatter.

All eyes went to him, and his cheeks flushed. "Sorry," he mumbled.

Jordan picked it up and handed it back.

"I mean, who knows how much time any of us have left, right?" Dody said. "In fact, just the other day Anita Parker spilled hot coffee in her car and nearly drove to her death right off the parkway bridge."

"That's morbid, Mom."

"It's just practical. People die every day, so none of us should waste one little minute. I, for one, am going to kick up my heels while I've got some kick left." She stuffed a forkful of noodles into her mouth. "I was thinking the second weekend of August for the party."

"Mom, that's in ten days," Fontaine sputtered. "I can't pull everything together in ten days, even if we could get the invitations out tomorrow. That doesn't give people enough time."

"If they can't come, then they can't come. But everyone loves my birthday parties, so I'm sure they'll try. We don't have to do anything too fancy. You and Sadie buy a few supplies and Jasper can make a cake. What else is there to do?"

"We need a theme! There's decorations, music, seating. We can't do something ordinary. People have expectations when they come to one of my parties." Fontaine was not going for it, but Dody was insistent.

"It's my party and if you don't have the time, then I can plan it myself." She took a bite of salad.

"Nobody wants you to plan your own party, Dody," I said. "It's short notice is all."

"Well, I should get to have it when I want it. Shouldn't I, Des?"

Des was bringing his fork to his mouth in rapid bites. Now he glared up at Dody as if her question insulted him.

"It doesn't matter what I think, Dody. This is your decision." He went back to shoveling in the food. He was acting so odd. He must be really exhausted.

Dody gazed at him for a second, an odd expression passing over her face but disappearing as soon as it came, making me wonder if I'd seen it at all. She turned to Jasper. "You can take care of the food, can't you?"

"Um, I guess. I'll have to take the night off work."

"I'll help too with whatever anybody needs," Beth said.

Dody smiled and patted Beth's hand. "Thank you, dear. Now, see? It's all settled."

"Nothing is settled!" Fontaine barked, pushing his plate away.

Jasper chuckled. "Don't get your panties in a bunch, Tim."

Fontaine huffed and crossed his arms. "Puh-leeze don't call me that. You know I hate that name."

"Why is that, Fontaine?" Beth asked innocently. "Tim is such a nice name."

Jasper chuckled again.

"It's not funny!" Fontaine scowled like an angry kitten.

"It's a little funny," Jasper contradicted, nodding.

It was a little funny. We all agreed.

Fontaine puffed out his bottom lip in a pout, and Jasper kept talking, explaining to Beth. "You see, when Fontaine was little, he was, like, freaky petite little. So when he was about ten..."

Fontaine jabbed him with an elbow. "I was eight!"

Jasper laughed. "OK, when he was eight, he sprained his ankle, and he had to go to school using this old crutch Mom had saved, right? This tiny little wooden crutch." Jasper gestured with his hands, demonstrating the tininess and doubling over with laughter.

I bit back my own smile.

"So the kids at school started calling him Tiny Tim. Everywhere he went, they were all, like, 'God bless us, every one. It's Tiny Tim. Bah, humbug.' And it stuck. For years they called him that. Tiny Tim!"

Murmurs of laughter circled the table. Even Fontaine's lips twitched, and he took over the story from there. "But when I switched to a new school in seventh grade, I told everybody my name was Fontaine."

"Thinking they would tease you less for that?" Des's doubt was genuine.

Fontaine had the audacity to look smug at his own cleverness. "I told my classmates I was working undercover with the FBI, trying to bust up gangs and organized cheating and stuff. Remember, those were the *21 Jump Street* days." Fontaine finally smiled.

"That's not the best part, though," Jasper interrupted, thumping his hand down on the table. "Tell them how you sprained your ankle in the first place. Really, this is the best part." He could barely contain his amusement.

Fontaine's smile broadened. "I fell down the stairs trying to walk in Mom's stilettos."

Dody smiled at him lovingly as we erupted with laughter. "I should have known right then."

*   *   *

As Beth and I cleared the dinner dishes, Dody and Des went out on the deck. Watching them through the window, I could see they were having more than a frivolous exchange. Des's hands were clenched as he leaned toward Dody. She looked all feisty too, with her hands on her hips and her jaw firm. Uncle Walter would say she had her Irish up. Whatever Des was selling, she wasn't buying.

"What are they talking about?" Beth asked, coming up behind me.

"I don't know. He's been strange all night. I think I'll find out what's going on." I went on the deck to find Des rubbing his temples with both hands.

"You can't put me in the middle of this, Dody. It's not fair to anybody."

Their conversation stopped abruptly when I appeared. They looked guilty, like my kids when I find them hiding in the closet with a bag of cookies.

"Put you in the middle of what?" I asked.

Des's face went blank. "I didn't like how she put me on the spot about her birthday party."

"Seriously?" That bothered him more than when she asked if he was circumcised? Or how old he was when he lost his virginity? This birthday party thing seemed pretty minor compared to that.

"Yeah, well, it's not my call to make. Listen, I've got an early shift in the morning and I'm beat. I'm going to head on home, OK?"

"I'll let you two say good night." Dody put her hand on his arm. "I'm sorry we disagree on this, Des."

"Yeah. Good night, Dody."

She went inside. The uneasiness stewing in me all evening began to bubble faster. This was not about her birthday party. And it wasn't about being tired. After last week, I thought we were past keeping secrets. Plus I was desperate to talk to him about Richard, but that would definitely have to wait.

"I'm sorry if she's bugging you."

"Look, I'm just…tired, OK? I've got lots of work stuff going on and I can't make decisions for her."

"Decisions for her?"

He hugged me fast and stepped away. "Never mind. I'll try to call you tomorrow, OK?" He practically sprinted through the house and out the front door, waving silently to everyone in the family room.

I went inside feeling queasy and needing answers. I found Dody standing near the dining-room table, staring at nothing.

"Dody, what the hell was that about? And don't try to pretend it's about your birthday. Something else is going on."

I had never seen Dody cry. And she was determined I wouldn't see it now. She blinked back tears and forced a smile.

My heart froze in place.

"Beth, dear, could you take the little ones upstairs and help them get into jammies? I need to talk to my big kids for a few minutes."

Everyone stopped talking. The air crackled with tension, warning each of us this was not one of Dody's whimsical announcements about taking up archery or entering the Miss Gorgeous Geriatric Pageant.

Beth nodded, scooting my kids from the room. The rest of us sat back down at the dinner table.

Dody stared at her hands for a minute before speaking. When she looked up, her eyes were rimmed with unshed moisture.

"Thank you, children, for such a lovely dinner. I'm sorry changing my birthday party has caused such a ruckus. That's what I was trying to avoid. But it seems I need to tell you all something." She breathed in. She breathed out. Seconds passed that felt like an eternity. "It seems I have a little bit of cancer and I want to have my party before I begin any treatment."

The air in the room turned toxic and heavy. I clutched at Fontaine's hand. Did she say what I think she said?

"What does that mean? A little bit of cancer?"

"It's some kind of duck filter something or other. I can't remember the name exactly. Oh, wait. I wrote it down in case I forgot. The paper is in my purse."

Forgot? She forgot? Who the hell forgets what kind of cancer they have? The room spun and shrunk as we waited for her to rummage through her bag. She pulled out a powder compact, a lipstick, and a cowbell, setting them on the table before producing a tattered slip of paper.

"Here we go. It says here I have infiltrating ductal carcinoma." She reached under her arm and pressed. "It's around here someplace. But the doctor tells me, in the scheme of things, this isn't one of the really bad cancers because they can treat it."

"All cancer is bad, Mom," Jasper gasped.

"Well, yes, of course, but it isn't the worst kind. With surgery and some chemo, I should be as good as new." Her lips trembled, betraying her optimistic words.

I didn't know what to say. None of us did. I thought Richard trying to steal my house and my kids was awful news. This was as bad.

Dody filled the painful silence with her usual sunny optimism. "So now you know. But don't you dare start treating me like some invalid, because I feel fine. And I'm going to stay fine. It's simply amazing what they can cure nowadays, so I don't want to make a big deal out of this. And I don't want to tell anyone outside of this room until after the party. Do you hear me?" She shook a finger at each one of us. "No one else knows. Except for Des, of course. He took me in for my biopsy. Sadie, I'm so grateful to him. Be sure to tell him that."

Tinier and tinier the room contracted, the walls collapsing toward me. He took her for her biopsy? How long had he known?

"When was your biopsy, Dody?" I asked.

"Three weeks ago. That must be when I lost my earring in Des's car. But I only got the results yesterday." She dropped the slip of paper back into her purse and opened the compact. She began to powder her nose, casually, as if she hadn't made the most dramatic announcement any of us had ever heard.

"Three weeks? Mom, why didn't you tell us?" Fontaine exclaimed. Jasper stared at her as if she were already a ghost.

"Because I knew you'd worry, and there was no point. Until we had the results there was nothing to talk about. But Des was so helpful. You really do get the movie star treatment when you bring your own doctor for a biopsy, let me tell you. I felt like Shirley MacLaine."

This was just sinking in. He took her for the biopsy? Des had known about this for three weeks and never said a word to me? How could he have kept this a secret?

Fontaine began to inundate Dody with questions while we all tried to absorb this unfathomable news. At last she held up both hands.

"Please, darlings, I have another appointment with my doctor the day after tomorrow. I'll know more then. And if you want to come with me, be my guest."

Fontaine's chair scraped against the floor. He stood up and walked over to the window, biting on his thumbnail.

"This isn't a tragedy, all of you. Do you hear me? This isn't the end of my life, and it certainly isn't the end of yours. But if you don't throw me the biggest bash this side of Lake Michigan, I might die just to come back and haunt you."

"This isn't a joke, Mom," Jasper whispered.

She patted his hand. "I know it isn't, dear. But if we stop laughing then the terrorists have won. So stop moping and start planning my party."

Time hung suspended while we exchanged disbelieving looks. Then Fontaine turned around, cleared his throat, and folded his hands behind his back. With the gravity of a judge he said, "I assume you'll want to invite all the usual suspects?"

Dody smiled. "Of course."

"And you'll want a big, obnoxious cake and lots of booze?"

"Definitely."

"I can arrange that."

Powered by the beauty of pure, raw denial, we started discussing party plans instead of treatment options. That would come soon enough. But right now Dody wanted to talk about balloon bouquets, mariachi bands, and if the silk dress Walter had bought her in Thailand might be too dressy for this party.

All the while we faked our acceptance, I was thinking of Des and how he'd kept this a secret from me for three solid weeks. That was unforgivable.

I tucked in Paige and Jordan that night, giving them kiss after kiss until they told me to stop. Dody's announcement had changed everything, suddenly bringing my life into focus. Family counted most. Being surrounded by the people you loved is what made life…well, life. None of the rest of it mattered. Suddenly I didn't care if Richard took that stupid house in Glenville. It was full of crap I didn't need and ugly memories that only held me back. But he wasn't going to steal away one moment of my time with my children. For that, I would fight him with everything I had.

Once the kids fell asleep, I checked with Fontaine to make sure he'd be around if they needed anything and then I walked down the street to Des's house. I was so angry with him for not telling me about Dody I was numb with it. I felt gullible and betrayed. Hadn't he said to Tom and Tasha he was no good at subterfuge? Sure seemed like he was! If he was so good at keeping secrets, what else might he keeping from me? Tears burned like acid in my eyes. This was a terrible day.

The lights were on at Des's so I knew he was still awake. He'd said he was tired and going to sleep. Guess that was a lie too.

I knocked rapidly on his door. When he opened it, I poked him in the chest. Hard.

"You knew? You knew for three weeks she had cancer and you didn't tell me?"

He stepped back, but I followed, jabbing at his chest again, harder this time. "How could you not tell me?"

He held up his hands in defense. "Sadie, we weren't sure it was cancer until yesterday. And ethically, it wasn't my information to share."

"Ethically? That's a load of shit, Des. You think it was more ethical to keep her family in the dark?" I tried to jab him again.

"Stop that!" He deflected my hand. "I didn't have any choice. I wanted to tell you, but she made me promise."

"Of course you had a choice! You could have told her no. Keeping something a secret is the same as lying."

Even I didn't believe that, but I was eager for a fight.

His jaw set stubbornly. "God damn it, Sadie. That's the second time you've accused me of being a liar. I respected Dody's wishes, and if you have a problem with that then take it up with her."

"But you're a doctor. She would have listened to you. Now we've wasted three weeks when we could have been planning some kind of treatment."

"Yes, I'm a doctor. But I'm not *her* doctor." He turned around and walked to the couch. He sat down heavily. "Look, I tried to help her out by taking her for the biopsy when she asked me to, and the oncologist she's seeing is one of the best. But there's not much more I can do for her. I'm caught in the middle of a situation I shouldn't be any part of. I didn't sign up for this."

My anger nearly gave way to tears. "None of us signed up for this. And I have a completely legitimate reason for being upset."

He sighed. "Yes, you do. Just not at me. At least not about that."

A puffer fish inflated in my gut. "What does that mean?"

He rubbed his forehead. "Sit down here a minute."

"I don't want to sit down."

He wouldn't look at me. What could he possibly say to make this day worse?

He ran a hand through his hair.

Something in his expression filled me with the worst sort of dread.

"Sadie, I know the timing of this sucks. But there's something I have to tell you."

I knew I didn't want to hear it. No matter what it was, I wasn't going to like it.

"I've had a job offer. A really phenomenal job offer. In Seattle. They want me to start as soon as possible."

Seattle. As in Washington? God, that was pretty fucking far away from Bell Harbor.

"For how long?" I heard myself whisper.

His eyes were dark and heavy when he looked my way. "Permanently."

The earth tilted on its axis and nearly knocked me to the ground. Permanent was a very long time. Permanent was longer than my marriage lasted.

"So you've told them yes?" The voice was mine, but the words were coming from nowhere. My brain had shut down. Breathing took all my concentration.

"It's a great job, Sadie. I'd be a fool to pass it up."

I nodded, my throat closing shut. I should have known this was how things would go. I was the fool to think this would end any other way. I wanted to be furious with him for lying, for leading me on. Only he hadn't.

And even if he had, none of it mattered now. My life would soon be consumed by a custody battle and helping out with Dody. I wouldn't have time for this silly, pointless fling anyway.

Des looked away. "I wish I could be here for you right now, Sadie. I really do. It's just not going to work."

I don't remember walking home. I'm not sure if I said anything else before stumbling out his door. All I know is I ended up back at Dody's, sobbing into my pillow. My heart galloping as if I'd run the race of my life but lost inches from the finish line.

Des was leaving, Dody was dying, and Richard was trying to take my kids. Everything inside me felt loose and unattached and covered in spikes.

Hours later, after my first round of tears had been shed, I climbed into bed with Paige. I breathed in the sweet, soft smell of her skin and prayed with all my heart that she would never, ever fall in love.

CHAPTER 24

MY ATTORNEY, JEANETTE, WAS THE sort of elegant, overaccomplished woman I normally disliked on principle alone. She was brilliant, fearless, and dressed with a panache even Fontaine could not duplicate. Her skin reminded me of a mocha latte, and her dark, soulful eyes saw through bullshit like laser vision.

In a single minute she could switch from demure and persuasive to abrasive and pushy, depending on the situation. She also dropped the f-bomb about as often as she blinked. She intimidated the hell out of me, but she was on my side, and so I loved her almost as much as I hated Richard.

She pulled a few papers from her sleek leather bag, setting them down on the table between us. We had agreed to meet at a coffee shop in Bell Harbor because I couldn't bear the drive to Glenville. Anything that brought me closer to Richard and farther from Dody was too painful.

"I talked to his attorney," Jeanette said. "I think he's trying to scare you. He pitched high so he'd have some bargaining power."

I shifted in my chair. "So what is it he really wants?"

"According to my inside source, he wants the house."

"That's it? He's threatening to take my kids because he wants the house?"

"You know Richard. It's all about the money and the prestige. His apartment is a fucking dump and he's paying the mortgage on a house you're not using. I'd give pretty good odds his lawyer convinced him to play the custody card to freak you out and make you malleable."

"It's working."

Jeanette frowned and adjusted her designer glasses. "Don't let him bulldoze you, Sadie. We can fight him on this."

I had thought about this a lot over the past few days. Incessantly, in fact, between crying jags over Dody's cancer and Des's abrupt departure. He hadn't even said good-bye. I'd gone to the Pullmans' house last night hoping to talk but he was already gone. There were cardboard moving boxes inside, from what I could see by peeking in the windows, but there was no sign of him.

Moving home to Glenville would have been the logical thing to do. I could pick up right where I left off, strolling around a big empty house haunted by the ghost of failure, surrounded by friends who were anything but. Or I could stay here and be useful. Dody needed me now, and frankly, I sort of needed her too.

"I don't care about the house. He can have it as long as I keep full custody."

Jeanette scribbled a few notes in the margin of the paper. "The housing market in Glenville is tanked right now. You could probably find a smaller, decent place to live, but what do you plan to use for money? I don't do pro bono."

"Actually, I've decided to move here. I can live with my aunt until I've figured something else out. I've started working, you know, and there are lots of rich, messy people in this town. I'm not making much right now, but I've got prospects."

Jeanette was disappointed at my capitulation. Me fighting with Richard was money in her pocket, plus she enjoyed putting the screws to him as much as I did. I think he reminded her of her own ex-husband.

"You need to think about this, Sadie."

"Trust me. I have. I'm certain moving here is the right decision. My aunt is thrilled, and so is Fontaine. And my kids think it's like moving to Disney World. You don't think it gives Richard another reason to demand custody, do you? Because if that's the case, I'll have to figure something else out."

"I doubt that will be an issue. Unless he thinks of something else he'd like to screw you out of. You don't have an awesome time-share or anything, do you?"

"I already gave him the time-share."

"Oh, that's right. You need a better lawyer," she teased. Her eyes darted around the kitschy coffee shop. "OK, if you're sure. I'll run the idea past Richard's guy and call you tomorrow. But we can't just *give* him the house. We should make him buy you out. I promise you, the custody thing won't fly. This business he's trying to stir up about your cousin is complete bullshit. Richard hasn't figured out that by taking your house he's basically forcing you to keep your kids in the living environment he says concerns him. I'll be sure to point that out when the time is right. Don't worry about this, Sadie. I've got your back."

That was the first good news I'd had in days.

· · ·

I threw myself into planning Dody's party with a vengeful desperation, glad for a project to occupy my mind. Fontaine enlisted Kyle's help, and it wasn't long before we had matching T-shirts declaring us Team Dody. Fontaine insisted every decoration be white, pink, or glittery. It was like coordinating a princess party for Paige. We bought miles of tulle to wrap around the deck, along with twinkly lights and dozens of tiny white candles.

For music, we reluctantly hired some friends of Jasper's. Their garage band had a local cult following, thanks to modest radio play of their one and only original song, "Salami Tsunami." I had my doubts about their talent, but they were available, they were energetic, and they played for beer.

Dody remained upbeat about her prognosis, encouraged by Madame Margaret's assurance that this was not the end for her this time around.

"She told me she saw feathers floating on a pond and two swans swimming side by side in a figure eight. That means I'll live to see eighty-eight."

"Or the feathers were from an angel's wings and you're a goner," Fontaine quipped.

Dody smiled warmly and caressed his cheek. "Thank you, dear. It means the world to me that you're still making jokes. I can't get Jasper to crack a smile no matter what I say."

"He's frustrated, Dody. He has a lot on his mind," I said.

I had a lot on my mind too, but was trying not to show it. No one needed to hear me crying about my romantic woes right now. They didn't need to know how devastated I was Des hadn't called to offer any closure whatsoever.

Or hope.

And I was so preoccupied with the reality of Dody being sick and the custody and house stuff with Richard I didn't have time to miss Des. Except in the evenings. And first thing in the morning. And sunny afternoons. And when I saw a sailboat or a convertible. Or a man.

I'd called Penny the day after he told me he was leaving. I wanted to cry on her shoulder, but she had a serious case of placenta head and was useless to me right now. Everything revolved around the baby. The baby was the size of a corn kernel, the baby could hear classical music through the uterus, the baby might develop allergies if Penny ate the wrong things. She'd even taken to watching foreign language films, thinking it might make the baby bilingual.

When she took a breath from baby talk to ask how things were in Bell Harbor, I desperately wanted to tell her about Dody's cancer but realized I was sworn to secrecy. Suddenly I found myself in the same situation as Des. Of course Penny should know, and so should my mother. But didn't I owe it to Dody to let her tell people on her own terms? Isn't that what I would've demanded for myself?

I wanted to be mad at Des because it was easier, but the truth was, I mostly felt sorry he'd gotten dragged into my messes in the first place. Yes, it was crappy of him to leave without saying good-bye, but then again, it wouldn't have made any difference in the outcome. And at least with no long, tragic good-bye, I didn't find myself clinging to his leg and begging him to stay. That would have been awkward. Predictable, but awkward.

*　*　*

Dody and the kids were playing a giggly game of Go Fish on the sunporch when I got home the next day after a meeting with Kyle. When I told him I'd decided to stay in Bell Harbor, he was nearly as happy as Fontaine. At least I had two men who loved me. Then I told him everything that happened with Des. I had to unload to someone who wasn't already overwrought about Dody. Kyle promised to keep my secret and to keep me so busy with messy, disorganized people I wouldn't have time to think about anything else. Fine by me.

"Who's winning?" I asked, plopping down on the chair.

"Me! I got the *K* and another *K*," said Jordan.

"Those are kings, baby," I told him.

"It doesn't matter which cards you get, Jordan. It matters how many pairs you get," Paige explained.

"But the *K*s are bigger than the *Q*s," Jordan argued.

"Darlings, go in the kitchen and color me some pictures while I talk with your mommy. I'd like one with butterflies and armadillos. Can you draw me that?"

They left the room, already in debate over what an armadillo looked like.

"How was your lunch with Kyle?"

I plucked at the fabric on the sofa cushion. "Fine. He's glad I'm staying."

She crossed her legs, unzipping the waistband of her poodle skirt. "Walter got me this, you know. Olivia Newton-John wore it in *Grease*. Goodness, she had a tiny middle. And that John Travolta? What a sexpot he was. Speaking of sexpots, where has Des been?"

I saw that one coming from a mile away and was ready with an answer.

"He's busy with some work things. He sends his best and hopes you're feeling well."

Dody's lips puckered in a scowl. "Sadie Turner, that's a big fat lie. I can tell by the way your aura is changing color. Where is he really?"

I feigned nonchalance. "Dody, my aura deceives you. He's busy with work, and that's the honest truth." Technically it was the truth. It just wasn't the entire truth.

She crossed her arms over her ample and righteous bosom. "Did you two have a fight because of me? Is he still mad I didn't tell you all sooner that I have cancer?"

Cancer was the new c-word as far as I was concerned. I hated the way it rolled over her tongue, as if she said nothing more provocative than "I have something in my tooth."

"He's not mad. And no, we didn't have a fight. Don't be silly, Dody."

"Sadie Turner, I did not fall off the tulip truck yesterday, you know."

"Turnip, not tulip," I corrected automatically.

"Oh, there you go again," she snapped. "Not seeing the forest for the breeze and missing the whole grand tamale."

"What?" She could make my head hurt faster than a shot of Jack Daniels.

"He should be annoyed with me. Just because I wanted to get my ball bearings before letting you all know, I was wrong to put him in that awkward position. I realize that now, but I suppose he got angry with you instead?"

"No, I got angry at him!" I snapped. *Darn it. Darn it.* Apparently I had the right to remain silent, but not the ability.

Dody almost smiled. She was a bloodhound on the trail. "Why are you mad at him?"

"I was upset he didn't tell me. It was practically the same as lying. But I'm over it." I flung myself back against the cushion.

"Oh, pish-posh, Sadie. A little white lie to protect me. You can't be mad at him for that."

"I'm not mad." The tears I'd held at bay for days burst forth and poured over my cheeks. "He's moving to Seattle."

Dody scooted closer, hugging me, patting my head like I was a toddler. And like a toddler, I pressed my face against her softness and let the tears flow.

"Seattle?" she said at last. "Well, that's simply ridiculous. All they have there is coffee and rain. Doesn't he realize how you feel about him?" She pulled the ever-present tissue from her cleavage and tried to wipe my nose.

I sat up. "It wouldn't make any difference, Dody. We both knew at the start this was short-term. He didn't trick me. And even if he'd stayed and I'd stayed, I bet we would've broken up eventually anyway."

"Oh, that's a fine attitude. You sound like your mother."

"That's mean to say. Don't you think I feel shitty enough already?"

"I'm sorry, but it's true. No one deserves to get cheated on, Sadie, and I think you were right to leave Richard. He is not a good person. But the truth is your mother started pushing your father away long before he did anything wrong. She's my sister, remember, and I could see their marriage was in trouble, but all she could focus on were his mistakes, never her own. Then he finally left, and she's been miserable ever since. Is that what you want? To mope around for the next thirty years?"

"What do you want me to do, Dody? He's moving to Seattle!"

"He hasn't moved yet, has he? You march your tushy down there right now and tell him how you feel."

"He already left. I went down there a couple days ago and the house is all closed up. And when I tried his cell phone, the message said it was out of service."

"One little phone call? That's the best you can do? Call him again."

♯   ♯   ♯

Dody's words bounced round and round in my head. Maybe I should call him again. Since I wasn't able to leave a message last time, it was possible he never knew I called.

He could've called me, though, if he wanted to talk. He was the one leaving, after all.

Still, I didn't want to end up like my mother, bitter and vengeful. I called his number and this time got his machine.

"Des, hey. It's Sadie. Listen, I was hoping we could talk. Give me a call, OK?"

I hung up, satisfied. At least I had tried. And when he called back? Well, I'd figure out what to say when that happened.

But it never did.

Three more days dragged by with not a word from him. It hurt. A lot. I deserved at least one more conversation, but I guess when he was done, he was done.

Missing him made me lethargic and empty. Once more love had tied little cement shoes to my heart and tossed me in the river of denial. The bluebird of happiness had crapped on my shoulder.

I tried to put on a good show for the sake of my kids and for Dody, but they were on to me.

The only bright spot that week came when Jeanette called.

"We have a deal," she said. "Give Richard the house and he'll drop the custody request."

An ounce of the burden weighing me down was lifted.

Jeanette continued, "And here's some good news: Richard has to pay you for your half. Like I said before, the market has tanked, but he has to give you fifty percent of its current value. That's not a huge amount, but it should be enough to get you settled in Bell Harbor."

Another tiny victory.

"That is good news, Jeannette. Thank you."

"You're welcome. I'm not sure how fast this will all play out. Richard is antsy to get in the door, but legally he can't enter the premises until you sign off on it, so his lawyer is drawing up the papers ASAP. As soon as I've gotten a copy and reviewed it, I'll give you a call. Don't let him in the house until I've said so."

So that was it then. It was all decided. Once again the flick of a pen would alter my entire future.

"That's fine. Whatever."

"I have to say, Sadie, you're taking this really well."

I was, kind of, wasn't I? Maybe I was finally learning which battles were worth fighting. Or maybe I just didn't have the energy to fight for anything at all.

CHAPTER 25

THE DAY OF DODY'S PARTY dawned clear and bright with not a cloud in the sky. It was a picture-perfect summer day in western Michigan. The decorations were up, along with a big white canopy and a makeshift dance floor made from painted plywood. Everything looked sparkly and elegant, as it should.

Jasper, putting the finishing touches on a tray of delectable goodies, said, "Sadie, could you please take the dogs over to Mrs. Schmidt's house? She said we could keep them there until after the party so they don't eat all our food. Fatso! Get down from there!"

The dog gave Jasper a doleful look and thumped down from the counter.

"Sure." I was glad for something to do. The fact that Mrs. Schmidt's house was next to the Pullmans' didn't bother me either. In fact, it was the perfect excuse to peek in the windows again to see if Des's boxes were gone. I still couldn't believe he hadn't returned my call. It wasn't like him to be so ruthless. But then again, maybe I hadn't known him as well as I thought.

Once outside with Lazyboy and Fatso, I recalled why I hated walking them. They were eighty-pound moving obstacles, jumping around in front of me as if I were a giant squirrel. Lazyboy dragged his head along my leg, leaving a trail of drool.

I could not get to Mrs. Schmidt's door fast enough. She opened it, wearing a peach housecoat and curlers in her hair.

"Oh, hello, Sadie. Do come in. How is Dody feeling?" For a moment I thought she'd found out about the cancer, but quickly realized she was just being cordial. The dogs bounded in, making themselves right at home. I heard a cat hiss in the other room.

"Dody is wonderful. Thanks for asking. She's very excited about the party, of course. Thank you so much for keeping the dogs."

"Oh, it's no bother. I'm like Dr. Doolittle these days," she responded. "With your doggies, and Phantom from next door."

As if on cue, Bitchy the cat jumped up on the counter and hissed at me. God! I hated that cat.

"Phantom? Is that her name? Why is she here?" I realized then I'd never asked Des anything about her. Maybe that's why he broke up with me.

Mrs. Schmidt nodded. "Yes, Dr. McKnight asked me to keep her while he's on his boat race."

Wait.

What?

"His boat race?" My voice came out in a strangled mumble.

"Yes. Didn't he mention it? I thought you two were quite an item." She wiggled her eyebrows, making the curlers twitch.

I shifted from one foot to the other. "Um, we're not. But what boat race are you talking about?"

"That big one from Chicago up to Mackinaw Island. He wasn't very excited about it, from what I could tell. But he said his friend called and insisted. Then he's going to visit his mother. What a dear boy."

The race? He went on the race? Could that be why he hadn't tried to call? Not that it changed anything, but still, it was an interesting morsel of information. At the very least, it could mean he hadn't officially moved yet. Could there still be a chance?

I tried to scratch Bitchy/Phantom behind the ears as if we were the best of pals. She bit me. "When will he get back?" I asked casually.

Mrs. Schmidt patted her heart. "Not an item, you say? But you'd like to be, right? Ahh…" She sighed and cast a dreamy gaze toward the ceiling. "Can't say I blame you. If I was thirty years younger and twenty pounds lighter, I'd be after him myself. Lucky for you I'm old and fat." Her eyes came back to mine. "I'm not sure when he'll be back. Sometime next week, I think."

"Well, thanks Mrs. Schmidt, for taking the dogs. I should get back home now. There's still a lot to do before the party."

"Of course. See you tonight."

I scurried back home as fast as I could, bursting in through the door.

Fontaine was slicing lemons at the island.

"He's on a boat!" I exclaimed.

"Who's on a boat?"

"Des is on a boat! Mrs. Schmidt just told me he's on the Chi-Mack race in the middle of fucking Lake Michigan! Do you think that's why he hasn't called?"

By now the entire family knew all the gory details of Des's abrupt departure. I hadn't been able to keep it a secret after all.

Fontaine raised his dark brows. "Maybe."

"Maybe?" My voice was unflatteringly shrill.

"I don't know, baby girl."

I clenched my fists, looking at Fontaine imploringly.

Come on! Couldn't he do better than that? I needed reassurance! I needed hope. If Des hadn't gotten my message, maybe there was time to tell him how I felt. Maybe it would make a difference in him moving away. Maybe it would make *all* the difference.

That was a lot of maybes.

And what if he never made it back? What if his boat capsized and they all drowned? I'd end up like the girl from that old seventies song in love with the sailor who told her she was a fine girl and what a good wife she would be. What the hell was the name of that song? Brittney? Bethany? Betty?

"Brandy!" I shouted, clenching my fists.

"What?" Fontaine's eyes went big.

"What if he drowns? I'll end up just like Brandy."

"The singer?"

"No, stupid, the tavern girl. From the song."

Fontaine set down the paring knife, slowly easing toward me with hands outstretched, as if I had my finger on the trigger of a loaded gun.

"Love bug, you have rounded the bend."

I giggled hysterically. He was right. The stress was making me nuts. What difference did it make if Des was on a boat, or the space shuttle or a hot air balloon? He was still moving to Seattle. Even if he did return my call, what could I possibly say to make him change his mind? Absolutely nothing. My momentary hope sank faster than the *Titanic*. Either way, I'd end up just like Brandy, standing alone on a windswept shore, waiting for a man who was out of my reach. Stupid sailors.

*   *   *

The birthday extravaganza was about to begin. Fontaine flitted around like a hummingbird on crack, spastically fluffing tulle bows and rearranging the floral arrangements. He had insisted Dody stay in the house all afternoon so she could have the Big Reveal moment. He'd even instructed all the guests to wear white so everyone would match our sparkly elegant palette.

Fontaine, Jasper, Beth, Paige, Jordan, and I were gathered on the deck when Kyle led Dody out from the house.

She gasped with pleasure. "Oh, look, it's delightful! Simply delightful. Oh, you children, you've done too much. It's so lovely. See the flowers and the bows and the lights. Oh, Jasper, the food looks divine. Oh, it's perfection." She hugged and kissed each one of us at least twice. My kids quickly tired of the attention not being on them and slipped away to run circles on the dance floor.

"That's a lovely dress, Dody," Beth told her.

Dody curtsied. "Thank you, darling. It's from the Marie Osmond Collection. I thought my silk might be a little too warm. And don't you look lovely too! Oh, my!" She gasped again, suddenly realizing we were all dressed in white. "You all look like angels. I'm not dead already, am I? Is this heaven?"

Fontaine shook his head. "That's nice, Mom! I go to all this trouble and all you can say is, 'I see dead people'?"

She giggled. "I'm sorry, darling. I'm teasing. It looks beautiful, really. Utterly fabulous."

"Thank you. Now let's get you a little wine spritzer, shall we?" Fontaine stepped over to the corner of the deck, where we'd set up an extensive bar.

Kyle came and stood next to me and leaned against the tulle-covered railing.

"It does look great, doesn't it?" He slung his arm around my shoulders. "Maybe we should add party planning extraordinaire to our list of services."

"We should. Thanks for all your help." I felt an overwhelming surge of goodwill toward Kyle. He'd been so kind and generous, stepping up to help us through this time of need. He'd become a true friend to me. I couldn't resist hugging him. "You're the best. I adore you."

"This must be Dezzzzzzzz."

Oh. God. You have got to be kidding me.

Richard's sarcastic drawl singed my eardrums like burning cinders. My head snapped around, and there he stood! I gripped Kyle so tightly he gave a little squeak.

"What are you doing here, Richard?"

Everyone turned in unison to stare. A silicone-enhanced *Jersey Shore* reject hung on his arm. She might have been twenty in real time but appeared older in skanky ho years. I'd had pimples that covered more surface area than the itty-bitty dress she was (almost) wearing.

Richard held up an envelope. "I have papers for you to sign, Sadie. House papers. Thought we should make this legal before your jackal of a lawyer tried to complicate things." He grinned at everyone around the deck and chuckled. "You guys having a party? Why wasn't I invited?"

Who had flipped over that big rock and let Richard crawl out? And how dare he? How dare he show up unannounced and start waving papers in my face? It was too much! And he brought a date? What kind of man brought a date to the figurative screwing of his ex-wife? I was speechless on the outside, but only because the screaming inside my head would burn my lips if those choice words came out.

"Richard, this really isn't the time," Dody said. "Why don't you come back tomorrow?"

Everyone's eyes darted between Richard and me.

Richard's smiled broadened, as if this were some chit-chatty visit with old friends. "Sorry. No can do, Doodoo. We are on our way out of town, but I want these papers signed before I leave since I can't step a foot over the threshold until Miss Ice Princess signs it over. So what do you say, Sadie? Sign the papers and I'll be on my way."

I could hardly breathe. "Richard, I'm not signing anything tonight. I'll sign it tomorrow, after I've had a chance to talk to my lawyer."

Richard shook his head. "Uh, uh, uh. I want these papers filed before next week. Don't make this hard. You agreed, so don't try and fight about it now."

"I'm not making this hard. You're being unreasonable. We are in the middle of a party, Richard. I'll read the papers first thing in the morning."

"Now would be better. Oh, by the way, this is Barbie. Barbie, Sadie."

Barbie smiled. I nearly expected teeth to be missing, she was so young.

Richard's drawl continued. "And aren't you going to introduce me to your friend, Dezzzzz?"

He gave Kyle a smug once-over. Damn it! Richard was so awful, so infuriating! That's what made me do it! That's why my mouth started talking independently of my brain.

I hugged Kyle tighter still. "Yes, Richard, this is Des. And we'd both like you to leave."

I heard the jaws of my family audibly dropping.

Fontaine whimpered in distress.

Ohmygod, ohmygod, ohmygod! Did I say that out loud? I stole a glance at Kyle.

He was wide-eyed with surprise.

Yes, it seems I did say that out loud.

After a lifetime, Kyle extended his hand. "Richard."

A collective exhale from my relatives followed.

Richard shook his hand. "I thought you were Scottish. Where's the skirt?"

Kyle, my brave hero, did not miss a beat. "At the cleaners. You'll have to chase somebody else's tonight."

Jasper laughed.

Fontaine whimpered again.

"All right, you've had your introduction. Now will you leave?" I snapped.

"Baby, I drove all the way from Glenville. And I'm not leaving without your signature.

"Richard, is that you?"

Un. Be. Lievable. My mother marched onto the deck, her dark hair perfectly sleek despite wind and humidity. Penny and Jeff were right behind her.

I gripped the back of Kyle's shirt so tightly I thought it might shred. He squeezed my shoulder.

"Helene," Dody called out, pushing Richard aside to welcome my mother.

Helene embraced her stiffly.

"Don't you look lovely," Dody said.

"White wasn't my choice, but the invitation was very specific," Mother responded. "Happy birthday, by the way."

Everyone milled around, greeting my mother, sister, and brother-in-law. I stayed glued to the deck rail and would not let go of Kyle's shirt.

Penny caught my eye and mouthed the word, "Cute!" She had no idea this Des was an imposter.

I started to shake my head, but it was already spinning so fast I didn't dare.

When Mother's gaze came my way, she lifted a cosmetically arched brow.

"Hello, Sadie. Who's this?"

She gave Kyle the barest flicker of a glance before directing her laser-beam stare back at me.

Richard snorted. "So you haven't met Sadie's new boyfriend yet either, Helene? This is Dezzz."

God, I really hated Richard.

"It's lovely to meet you, Mrs....uh..." Kyle faltered.

"Harper."

"Mrs. Harper. I'm..." he stuttered slightly. "I'm D...Des."

"Penny's pregnant," Fontaine blurted out.

Exclamations of congratulations erupted, and suddenly everyone was milling around again, hugging my sister and her husband. Penny managed to embrace each one of them while casting livid daggers my way. So much for keeping that little secret.

In the chaos, Fontaine jumped to my side, grabbing my wrist and Kyle's and dragging us inside.

"What the hell are you doing?" I hissed. "Penny didn't want anyone to know yet."

"What the hell am I doing? What the hell are you doing? Why did you say Kyle was Des? That's idiotic."

"I don't know! Richard shocked me, I guess, showing up here with that Pussycat Doll. It slipped out."

"What are we supposed to do now?" Fontaine demanded.

"Guys, guys, relax. It's not a big deal. I can be Des for a little while," Kyle whispered.

"You can?" I asked.

"You can't!" Fontaine answered.

"Sure I can. It'll be fun. I haven't pretended to be straight in ages. Here, watch my straight-guy walk." Kyle lurched awkwardly across the living room.

"You look like John Wayne with hemorrhoids," Fontaine sputtered. "This is not going to work."

Kyle laughed. "Come on, I'm kidding. I'll be fine. It's only until Richard leaves."

"But he could be here all night. I'm not signing those papers until my lawyer reads them. Plus you'd have to be Des until my mother leaves too. I am not explaining this charade to her."

"Oh." He thought about that for a second. "OK. Whatever. I can still do it. You guys are always saying what an asshole this Richard is, so let's mess with him a little. Besides, how would we undo it now anyway?"

He was right. Without confessing to both Richard and my mother, there was no other solution.

Fontaine looked at Kyle with new admiration. "I had no idea you were so sneaky. It's very sexy."

Kyle preened. "Why, thank you."

"Wait, what about my kids?" I exclaimed.

Fontaine bit his thumbnail. "Oh, yeah."

"What the hell, bigmouth!" my sister shouted, coming inside from the deck. Her cheeks were flushed pink.

I held my hands up in self-defense. "I'm so sorry, Penn. Really, but let me fill you in."

Our little Axis of Evil huddled in the kitchen, whispering details to Penny. She forgave me instantly, if for no other reason than she couldn't wait to see what happened next. She offered to run interference with my kids. I hated dragging my innocent children into my tawdry business, but it would provide interesting fodder for their future therapists.

And so *Operation Desmond Storm* was launched.

*   *   *

"Sadie, just sign the fucking papers so I can get out of here," Richard snapped as soon as I went back outside.

"I just called my lawyer, Richard. She got a copy this afternoon and she's reading it now. As soon as she calls and says it's OK, you'll have your stupid papers. Until then, stay out of my way and don't be rude to my family. Now, I have party guests to attend to and you're not one of them."

"Can I at least get a drink and see my kids?"

I gave him the finger and went on down the deck steps to the beach.

The party was picking up steam as more friends and relatives arrived. Fontaine scuttled like a sand crab, greeting everyone and ushering them over to Dody, who sat in a tulle-draped chair. She looked like she was floating in meringue. My mother sat next to her, her posture as impeccable as her manicure. Two sisters could not be more dissimilar.

Paige and Jordan said a brief, and well-monitored, hello to their father before Penny tugged them away. Now my kids were running around on the beach with a dozen of their cousins. That would keep them occupied for a bit, at least long enough to get Richard out of here before they gave away my diabolical secret.

Kyle played the role of solicitous boyfriend to the hilt, keeping his arm around me and patting my butt so often I finally told him to stop.

"Sorry," he whispered. "Isn't that what straight guys do?"

"Yes, but that doesn't mean straight women like it."

He shrugged and took a sip from his glass.

As the sun sank low on the horizon and copious amounts of alcohol diluted old family grudges and made strangers into friends, the party grew boisterous. The age range on the makeshift dance floor expanded to include the very young to the very young at heart. Harry had arrived, and I watched as Dody tried teaching him to tango with a carnation in her teeth.

Off to the side of the crowd, Jasper, Fontaine, Kyle, and I stood congratulating one another on a party well planned.

"I think we're a success," Jasper said, raising his glass.

"I agree. Dody looks so happy," I added.

We clinked glasses.

"And thanks to the new Des, we've even managed to pull off quite a little caper," Fontaine added, smiling at Kyle.

"Pulled off a cape, huh? Are you wearing a cape these days, Timmy?" Richard said, coming up behind us. He was like death, so silent and feared.

"Where's Bambi?" Fontaine responded.

Richard snickered, gulping from his drink. "Barbie. She's in the house watching TV. Sadie, hasn't that fucking lawyer of yours called back yet?"

"Not yet, Richard. Why can't you just leave? You're getting what you want. Do you have to ruin this party for me?" If I sounded petulant, it's because Richard reduced me to it.

"Believe me, nobody wants to blow this Hicksville party more than me, but I didn't drive all the way from Glenville to leave without the keys to my house." He took another drink, sucking an ice cube into his mouth. He nodded at Kyle. "You're a doctor, huh?"

Kyle glanced around before realizing Richard was talking to him. "Oh, um, yeah."

"Podiatrist or chiropractor or something?"

"Emergency medicine?" Kyle looked at me furtively, like *"That's right, isn't it?"*

I started to perspire. I didn't want Richard chatting up my fake boyfriend. If he caught on to our ploy, I'd never hear the end of it.

"Richard, shouldn't you be sitting inside with Bambi?" I asked.

"Barbie. And I'm trying to be sociable with your new friend here. Remember, I care who my kids are around."

I could not miss the thinly veiled threat. If I didn't sign those papers soon, he'd start mouthing off about being offended by Fontaine. Oh, the irony.

Richard turned back to Kyle. "You're from Scotland, right? Why no weird accent?"

Oh. We'd forgotten that little detail! Kyle had a distinctly Midwestern monotone.

"I've lived in the States most of my life. But speaking of weird accents, you've got quite the hillbilly twang there yourself, Dick," Kyle said.

I smiled with relief. *Nice response, fake Des.* Kyle was the best phony boyfriend I'd ever had.

Sensing an inevitable loss in this verbal duel, Richard turned to Jasper. "You still flipping burgers?"

"Yep."

This was getting tedious. I needed Jeanette to call so Richard would go away! I surveyed the crowd. Wasn't there some dislikable and unsuspecting relative I could foist him off on? Looking toward the beach, I noticed a lone figure walking our way. He was tall and broad and distinct. My heart stopped. It didn't just skip a beat. It came to a full-on, tires-screeching, pull-your-children-out-of-the-way dead stop.

It was Des.

He was back in Bell Harbor.

No, better than that, he was here! He was coming to Dody's party! He looked tan and magnificent, with his white shirt untucked and billowing in the breeze. He was even more devastatingly handsome than I remembered.

How was that possible? The urge to run over and cover him with kisses overwhelmed me.

"Des," I breathed his name involuntarily. He was too far away to hear it, but Kyle was right next to me.

"What?" Kyle asked.

I looked up at him, startled.

Wait.

What?

Oh, shit. Shit.

Kyle!

And Richard!

And Des! The real Des.

What was I going to do now?

"Des," I said again, my voice strangled. I tipped my head ever so slightly so Richard wouldn't notice.

Kyle and Fontaine caught my cue. Following my gaze, Fontaine stifled a gasp and Kyle's eyes darted from Des to Richard to me and back to Richard again.

Jasper noticed our silent panic too, and turned to look. He made a noise with his tongue like the sound Fatso makes with peanut butter in his mouth. He abruptly turned to Richard, blocking his view of the beach. "So who do you like in the Mayweather fight?"

Thank you, Jasper! Thank you! Talking about his most revered boxer would keep Richard occupied. But only for so long.

What was I going to do? Des was twenty feet away and approaching fast. There was no way out. I was doomed, destined to be exposed. I suddenly understood how a wolf could chew off its own paw to be freed from a trap.

Well, no. I didn't really, because that was completely bizarre. But at least now I understood the wolf's perspective. I wanted to be free of this trap. A trap created by me, out of pride and stubbornness. And, quite possibly, stupidity.

What *should* I do?

What could I do?

I was going to have to tell the truth, fast, before Des could hear.

"Richard, I have to tell—"

But my words were drowned out by Fontaine's screech. "Darling!" he sang, flinging wide his arms and running toward Des. "What took you so long? I thought you'd never get here."

Des halted in his tracks, eyes widening at the sight of Fontaine bearing down on him like an attacking swan.

It was like watching a car crash in slow motion, as Fontaine leaped into the air and collided with full frontal contact against Des. Then he wrapped his arms around Des's shoulders and kissed him hard, right on the lips.

Des took a giant step back, as much from the force of Fontaine's momentum as from his own shock. If the moment hadn't been so brutally painful to me on so very many levels, it would have been the funniest thing I ever saw.

"What the fuck, Fontaine?" Des exclaimed.

My heart gave one last, convulsive thump and I reconsidered chewing off my own paw.

"You're naughty to keep me waiting here without a date, baby boy," Fontaine giggled, pulling a bemused Des toward the cluster of onlookers. "But lucky for you I've had people to talk to. See? Sadie is here with her new boyfriend."

316 / Tracy Brogan

"Her new boy—"

"His name is Des," Fontaine said emphatically.

"What?"

"Look." Fontaine grabbed Des by the jaw and manually turned his face toward us.

Des saw Kyle's arm clutching me possessively.

Des pointed. "That's Ky—"

"Kind. Yes, it's so kind of him to be here, but of course it's Dody's birthday and we all want her to be happy. Now, you know Jasper and Beth, of course. Oh, and that's Richard. He was Sadie's husband until she realized he's an asshole. He wasn't invited to this party. He just showed up."

Fontaine could not have been more obvious in his explanation, his delivery so flamboyantly outlandish, I couldn't believe none of us started laughing. We were all too dazed. Meanwhile Richard remained oblivious to the drama unfolding totally for his benefit. He was too intent on sucking a poppy seed from his teeth to pay attention. Since he considered Fontaine beneath his notice, he certainly wasn't going to feign interest in meeting one of his paramours.

Des's gaze skittered around the group, finally locking with mine.

Oh, what a feeling, to be gazing into those beautiful green eyes again.

What a moment.

What a pleasure.

What a fucking disaster.

This was absurd. This needed to end. "Richard," I said again, but Fontaine would have none of that.

"Sadie, Sadie, let me finish introductions. Richard, this is…uh, Gerard. Gerard, this is…everybody."

Des blinked, like an alien waking up in a laboratory on another planet. He stared down at Fontaine, bewilderment in every line of his face.

Fontaine shrugged and rolled his eyes.

Des sighed and turned his head away for the briefest moment.

This wasn't going to work. He wouldn't go along with it. And why should he? He'd had a taste of the carnival freak show that was my life and had decided he wanted no part of it. At the moment, I could hardly blame him. I was so not worth the bother.

Then Des looked back at me and nodded almost imperceptibly.

My heart resumed beating, but barely.

"Seems like I've got some catching up to do," he said.

"Who are you?" Richard asked, as if noticing this newcomer for the first time.

Fontaine clung to his arm. "He's my fabulous new lover."

Des's face went remarkably void of expression, as if struck by sudden-onset amnesia. He extended his hand to Richard, who reluctantly responded with a perfunctory, testosterone-laden, he-man one-pump.

"Dick," Real Des said.

"Uh, it's Richard, actually."

Des shrugged. "And I'm Gerard. Apparently."

"You Scottish too?" Richard asked.

Des glanced at Fontaine.

"Yes!" Fontaine answered emphatically. "What a coincidence."

I pressed my face into Kyle's arm, not sure whether to laugh or confess or just observe as my own horrendous judgment ran its course. Either Des was the best sport ever or he was so confused he didn't know what else to do.

Richard sneered, "He's a little macho for you, isn't he, Fontaine?"

"Jealous?" Fontaine hissed.

Richard gave his most condescending smile, the one that always made me think of Hitler. "Yeah, whatever. Sadie, how much longer do I have to stick around for this gay-pride parade?"

Des slipped his arm around Fontaine. "Dude, that's uncalled for, don't you think?"

Richard stared as if they were cockroaches at the bottom of his drink.

"Uncalled for? Listen, *dude*. What's uncalled for is guys like you hanging around my kids."

"Des! You're here!" It was Dody, trotting over from the dance floor, her full skirt swirling around her.

Des took a step, then turned and looked at Kyle.

"Oh!" Kyle gasped. He strode toward her, cutting her off at the pass. "Yes, Dody. I'm here for you." He steered her back to the dance floor whispering into her ear while she looked over her shoulder. They began to dance, watching us all the while.

I didn't dare look at Des, or Richard either. I stared into my drink, wondering how it had emptied so fast. Was there a hole in my glass? I held it up but could not find one.

After a long, silent moment, Des cleared his throat. "Well, I think I'll cut in. I'd like to say hello to the birthday girl."

He walked over, he and his proxy exchanged a few words, then Des took Dody by the hand, leading her away to sit down in some empty chairs. Kyle sauntered halfway toward us before remembering he was straight. Squaring his shoulders, he walked the rest of the way to rejoin our group.

"I need a drink," Richard huffed. He headed toward the deck, calling over his shoulder, "Unless she can't read, Sadie, your lawyer should be done by now."

"Well! That went about as good as it could have, considering," Jasper chuckled once Richard was out of earshot.

"What is Des doing here?" I asked. "He's supposed to be on a boat race. He's supposed to be visiting his mother or on his way to Seattle. Why is he here?"

"Maybe he stopped by to wish Dody a happy birthday," Fontaine said. "Or, more than likely, he's here to make up with you."

I trembled, hoping beyond hope that my cousin was right.

Penny came up beside me and tipped her head toward the chairs near the dance floor. "Who's that with Dody?"

"Des," I sighed.

"The real Des? Wow."

"Hey, I resent that," said Kyle.

I slipped my arm around his waist and gave a squeeze. "You're every bit as *wow*, Kyle. In fact, tonight, you are my hero."

He hugged me back. "You're my first girlfriend. Real or fake."

I watched Des and Dody chatting like old friends. He laughed at something she said. She reached over and patted his knee. I considered interrupting, but honestly, if she was pleading a case on my behalf, I was OK with that. Paige and Jordan skipped over to them and climbed into Des's lap as natural as could be. Paige kissed his cheek. It made my heart sore. They adored him. They'd be hurt too when he said his last good-bye. I guess I should have thought of that three months ago.

I heard a familiar ring tone, and Kyle pulled my phone from his pocket and handed it to me. I'd asked him to carry it since I was waiting to hear from my lawyer and had no pockets of my own.

I glanced at the screen. "It's Jeanette. Thank God." I walked a few yards down the beach to get away from the music.

"Hi, Jeanette."

"Hi, Sadie. Just wanted to let you know the paperwork looks fine. I made sure it included a provision stating if he doesn't come up with your share of the money within ninety days, possession reverts back to you. That way he can't move in and never pay you. I also added a clause stating you can live anywhere in Michigan without him using that as foundation for future custody challenges."

"What if I move to Seattle?"

"What?"

I shook my head. "I'm kidding. I'm not moving to anyplace but Bell Harbor."

"OK. But you still don't have to sign this, you know. You could keep the house. This abandonment ploy of his would never hold up in court."

I could keep the house. I could pack up my sandals and beach towels and kids and go back to Glenville, to my big, expensive house in the ritzy neighborhood. I could lunch at restaurants with stiff cloth napkins and valet parking with so-called friends who hadn't contacted me in months. I could drink my coffee in peace and quiet every morning, without Fontaine and Dody buzzing something ridiculous in my ear. I'd have my own bathroom.

No thanks.

"Thank you, Jeanette. He can have the house. I'm actually very excited about moving here. I think it'll be fun."

I hung up the phone and pressed it to my heart. Fun, yes. I could use a little fun right about now.

Everyone seemed to be on the dance floor in mixed-up couples. My mother was dancing with Jeff, Penny with Des, Fontaine with Beth, Jasper with Paige, and Kyle with Anita Parker. Even Richard and Barbie were dancing.

I went past them all and on up to the house, where the papers were sitting on the dining room table. I took a pen and scrawled my name on the dotted line, again.

I waited for a feeling of remorse to descend, for sadness to flood my heart, but it didn't. Waves of relief washed over me instead. That house, and Glenville, were my past. My future was here. Here in Bell Harbor, where the sun rose over the lake and each day was filled with possibility.

I skipped back down the deck steps. I found Fontaine and Kyle standing with Penny and Jeff. Jasper was climbing up on the makeshift stage, in front of the band.

When the crowd quieted, Jasper said, "Thank you all for coming. We are here tonight to celebrate the most magnificent woman. A simply delightful woman."

Faint laughter rippled through the group.

"My mom has so many wonderful qualities, I can't list them all—although I'm sure she'd like me to try. But let me just say that every day, in a million little ways, she has taught me to live my life with honesty, with purpose, and most of all, with a sense of adventure. I love you, Mom. Happy Birthday!"

Feet stomped, hands clapped, and voices sang the birthday song while Jasper helped Dody up onto the stage next to him. She blotted at her eyes with the sleeve of her Marie Osmond dress. Des caught my eye from several feet away. The expression on his face made me tremble with hope. He made his way through the cluster of people to stand right next to me. We exchanged tentative smiles before returning our attention to the stage.

"Thank you all so very much," Dody said. Her voice trembled with emotion. "It means the world to me that you came, especially on such short notice. You all look so lovely, just delightful, really. I'd like to thank my darling children, Jasper and Fontaine, who put so much work into this party. And my niece, Sadie, and our dear friends Kyle and Beth, and Des too. I love you all so much. You've all made this a very happy birthday! Now, as that great lady Eleanor Roosevelt once said, let them eat cake."

More cheering, clapping, and stomping occurred as Jasper helped her down. Then he held up his hands to quiet us again. "Beth, would you join me up here? If everyone could wait one more minute on that cake, I have something else I'd like to say."

Beth stepped up, blushing bright pink and looking a little bewildered.

He took her hand. "Most of you have met my girlfriend, Beth. For those who haven't, everybody, this is Beth." She blushed even deeper. "She's been my girlfriend for a year now. She's also my best friend, my partner in crime, and the love of my life. I don't want to spend a single day without her." He dropped down on his knee and pulled a velvet box from his pocket. "Beth, I love you. Will you marry me?"

Her eyes went wide, her hands pressed against her cheeks.

A surprised hush descended over the group. You could have heard a pin drop, even in the sand.

"Holy matrimony, Batman!" Fontaine gasped in my ear. "I didn't know he was going to do that. Did you?"

I shook my head, not wanting to look away.

Her answer came out as a tiny squeak, but was accompanied by vigorous nodding, and Jasper jumped to his feet to hug her. The family erupted with cheers and whistles. Dody sprang back on the stage like a kangaroo to kiss them both.

"Isn't that the sweetest thing?" Richard drawled sarcastically behind me.

"They're much too young. It will never last," my mother said.

I hadn't realized either one of them was behind me. Amazingly, I was feeling so good, the sound of their voices hardly made me flinch at all. I turned around to face them. "It is sweet, Richard. And it will last, Mother, because they love each other. Honestly, what's the matter with you two? I'm tired of all your negativity. Take your doom and gloom and sell it someplace else. And, Richard, the house is yours.

I signed the papers. I'm moving to Bell Harbor. So take Bambi and go away now, and don't let the door hit you in the ass on the way out."

My mother's brows crashed together. She tossed her shoulders and pointed at Kyle. "For him, Sadie? You're uprooting your children and moving here for a man you hardly know?"

My smile was genuine. "No, Mother, I'm moving to Bell Harbor for me, because my children and I love it here, and it'll be good for us." I patted Kyle's arm. "And anyway, this isn't really my boyfriend. He's sort of my boss. Although he'd make a great boyfriend. For Fontaine."

Kyle blushed and stole a glance at my cousin.

My mother's eyes narrowed. "Are you trying to make a fool of me?"

"No, Mother, I'm not," I said, not sounding the least bit remorseful. Because I wasn't. "We were playing a joke on Richard, and you sort of got caught in the middle."

"What?" Richard spat.

I shrugged. "Yep. Sorry."

Fontaine, Kyle, Penny, and Des leaned in close, cocooning me in safety.

My mother's face flushed. "Sadie Turner, that is the most ridiculous thing I ever heard! Playing a trick like that. Shame on you. Why that's…that's the most totally Dody antic I've ever heard of!"

I smiled. "Yes, I guess it is. And that's about the nicest compliment you've ever given me."

Mother harrumphed like Miss Piggy with PMS and flounced away.

Richard was still glowering. He jerked a thumb toward Kyle. "That's not Dezzzzz?"

I smirked and leaned against Des. "Nope. This is."

Des put his arm around my waist and my heart swelled with gladness.

Richard scowled. "What the fuck, Sadie? You owe me an explanation!"

Now I laughed right out loud. "No, Richard. I don't. I don't owe you anything. Now please take Bambi out of here before I rip up your precious house papers."

"It's Bar…oh, whatever." He spun around and stomped away.

We watched my mother and ex-husband fade away into the crowd.

"Wow, Sade. That was awesome!" Penny laughed from behind me. "You shut them both up. Good job."

Fontaine gazed at me with the pride of a parent watching a baby's first step. I think I may have seen a little tear in the corner of his eye.

Des's arm tightened wonderfully around me, sending a warm, shimmery glow through to my bones. I still didn't know what his being here meant. But I was glad for his presence, no matter how long it lasted.

The band had started up again, playing something slow and romantic.

I tugged Des by the hand. "Will you dance with me?"

He smiled. "I'm pretty good, you know."

"So am I."

Sliding into his arms felt like Christmas morning. We had lots of things we needed to talk about, but not just yet. I wanted to enjoy this moment without worrying what it meant. Or what it didn't mean. Des was mine for the next few minutes, and that was good enough.

We danced for a song, and then another, swaying cheek to cheek.

Dody caught my eye and gave me two thumbs up. I giggled at her, feeling precious and girly.

"What's funny?" Des asked.

"Dody's glad you're here."

Our swaying slowed. He looked into my eyes.

"And what about you? Are you glad I'm here?"

"I'm glad you're here for the party. But I'm also kind of wondering when you'll leave again. It was really shitty of you to run out of town without a word. I think I deserve a proper good-bye, don't you?"

"No."

We stopped dancing. My heart tumbled over his single word. That wasn't true. I did deserve a proper good-bye. I deserved respect. The respect paid to a friend if nothing more.

His face relaxed and he smiled as he pulled me from the dance floor. We moved away from the crowd, until we stood in the sand, under the moonlight.

"Sadie, I don't want to say good-bye."

"Well, good for you, Des, but I could use a little closure."

He chuckled and shook his head. "No. I mean I didn't take the job in Seattle."

Wait.

What?

"You didn't? Why?"

He pulled me close. "Why do you think?"

I racked my brain for a logical answer. Because his parole officer said he couldn't leave the state? Because he'd been nominated for surgeon general? Because his Argentinean girlfriend was taking him to Bora Bora? Try as I might, I could only come up with one good reason. Because he was crazy about me and couldn't bear to leave my side.

Just to be on the safe side, I said, "Why don't you tell me?"

He sighed and brushed the wind-whipped hair away from my face. "I just wasted five days of my life on a sailboat with a bunch of guys. We spent the first couple of hours thumping our chests and talking about how great it was to be us, to be men out on the open water. But honestly, Sadie, by the second day all anyone talked about was their wives and their kids. It made me realize what I had back here in Bell Harbor."

That was hardly the declaration of love I was hoping for. "In other words, you got lonely out at sea and now you want some company?"

He chuckled at my dissatisfaction. "No, Sadie. Not just any company. Your company. I want you. I want to make a life here, with you." He squeezed my hands, stirring up a flock of butterflies deep inside my belly.

"I'm sorry I left without telling you," he said. "I guess I panicked a little. I'm not very proud of that, but it's been a long time since I needed somebody. I need you, and it makes me...flustered. You know what that means, right?"

He was teasing, but I didn't mind.

"Yes, I am familiar with flustration."

He smiled. "You do realize that's not a word, right?"

"It is in my world."

"All right. Well, I like your world." He pulled me closer. "I like all the stuff in it. I like all the people in it too." He gazed down, as if searching my face for his answer. "God, Sadie. I missed you. I missed you like crazy."

I breathed in the smell of the water and the cooling sand, the smell that always brought happy memories. And here was a brand new memory in the making.

"I missed you a little bit too," I said.

"Just a little bit?"

"Mm, maybe a lot. I can't remember. I was pretty busy with the party."

Des laughed and pulled me tightly into his wonderful arms. I smiled up at him and at the stars, and at last we shared a glorious and much-needed kiss. And then another and another. The moment was sublime, like lying on white sand beaches near blue Caribbean waters, with a piña on one side and Des pressed up against me on the other.

My heart went pop, pop, sparkle, sparkle, shimmer, shimmer, sigh...

᠅ ᠅ ᠅

The party momentum slowed until at last only a few of us remained. We gathered down by the water's edge, sitting on beach blankets and listening to the waves. Penny and Jeff snuggled together with Jordan snoozing between them. Dody sat next to Harry with a fluffy new barrette in her hair. It was his birthday gift to her, purchased from the Audubon Society and made entirely from goose feathers. Beth and Jasper were there too. Every few minutes she would hold out her left hand and watch her engagement ring sparkle in the moonlight.

Off to the side, Des and I shared another spot, leaning against each other with Paige curled up and resting her sleepy head on my leg.

Fontaine brought down a tray of drinks and passed them all around. Then he plopped down next to Kyle.

"Sadie says you make a pretty fierce boyfriend," I heard him say quietly.

Kyle smiled. "Yeah, but she dumped me. Looks like I'm available again," he murmured back.

Fontaine shook his head. "Not if I have anything to say about it."

They tapped their glasses together and drank. Love might be inconvenient, but it was also persistent.

Dody sighed happily. "Thank you again, darlings. I don't imagine a party at the Taj Mahal could have been any more magnificent. What a simply delightful evening. Jasper, you coy, romantic devil, I had no idea you were going to pop the question. And I'm usually so astute about these things. Beth, did you know he was going to do that?"

Beth wiped the corner of one eye. "No. But I'm sure glad he did."

Jasper leaned over and kissed her cheek while she looked at her ring again. He'd gotten the one he wanted, and it suited her perfectly. Joy for them fluttered over me. They'd be happy. I could see it. And how nice that Richard's gift, which had lost all its luster to me, could be recycled into a brand new future.

"I knew I could trust Madame Margaret," Dody added. "She said this night would be beyond compare."

"Madame Margaret? Is that the psychic you went to?" Des asked.

I nodded. "Dody made me."

He chuckled. "Dody is very persuasive. So what did this psychic tell you about your future?"

I wove my arm through his and snuggled closer. "She told me I'd meet a tall, dark, handsome doctor and my future looked simply delightful."

"Did she really say that?"

"Maybe I'm paraphrasing."

He smiled at me, his dimples shadowed in the moonlight.

I smiled back, thinking how the life before me looked full of wondrous possibilities.

The moon was high, the night was dark, but deep inside, I was the sunshiniest girl around.

THE END

Acknowledgments

IF I COULD PERSONALLY THANK each kind person I have encountered along this journey, I would do it, but for the sake of brevity, I've whittled down the list to a few very special individuals who have helped make this dream come true.

First and foremost, thanks to my husband and our children for supporting me in innumerable ways, from sharing my joy over each tiny victory to bringing me toaster waffles and (more) coffee. Without you, none of the rest matters.

Thank you to my sisters for their endless encouragement, which they give freely even while disagreeing with me about how to build a snowman. And thanks to Jim and Joan for their boundless support and generosity.

To my *Three Cheeka Honey Badgers,* Kimberly Kincaid, Alyssa Alexander, and Jennifer McQuiston. You are the awesome-sauce on my sundae of life.

To Meredith, whose glowing endorsement of the first draft of my first novel was "Hey, this totally doesn't suck," and to Kris, who doesn't really like books but promised if I published one, she'd read it. You two have been my dear friends for most of my past, and will be my dear friends for all of my future. Thank you for each and every laugh.

To Jane, who read every word of every draft with her red pen poised and at the ready. Thank you for spending endless hours with me discussing the merits of Desmond's stupid awesome hair.

To Jenny, whose excellent professional advice was, "I know you like that *Gone with the Wind* stuff, but you should write something funny."

To Hillery, Peggy, Heather, Scott, Sue, Jeff, Samhita, Kim, Dave, Marti, Ted, Mary Beth, Ashlyn, Andrea and Tracy. Thank you for your words of encouragement. They always came at just the right time.

To Marc Graham, Sharon Kendrew, and Jeanette Schneider Vollstedt, a.k.a. Kilt Guy, Boston, and Miss J. Meeting you changed my trajectory and I am forever grateful. See You @ Arno's. I'm buying.

To Dr. Gil Padula, thank you for graciously sharing your medical expertise so I might include a smidge of it in this story. I appreciate your generous spirit.

To my wonderful friends from Romance Writers of America, the Mid-Michigan Chapter, the Starcatchers, the Firebirds, the Dashing Duchesses, and to all the awesome authors who've offered their knowledge and support (Kristan Higgins and Delilah Marvelle, I'm looking at you), thank you, thank you, thank you.

To my agent, Nalini Akolekar, who has always believed in this book. My gratitude to her is boundless.

And finally, thank you to my amazing and tireless editor, Kelli Martin at Montlake Publishing. I will gush my full appreciation to her in private so as not to embarrass myself. For now, suffice it to say, working with her is an honor and a joy.

About the Author

Photo by Allie Gadziemski, 2012

PAST OR PRESENT, TRACY Brogan loves romance. She spends half of her time writing funny contemporary stories about ordinary people finding extraordinary love and the other half of her time writing sexy historical novels full of political intrigue, damsels causing distress, and the occasional man in a kilt. She is a two-time Romance Writers of America Golden Heart finalist, and she has won several RWA awards. Like most people born in Michigan, she has a tendency to point to the palm of her hand to indicate where she lives.

During the rare moments when she's not writing, or thinking about writing, Tracy enjoys time with her family, traveling, and avoiding exercise at all costs.

Tracy loves to hear from readers, so please visit her website at tracybrogan.com or find her at facebook.com/author-tracybrogan or twitter.com/@tracybrogan.

Made in the USA
San Bernardino, CA
08 May 2013